THREE DEGREES

The Tempestas Series
BOOK 1

JIM WURST

TITLE: Three Degrees, The Tempestas Series — Book 1

ISBN: 978-1-7345724-6-9 (e-book)
ISBN: 978-1-7345724-7-6 (paperback)

Library of Congress Catalog Card Number: 2020918833

2nd Edition

For Elena, who will be 55 in 2052

Early in the 21st century, the scientific community reached the unanimous conclusion that climate change was inevitable. To avoid large scale and irreversible damage, the warming of the planet had to be halted at less than two degrees centigrade.

SEPTEMBER – NOVEMBER 2052

CHAPTER 1

An elderly couple sat on a bench near the Jefferson Memorial, the morning sun not yet becoming uncomfortable. They reminisced about the Tidal Basin and the cherry escalade of their youth. The Potomac had swallowed the Basin. The 2035 blight finally killed all the trees.

The couple watched a young couple stroll by. As is natural, the old noticed the young more than the other way around. A fine match, they thought. The man was tall and thin, his skin a deep mahogany, and he moved with an air of confined Washingtonian authority. The woman as if she'd walked off a Diego Rivera mural had mocha skin, straight black hair and Hispanic origins.

"What a lovely couple," the elders thought together as 40 years of unity will allow, "I wonder if they have any children? What lovely children they would be. What a mixed palate. I wonder what color our grandchildren would have been if Richard and Mary had been able."

The young couple walked on.

"I better hurry," he said, "The senator said wants an early briefing. When do you leave?"

"This afternoon. We have to start early in Seattle."

"I hate it when you fly, Elena."

"How do you campaign without flying sometime? Holo-conferencing gets you just so far. Sometimes you have to make personal appearances. You have to... what's the old expression?"

"Press the flesh."

She grimaced at the thought. "Lilly hates that." Touching strangers. Then she noticed the strangers on the bench. Not too many left of that age, she thought. Elena had a generous nature, but she shared a common reflex of her generation when she happened upon that generation: what did you do to stop this?

CHAPTER 2

Sensors attuned for color, density and motion picked up an image. From 3,000 kilometers up it looked ugly. The young technician taking the readings called her boss to look at it. "Well, I'd rather be above that then under it."

"Or in it."

They were looking at a sludgy brown cloud, roughly 200 kilometers long and 30 wide. Its origin, the Chinese mainland and at a heading of 35 degrees Northeast; it would cross Japan by the next day.

"We tell Tokyo?"

"Yes, that's protocol. Tokyo has to be aware of it but transmit the data anyway. They'll have a better idea of what is in the cloud. Besides, it'll be up to them to ask Beijing about it. Any chance of it missing the mainland?"

"Not without a radical wind shift. She pointed to a storm gaining strength north of the Philippines, "the most likely source is that storm center. The winds could push it closer to Japan but it's on the same heading as the cloud and far enough south to miss it."

The Lucky Dragon 8, equipped with the most modern communications system and one of the last, large fishing ships was not in Japan. It was out at sea and the captain knew it was in the direct path of a storm.

He only had terrible options to consider. He could reverse course and head back to Japan. That was the safest but also the worst economic one. He could stay the course and ride out the storm, which would allow him to follow the fish but put the ship at risk. Or he could head south, try to get out of the storm's path and still find fish. The fish were important, so he gambled on the latter.

The Lucky Dragon was as successful as it was because it was designed to sweep up whatever was left down there. The giant nets that hung down from extensions on either side of the ship were large enough and strong enough to snag even a small whale. It could also snag a large whale if there were any left, which would have been a problem. The captain could fight the whale and follow the tradition of the Pequod or release the net and lose half a billion dollars of equipment and fish. Some would call that revenge, but despite the name of the ship, the captain was not superstitious. But he could count, so he ordered a southern setting. It was all about the fish.

CHAPTER 3

O h, he loved the feel of wood. Fewer things made of wood meant the old pieces were in high demand. He could afford it, but in his public space, there was no need to remind people that he could have what they could not. But the desk had to be wood. Cherry, from a time when cherry grew thick enough to make furniture. It was his father's first desk, and Senator George Cranston brought it with him with every victory. I'll use the Resolute desk in the Oval, he thought and save this one for my private office. "What confidence! What vision!" the campaign advisor in his head said. "What an ass," said the rest of the choir.

Reality came from the intercom. "Senator? It's time for your daily briefing."

"Send him in, Nancy."

His assistant, Nancy Liu, promptly entered with a young man by her side. He had made this visit many times before but still was ill at ease. Not because he was in awe of this man who wanted to be president (that would have been ridiculous) but because he was on official business and anything like relaxation was inappropriate. He carried a small, thin metallic attaché case close to his side. Nancy directed him to a chair directly in front of Cranston while she took a chair to the side. Rogers was a severe young man, severe suit, severe haircut, severe posture. A half-dead dog across the street would see him and think "Fed." Rogers was a young and ambitious Secret Service agent. He had no field experience but was angling for something special. He was an armed bureaucrat. Rogers sat down so fast that Cranston didn't even have time to get up and shake his hand. So there was Cranston, half-standing with his out-stretched hand unshaken. Rogers did his best imitation of someone with social graces and jumped up and shook the senator's hand.

"Good morning, Senator."

"Good morning scanned the news today and have seen nothing special. What's secret?"

"Senator, please, you know the protocol." Cranston did this every time and every time Rogers never learned. He opened his case and took out a small computer with a screen camera but no keypad. "Agent RR, reporting. 08:45, location Bruin station," he said to the device, "All secure."

"Should I tell you again how much I dislike my codename?"

"I'd rather you didn't, sir."

"I mean, seriously. Who's that supposed to fool? I went to college at UCLA. How long is some genius going to take to add two and two?"

"Senator, please, this has been protocol for decades. You are cannot change it."

"If I'm elected president, can I pick my codename?"

"No, sir, that is the prerogative of the Secret Service."

"Well, I don't want to be president then." Even Rogers found this amusing, which was something Cranston couldn't allow. "So what's Dr. McDowell's codename, Dragon Lady?"

"Sir! We would never..." Now Nancy was grinning too. That was the last straw. "I am on a schedule, sir, this material is time-sensitive."

"Go on, go on. When I'm president, I'll request you for my detail so I can harass you every day. How about that?"

"I'm not in the personal protection unit, sir, I..." Rogers finally went on the offensive, playing the only part of the game he could control. "National Security Weekly Briefing, September 21, 2052. Briefing by RR. Present, Senator George Cranston. Voice and biometric recognition, please." He turned the computer towards the candidate and with professional seriousness, he said, "George Cranston."

"Present, Nancy Liu, special assistant to the Senator. Voice and biometric recognition, please." He repeated the procedure.

"Nancy Liu."

"Recognitions confirmed."

Satisfied with the results and comfortable that the terrain now favored him, Rogers began reading from his tablet.

"The Siberian fire appears not to have spread. There is still no confirmation as to the cause of the fire. Particulate matter will drift over the Arctic and Alaska within five hours. Methane levels have peaked at orange. We will know by then if it is a solely a forest fire as claimed by Moscow or some industrial accident that set off the forest fire."

"The border between Iran and the Caliphate is calm. Severe sandstorms continue to make troop movement and flights hazardous. Nothing new of significance to report."

"They will announce first reports on the European harvest tomorrow, 0800 GMT. Our estimate is that the harvest will not be below expectations in the key food groups. We do not expect major changes in the stock markets or social indicators."

"There are several weather conditions forming in the Northern Hemisphere: one hurricane is forming southeast of Cuba, another west of Grand Bahamas. Neither appears at the moment to endanger the US mainland. Three storms are forming in the north Pacific it is too soon to know where it will land but the Yukon is the best guess. The North Atlantic is quiet."

"In the Southern Hemisphere, two storms are forming in the South Pacific, one in the Indian Ocean. Typhoon 14 made landfall at 0430 GMT 200 kilometers north of Santiago de Chile. Damage was minor."

"Accra is in its 23rd day of plus 35 degrees Celsius temperature. The WHO is detecting signs of a waterborne disease spreading, possibly a strain of SARS. This is worrying. If this does progress as predicted, we will face the possibility of a pandemic, panic and attempted flight. The African Protection Force is mobilizing to seal the city.

"The voluntary migration in Kenya is nearly complete. 250,000 people have moved from the Kenyan desert to Tanzania. We estimate that 20,000 people died this past week. They have reported no significant incidents."

"This concludes the national security briefing for Senator George Cranston, presidential candidate for the Federalist Party."

He turned off his computer, satisfied with a job well done.

"That's it? Nothing from China, Mexico?"

"No sir, were you expecting something?"

"What's that stinker coming out of China I saw this morning?"

"Routine industrial pollution. Nothing but wind currents is causing the cloud to have that oblong form."

"No radiation?"

"No, sir."

The agent trained to say only what was necessary and the politician who always wanted more stared at each other silently, one knowing that he had to stop and the other refusing to acknowledge it.

"Well, okay," Cranston said. "Thanks."

Rogers stayed as stone-faced as possible, collected his

gear and bade a formal goodbye to the candidate. Nancy escorted him out. Once the door closed, Cranston remained seated, calm, unhurried. It was less than two minutes before Nancy reentered with Sean. Cranston pointed to the chair Rogers had just vacated. All stayed silent until Cranston said, "Ok, Nancy, I've got three speeches to go over this morning, right?"

"Yes, sir," she answered.

"No recent additions? Nothing before my 11am call with Dr. McDowell?"

"Nothing, sir."

"Fine, show me the speeches."

The disconcerting thing about this routine office conversation was that neither one of those moved nor did anything matching their words. Nancy had no speeches, Cranston wasn't reaching for them. It was as if they were practicing lines from a play. Only Sean – Cranston's 360 – was mobile. He went to the chair, took out a small box and pen from his pocket. Carefully examining the chair, he pulled out from the seat cushion a small, metallic wafer. Waving the stylus over the wafer, he put it in the box. For the first time, someone said something that matched their actions: "All clear."

With that, Nancy relaxed and slumped in a chair. Cranston, the public politician with the glad hand and ready smile, gone. Cranston, the private politician with the short knife and claws, spoke. "Anything new on that son-of-a-bitch?"

"No, sir," Sean said, "He's clearly not acting on his own, we have to assume he is following instructions from higher ups." He replaced the wafer.

"Yeah, assume" Cranston said as he mentally sharpened his knife.

CHAPTER 4

Zhidoi mattered. It never smelled nice. Air still burned the eyes; there wasn't much to look at. But as an industrial city in the central Chinese highlands, it had always been important to the country. If the word lyrical could ever apply here, it could apply only because of its important to history's imagination. It stood at the headwaters of two great rivers: the Yangtze and the Mekong. Those storied waterways that helped define the peoples and history of Asia began their lives as humble streams in these mountains. Otherwise, it was a grim city, sacrificing whatever beauty or elegance it might have on the altar of greater production.

The engineer's apartment was a weakened version of the impressive constructions of the 2010s. His skills meant he had certain privileges, but he lacked the family and political connections to do better than the minimum. Minimum in this case meant a one-bedroom apartment with a kitchen suitable for boiling rice and tea and not much else. There were windows, but no one would care what they looked over.

The engineer tried to swipe the key card precisely right so he could get into the apartment quickly. With his hands trembling, it took three tries. Not bothering with the light but concerned with the locks, he pushed a chair against the door and ran to the bedroom. From a panel in the headboard, he removed a thin computer and turned it on. Carrying to the kitchen counter, the closest level surface, he heard the footsteps he knew were coming.

As long as there have been boots - probably longer, really, Romans had sandals - the running stomp of the boot meant the same thing to hunted humans as did the howl of the wolf to a hunted animal. Stomp, a crash at the door, more stomps. "Ready to transmit" finally appeared on the screen. The engineer removed a tiny chip from his glasses frame and worked it into a special slot in the computer. Despite being much more delicate than the key card, he succeeded on the first try. No more stomping, just crashing.

"Loading," the computer announced.

Another crash. Their battering ram, a good deal stronger than his door.

"Transmitting," the computer reported.

The door was now splinters. The chair, toothpicks. The engineer scrambled to the bedroom, leaving the computer to its own devises. He forced the window open but had only one leg when the soldiers with night-vision goggles rushed in and fired. Rather than bullets, a stream of goo shot out. The shooter directed the stream up and down the engineer's body as if he was watering an uncooperative lawn (not that the soldier had ever seen a lawn). The engineer fell to the floor, his arms pinned to his sides, unable to reach up to his neck to relieve the stranglehold of the now solid goo. A soldier came over and cut the goo from his neck. Death was not part of the orders. Meanwhile, another soldier spotted the computer and with his laser pistol fired at the keyboard. With a fiery phsst, the computer stopped transmitting.

CHAPTER 5

He was the only president most Americans knew. Because of the assassination of President Branson in 2041 less than one year into his term, Vice President Thomas Ailes became president and reelected twice, thus having served longer than any president other than Franklin Roosevelt. And now, finally, he had to step down. But stepping down and leaving were not the same things. President Ailes had had more than ten years to shape the federal government into his image, so he wasn't going to just walk away. The Doctrinists controlled Congress, most state houses and the courts. He had more than a few options in his pocket.

Ailes was in his second favorite room. The Oval was first, but the Situation Room was where a president got to be more than a head of state. He was a god, the world one computer command away. He ruled here even more than he ruled above ground. Even the chairman of the Joint Chiefs hesitated before raising his voice. Ailes gloried in the power of this room. He had no interest in sharing it with anyone. Only Ailes' Chief of Staff would not hesitate to speak, but he rarely saw the need. He was Ailes' fixer and right-hand man from the start. His silence was legendary, his power more so. Serene, silent. He could have been a Buddha if Buddha's father was a golem.

Here, everyone was silent except Ailes and the general conducting the Situation Room briefing. The brass in the room had no interest in contributing any comments and the civilians knew that no one intruded on the President's domain.

"So, what is it?" Ailes asked.

"It" was a projection on the main screen of the room. It was a simple schematic of... something. A two-dimensional diagram without the normal holographic add-ons, colors, rotations, sounds. Someone designed this with the need for rapid transmission in mind. Simple meant fast. But it was also too simple to understand.

"We don't know," the General said, "Transmission was interrupted before we could download the full schematics. We're not even sure how much of it we have here could be the beginning, could be nearly half, but it is definitely not complete."

"Could it be a weapon?"

"Yes, sir. A definite possibility."

Choosing to focus on the schematic and not the man, Ailes continued, "But not a certainty. Other possibilities are?"

Directing a laser pointed to a blockish part at the base of the drawing, he said, "This unit here is undoubtedly a power source, but since it is so incomplete, we can't be sure if it is a power source for this device or if the device is itself a power source. It could have industrial applications Zhidoi is heavy in minerals. This could be a new extraction or refining device..."

"And what about that thing? It looks like a cannon." The appendage looked like a cannon barrel. Ignoring all the electronics in the schematic and anyone would think it was a World War I howitzer.

"It's obviously a key component, possibly the *key* component to the device. A cannon, sensor. We know it's hollow, but it could introduce other components to make a telescope or..."

"How many times are you going to use 'could' in this briefing?"

"We would be negligent in our duties if we gave you

unequivocal answers when we don't have them, Mr. President. We speculate that it is a weapon because prudence demands it, our agent thought it urgent to get this material out, and obviously the Chinese are going to great lengths to keep it secret."

"You already had this man in place, you had to have had some suspicion before today."

"We have agents in many such facilities. It's not a pinpoint operation, more of a fishing expedition. We found a correct point."

"Do the Chinese know that we know?"

Avoiding that dreaded phrase, he said, "Depending on what's left of the computer, they may trace it to its origin. It's a standard issue covert system, so there are false trails and links that could track it to Russia or Europe or Japan, and us. If it's relatively intact and they have a capable engineer working on it, it'll take days for them to be sure where it came from."

"Unless they work on the guy faster."

"True. His implant is registering life signs, weak but life signs. They could work him over when they want to."

"Implant? Why are we wasting an implant, a traceable implant, I assume on a factory worker?"

"He's not a simple factory worker he's an electrical engineer. The implant is 85 percent biometric. He has a legitimate titanium knee replacement. The implant is between the organic bone and tendons attached to the metal knee. It won't be easy to find."

"Do we have any other assets in the region?"

"No HUMINT, they have already moved the satellite over China into position over Zhidoi. We're slowly moving some resources out of Beijing and Shanghai, but we can't do it too fast and even when they get there, they will only be able to operate on the periphery: observe movements of trucks, monitor power surges, that sort of thing."

"Weapon, power source, mining tool. Anything else?"

"Possibly a space use. Zhidoi is the highest elevation in China outside Tibet, this argues for a space use, but it's so far from the Chinese population centers that a defensive space weapon would be of dubious use. An offensive space weapon would be a massive treaty violation, which would account for the secrecy. There could be other non-military industrial uses, but that really would be an unhelpful speculation with so little concrete information."

"So we consider this device a potential threat?"

"Definitely."

"Does this mean we have to tell Cranston about it?"

"Excuse me?"

"Cranston, the Federalist candidate. Aren't we obliged to hand this information over to him?"

"You're referring to the daily security briefing?"

"I am. When else do we deliberately leak sensitive intelligence?"

"That's really outside my responsibilities, sir. There are laws covering that..."

"*And* McDowell? We have to tell that useless little chi...."

Buddha spoke. "Mr. President, I believe the general has more to say."

The President looked around the table, no one dared tried to make eye contact. He willed his last sentence out of existence. "We'll continue this conversation later."

CHAPTER 6

Now it was time to find out if the Lucky Dragon 8 deserved its name. The ship headed southwest out of the path of the storm. But the captain left the nets deployed, hoping to catch something. This naturally slowed down the ship. By the time he pulled in the lines, with little to show for it, he didn't need a radar to see the thunderous grey and black moving in on him. The computer said it was a Category 5. When he was a boy, there was no Category 5. The only thing left to do was to steer into the storm, cut the engines and do the best imitation of a cork as he could.

The first waves were babies, nothing the ship hadn't handled before. Love taps. Then they started building and the winds that drove the water were soon licking the sides of the ship. The captain and helmsman were the only ones on the bridge, everyone else, including the first mate, stayed secured below deck. Then as the waves fully embraced the ship, sending water over all the deck, the sky became a grey liquid. It barely qualified as air. Neither of them could breathe. The air was stifling and none of them could breathe.

Gripping whatever was solid enough, they stared out into the void. It was the most solid nothingness they had ever seen. A wave like a giant whale's tail flipped the ship into the liquid air. They had the sensation of flying while still wedded to the waves. And then they crashed. How could the ship crash when it was never free of the ocean? Yet there it was, a hideous cracking and screeching as the ship surrendered. The radio tower flipped like a used toothpick into the deep. The secured arms of the nets were no longer secured. They were swinging about the deck like the broken wings of a bird. It was almost a mercy when they too disappeared into the grey. The sun had to be up there; it had to be, but it seemed so long ago that it might have just given up. It was now black, not even grey could survive this. It wasn't even right to speak of waves now. Waves suggest separate, individual movements. This was one solid world of water. No bobbing, no thrashing, just the primordial existence of all water in the world encasing the ship.

It was as if the Akkorokamui of ancient Japanese myth had grown so large over the centuries that one tentacle rising from the seabed had curled itself around the ship, bored with its resistance, not even bothering to rouse another tentacle. So puny that it was beneath it to exert the energy to crash them. The captain had long ago closed his eyes and surrendered to the fates while his crew lay covered in vomit. The heaving, the deafening winds, the water in the lungs, the blackness was now normal. Just the sights and sounds of impenetrable death.

Later, the captain swore he did not remember the end of the storm. Just like when you have a headache, you don't register the moment it disappears, just that it's gone. He insisted this was the same. He had no idea when the wind and the water had become embedded in his soul. He just lifted himself from himself, looked out at the calm sea and what was left of his ship. The black gone. The sky still grey, but it was a grey he could live with.

CHAPTER 7

In the quiet of dawn, the kitchen silently and methodically came to life. Even before anyone was there to smell it, the aroma of coffee filled the room. A warming cabinet began its program. The thin, photosensitive shades slowly lightened to let in the first light of the day but stood ready to darken again when the heat started cooking the fabric. The moment Carlos Lopez entered the kitchen, the ceiling lights sprung to life and the near-transparent screen against the wall lit up with the day's news and weather report. It's 5:30 am. This was modern Albuquerque. The sun had the last word, even before it rose.

He looked at the monitor, thought better of it, and poured his coffee first. This was one of his few indulgences real, imported coffee, which was more expensive than meat, but he allowed himself and his wife one cup every morning. The tortillas were easy, but not as tasty as the ones of their youth. Beans were also easy. Eggs needed imagination.

The kitchen was the definition of efficiency. All appliances were just the right size, no super double oven here and run with the highest energy savings. Everything was metal, plastic or alloys. No wood. Traditional Mexican touches, a terracotta bean pot, and Talavera tiles offset the sterile efficiency. He opened the warming cabinet and took out a small stack of tortillas and a bowl of refried beans. He rolled some beans in the tortilla and sipped his coffee.

Thus fortified, Mr. Lopez turned to the monitor. He didn't need to touch anything, no button or remote. They had programmed the screen to react to his voice and routine need.

"Predicted high for the day." The screen shows a high of 102 by 1340 hours. "That's not good. Send mail." The writing screen appears. "To Advanced Horticultural Seminar 3: Weather not favorable for a trip to the field station at 1500 hours. Please meet in the seminar room at 1700. You are excused from midday exercises but experiments 21 and 22 must be completed in full before the trip to the field station. Signed, Professor Lopez... Send." The screen reverts to the weather page. "National news."

What appeared next is not what he programed. There were a few smaller outlets he preferred, and the computer would load the most trafficked site, or what was now the "national standard." President Ailes appeared, meeting with some head of state. "Next page." President Ailes appeared, addressing a cabinet meeting. "Next page." President Ailes campaigning with his heir apparent, General Hayden. "Next page." President Ailes... "Oh, for God's sake. News on Federalist Party campaign." After all these years, he still hoped what he programmed would actually appear. Somehow, he felt it was a defeat to keep asking for the news he wanted. Senator Cranston now made an appearance, but it was a static muddy shot with no audio.

"Goldstein vlog." Not his favorite site. He knew Goldstein did not follow the party line, but Mr. Lopez worried about what voices might be in the young man's head.

"... Despite official reports, the Cranston rally in Richmond was actually 50,000, not 20,000, people. The 'disturbance' at the rally was actually a fight on a food line three blocks away..."

Mrs. Lopez shuffled into the kitchen, giving Mr. Lopez a reason to stop wrestling with the computer. She was the same age as Mr. Lopez, but she wore the years badly. The child becomes the parent to the parent if they are lucky, but sometimes the luck lasts too long. She had been the parent to the parent for a very long time. First, she poured herself a coffee, performed the same ritual with the beans and tortilla, then looked at the screen, absorbed that it showed the news and only then did she address her husband.

"Have you checked the weather yet?"

"Yes, it's going to be too hot this afternoon to go to the field station."

"No local weather, national. Elena is flying today."

She hadn't put enough strength into her voice for the computer to register, so Mr. Lopez repeated "national weather." But the screen went blank and then exploded into garish colors and even worse music, as if an armadillo was trying to play an organ. The colors gave way to screen filled with the most obnoxious clowns imaginable. Someone had put in a lot of effort to drive every four-year-old into pants-wetting panic. The clowns started yelling, "Elections are approaching! Elections are approaching!" Bloodshot eyes and rotten teeth. "Don't forget to vote for the clown of your choice!" Smacking lips and spittle-specked voices. "As if you had a choice!" And then the screen went blank again and the weather map appeared.

"I loathe those people," Mr. Lopez muttered.

Mrs. Lopez was too tired to be outraged. "I can't understand why the government can't catch them. They've caught enough innocent people."

"Maybe they're the right kind of guilty. If their goal is to mess with the elections, we'll be seeing a lot more of them."

"Can't wait." Finally, working up the energy to speak to the computer, she said, "Weather and travel conditions, Washington, Seattle, beginning at 1300 Eastern time." This time the computer responded promptly and accurately. "Five percent chance of lethal turbulence!" she cried, as if she had never seen this before.

"Please calm down, you know the statistics are never better than that."

"Our daughter is going to fly today with a 5 percent chance of dying, and you tell me to calm down."

"It is a fact of life," he said, trying to suppress his irritation, "They all fly only when they have to. Besides, remember the next campaign stop is here. Want to check the odds?" He immediately regretted saying that. Mrs. Lopez fell silent. She had no response to that, and he knew it.

In his darkest thoughts, he sometimes wondered if he did this to her deliberately. He didn't think of himself as cruel. Was it guilt that he didn't feel the same? Anger at her weakness? Projection that he felt the same and was angry with himself for not showing it? He left the kitchen. "I have to get to work."

She didn't acknowledge his absence and instead turned to the computer. This time her voice was steady. "Papi."

The screen now showed another room. Like the kitchen, it had state-of-the-art technology and was decorated with traditional art, the Lady of Guadalupe being the most prominent. A small case with military decorations hung on a wall. What was most obvious in the room was the bed. It was a single hospital bed encased in a 21st century version of an iron lung: transparent, connected to numerous machines and monitors, including an oxygen tank and IV drip. All of this was in place to aid an elderly man, still and wasting away, laying in that bed. Mrs. Lopez looked at the picture and studied the data being supplied by the monitors: heart rate, caloric intake, depth of breath, bowel activities, and a countdown clock showing when next the man needed to be changed and rotated. The vision was the best Mrs. Lopez could expect. "Off," she ordered the computer. That was enough for one morning.

Mr. Lopez finished dressing in his usual attire of long, lightweight slacks and shirt and his broadbrim hat, styled in the Mexican tradition but constructed of the latest fabric for protection against the sun and for the retention of body moisture.

He walked out of the house onto the mostly silent street. On either side, he could see a few people walking towards his destination, the monorail station. Few people here had cars. And those who didn't waste them on commuting to work. In fact, living in this neighborhood was a reason not to have a car. Albuquerque went through a massive housing boom in the 1990s, nearly doubling the size of what people would consider Albuquerque. Stretching deeper into the desert, the reach of modern infrastructure followed roads, electricity and water. Most of all, water.

The water that magically appeared from every faucet in the city, easily wasted, no more a concern than air. And then it wasn't there. The city contracted, suburbs wilted, swimming pools emptied and even filled in, grass replaced by rocks and cacti. "Brown water" entered the vocabulary.

The Lopezes were better off than most, they knew what to do before most people understood. Now only about a quarter of the houses in their neighborhood were occupied. The majority were empty shells, some missing roofs and windows, all missing copper wiring and plumbing and porcelain products. Mr. Lopez, leveraging his experience in agriculture, staked a claim to the backyard of his now absent neighbor to build a greenhouse. which he redesigned to trap water rather than warmth. It included a wind tower, a catchment system and a small field of corn where he could conduct his experiments. It was an oddly vibrant compound where the majority of the activity was the wind whistling through empty houses.

Shortly after, the magnetized, solar powered monorail slid down its tracks in the center of the street. Mr. Lopez got on, nodded to a few familiar faces and decided that today, he didn't want to look out the window.

CHAPTER 8

It was time for Cranston's daily security briefing. No banter this time. He knew something was coming and wanted to know what it was. The three of them the senator, Nancy, Rogers were sitting in their usual seats. No one was especially comfortable when Rogers stopped talking.

"Are you sure it's a weapon?"

"No, sir. We're not sure of anything at the moment. In these situations, we err on the side of caution. We assume hostile intent until they can prove it otherwise."

"And your opinion?"

"I have no opinion. I have not seen the schematic. I am only repeating what I am authorized to tell you."

"What are the realistic non-hostile options?"

"Power source, industrial equipment, some kind of mining or refining machinery. Space-oriented."

"Space-oriented is not hostile?"

"Sir, my briefing must be within strict guidelines, I can't engage in interpretations or speculations beyond my orders."

"What else are you authorized to tell me?"

"Only that you will receive periodic briefings in addition to your daily briefing. The scheduling and means of communications will be dictated by need and conducted by people far above my level."

"Thank you." He was also saying goodbye.

After Nancy returned after escorting Rogers out, she saw Cranston had not moved. She mouthed "Sean" and the senator waved her off. "Nancy, find out if Dr. McDowell has had her briefing. We need to talk. Where is she right now?"

"On her way to Seattle."

"Well, she can't turn back, and I can't go there. She must come here as soon as the Seattle rally is over."

"She's due in Albuquerque next."

Shaking his head, he said, "Here."

CHAPTER 9

There was nothing about this experience that Lilly McDowell liked. Well, except for the seat. That was much nicer than the average airplane seat. But she hated flying, so the comfort of the seat didn't count for much. Elena Lopez was sitting across from her, facing backwards. The other two seats were empty. This was a private cabin, but the rest of the plane was not much larger. Only 20 people could fly in this state-of-the-art aircraft. This was the elite of the elite, only the richest and most powerful people could have access to the luxury and safety it offered. Absurd, Lilly thought every time she boarded this thing, that I have any business on such a craft. It would be over in a few months and she would have her normal life back. But for now, she traveled in luxury, had a staff and was, generally, listened to. Absurd.

As a scientist and tenured professor, she was the least likely politician to come onto the scene in decades. Lilly was in her 50s, about the same age as Cranston, but that was where the similarities ended. She was born in China, adopted by American parents, and had little use for the public and private machinations of politics. She was shy, all intellect and no passion, and was running for vice president of the United States.

Absurd.

Elena was briefing Lilly about the rest of the itinerary. Lilly was not looking at her but at some distant point, probably in the past, she wasn't a big fan of the future at the moment. Elena knew well enough not to mistake lack of eye contact for lack of attention. She could read Herodotus Histories, and

Lilly could repeat it back to her. Her casual intellect was what Elena liked most about her. Lilly liked Elena's enthusiasm. They were comfortable together.

"... You have an interview with the Post in ten minutes. A press conference at the airport before the motorcade to the hotel. After the speech, you have a private dinner with five donors..."

"How private?"

"Just them and spouses. No aides."

"That means chitchat. I hate chitchat."

"Well, one is an oceanographer, so it would be possible to raise the level of conversation a bit."

"Can we talk about deep sea drones?"

She wanted to say, "but it's a fundraiser," but stopped herself. "You can try..."

As much as she hated chitchat, she truly loathed large crowds, so this evening would not be the worst thing imaginable. "Pressing the flesh" was still an expression, but few did it. The fear of communicable diseases made even the thought of it repulsive. Politicians would still make public appearances and even sometimes walk through a crowd, but it wasn't common. The public no longer expected that. For Lilly, this was a minor relief.

There was a knock on the cabin door. An aide walked in without waiting. He was even younger than Elena. He had survived his teens in Florida. Determined never to return to a state that committed itself to suicide, he signed on to the first opportunity that promised him escape. No promise of wealth, security or success of course, just escape. That was enough. Working for a loser wasn't the worst job in the world he was from Florida. At least McDowell never yelled at him. She never yelled.

"Dr. McDowell, we just received a communication from Senator Cranston. He says you have to come to Washington after Seattle. It's urgent."

"Meaning?"

"There seems to be a security issue involved. He didn't want to go into detail. The senator says Sean has sent a message to Elena." Elena immediately reached for her pocket computer, but the aide interrupted. "Um, the instructions are that you are not to open the message until I leave. Only the two of you can see it."

This was beyond odd. "Anything else?" Lilly asked.

"No, ma'am." And with that, he dismissed himself. Elena immediately took out her computer and started reading. A small smile crossed her face.

"This better not be a love note."

Elena sputtered. "What? No, ma'am! It's just that it's in a kind of personal code. We designed it for use on unsecured lines."

"Well?"

"Oh, yes. Well, it's about my aunt visiting that's you and, well, the senator needs to brief you on a national security matter that impacts on the campaign and it involves, um, an Asian country, probably China or Japan. I mean, it's not exactly a sophisticated system."

The aide poked his head in again. "A message from the White House. You will receive a security briefing after you land in Seattle but before you speak."

"Obviously not a coincidence."

"No, ma'am." And he left again.

"Elena, as soon as you can, please devise a more specific set of codewords with Sean, and for God's sake, could you please make a distinction between China and Japan?"

"Yes, ma'am."

"You realize that means we're not going to Albuquerque."

Yes, ma'am."

Elena's computer pinged. "Oh, the interview. Are you ready?"

"If I must." Elena pressed the intercom button. "Send the reporter back."

The aide brought in the journalist, also a young man. "When did I become the old lady?" Lilly said to herself.

He sat down opposite Lilly, while Elena pressed another button on the console and a small computer descended. He removed a chip from his pocket and inserted it into the panel. Elena pressed another button and a screen lit on the journalist's side, showing Lilly in her seat. He settled in, barely looking at Elena other than to judge the length of her skirt. He clearly found it regrettable.

Protected by party and parents, he slid up the ladder. He was very easy to read but he didn't care. They set him up for life.

Elena took on the ridiculous role as enforcer. "Remember, you have ten minutes."

"Right, so shall we get started?"

"Please," Lilly said, barely disguising her boredom.

"Ms. McDowell..."

Elena interjected. "*Doctor* McDowell, please."

He looked at her with that "girly, why are you still here?" expression that Elena had seen a thousand times before and had ignored a thousand times before. "*Doctor* McDowell, as a leader of the Expendables, do you feel equipped to represent all the people of the United States?"

Elena tried not to grimace as Lilly immediately took the bait. "I am not a leader of the Expendables. The Expendables are not an organization. I am the Federalist Party candidate for vice president of the United States, and I am perfectly qualified to represent all the people of the United States."

Could have been worse.

"You deny being a leader of the Expendables?"

"There's nothing to deny. The Expendables is an expression. For nearly 30 years it is how we've referred to US citizens who were born in and adopted from China. It was simple irony at first, nothing more. It is not a secret society with rings and secret handshakes."

Still ok, but now Elena was fantasizing about whether to slug him in the nose or his big mouth.

"But you coined the phrase..."

"No, I did not. True, it was first used at Columbia when I was there, but I was not the one to call Chinese orphans expendables. I used the phrase then, true, as did most of us. But it was in a youthful fit of defiance. A way to define that moment in history, but it is not now, nor was it ever, what you imply."

"So, was it an act of defiance against the American couple who saved you?"

"I will not allow you to make this about my parents."

Boom!

Realizing she had done it again, she added, "Do you have *any* policy questions?"

"Seeing that China is the great rival of the United States, can the American people trust you not to harbor some sentimental attachment to our enemy?"

Elena interrupted. "Interview's over." Why should only one side be subtle?

Rather than protesting, the reporter grinned at her and took his chip out of the monitor. He had what he needed, no reason to make more work for himself. "Thanks, truly enlightening." With a 'you-don't-dare-do-what-you're-thinking-of-doing' grin, he turned to Elena. "Mucho gracias."

After he left and the air became less toxic, Lilly asked, "Does every journalist covering this campaign work for the Doctrinists?"

"Pretty much. Even if they're not officially on the payroll, they know the lines. Cross the president and your bandwidth starts to shrink or reception drops. Everyone remembers what happened to Goldstein. Lost 80 percent of his bandwidth in less than a month. If those hackers hadn't boosted him just to annoy Ailes, then he would have disappeared even faster. No one wants to shrink like that. I can get the unedited version on our site before his version comes out."

"I'm not sure the unedited version is going to help us any."

"They're going to make this an 'us against them' story with you as the 'them.' The unedited version has to be better."

"Remind me again why I'm running?"

Elena repeated the party line. "Because you're uniquely equipped to represent all the people of the United States in these troubled times."

"George is going to kill me, isn't he?"

Nodding, she answered quietly. "Yes, very slowly."

CHAPTER 10

Bureaucracy is always a growth industry, especially when the leaders who hate bureaucracy need it. A clever politician can fob off decisions to bureaucrats and then rail against bureaucrats who impede the people's will. The trade-off for the bureaucrat is that he has a job, a considerable factor. Mr. Anderson was a bureaucrat for the Minnesota Bureau for Internal Migration. His primary responsibility was to say "no." He looked straight ahead. Unfortunately, there was a face staring back.

"You're too old for an A Visa." Mr. Anderson stared into the screen looking at a man not much younger than himself. He didn't pretend he was interested.

The tired man stared into his computer screen, trying not to look tired. "I have a long and unblemished work history."

"You understand, an A Visa, permits you to migrate to Canada. How am I supposed to justify giving you a ticket to Canada?"

"I don't want to go to Canada, I have family in Minnesota, and I have plenty of skills you need."

Mr. Anderson glanced at a side screen displaying the applicant's dossier. He didn't have to; he knew what it said, he just wanted an excuse to look away. "I'm sorry but you don't."

"The wind farms need repair staff. I'm a skilled mechanic."

"There is a three-year waiting list for working on the wind farms. Sorry. And besides, there is another problem."

Like a falling man grasping for a branch he passed ten seconds ago, he asked, "What?"

"You were working in Louisiana four years ago…"

Another branch came within reach. "Exactly, on industrial cleanup. That is a valuable skill. That requires judgment, attention to detail, and…"

"But you didn't list it on your work history. I found that in your official record. Why did you exclude it?"

"Must have been an oversight, I'm proud of the work I did there…"

"Frankly, sir, were you exposed to Texas Cholera?"

Forget the branch, the whole damned tree just snapped.

"What! No, of course not. Never."

"I'm sorry. I have to reject your application. Check your screen, you'll see the address of the Appeals Office. But I seriously doubt my decision will be overturned. I'm sorry…"

"But you have to hear me out."

"I have heard you out. You've used your allotted time. Good day." With that, Mr. Anderson reached for his best friend, the off button.

With a groan and a useless rubbing of his temples, Mr. Anderson leaned back in his chair. Recognizing that sound, his neighbor McKinnon peeked over the common wall of their cubicles. "Rough one?"

"By all criteria, he should not even have applied. He's too old, lied on his application, and was likely exposed to the Texas Cholera. He has the nerve to think he can move north. They should have screened him out at Level One. I'm sick to death of being the one who makes the hard decisions. Sometimes I just want to quit and go to Canada myself."

"Why don't you?"

"They'd hold it against Ron. It's uphill enough for him as it is. If I leave the Bureau, leave the country, they'd be able to say his family isn't loyal enough."

"Seriously, I'm sorry, but do you really think Ron has a chance?"

"He was in the top ten percent of his class. He's gotten nothing but excellent evaluations from his superiors on the station..."

"He's the son of a clerk, a member of the wrong party, the wrong kind of Evangelical. Besides, he has to complete his rotation at the station and then he'll be rotated to Earth. God knows what kind of crappy assignment he'll get. By the time he gets his Moon assignment, if he gets it, they will have selected the crew. His chances are next to nothing."

"And nothing if I quit. Besides, there'll be other missions."

"Sure, for *his* son."

A reminder bing from Mr. Anderson's computer interrupted the depressing imaging of the life of Ron's unborn son.

"Next one up." His expression changed to one of relief. "Oh, good. She's 23 years old and applying for a C Visa. This'll be easier."

CHAPTER 11

The mother screamed and flailed. The father fretted and bit his lip, clenching and unclenching his fists. Soon a head appeared, shiny and red. Then the rest of the body, matted with fluid. Ruth watched it all on a monitor. She was aching be to there, to mop the mother's brow, to make a clean, quick cut of the umbilical cord, and yes, to hold the baby as soon as the mother would allow or more likely the father. He would undoubtedly be ready to break Ruth's arm, seeing the agitated state he was in. The baby screamed, a shrill bellow that relaxed the father some, but did little for the mother who was still thrashing about. Ruth could see it was a boy. The father reached down, picked up the baby, and brought it up to his mouth so he could bite through the umbilical cord.

Ruth turned to Jamal, the captain assigned to her station, and smiled. A trained solider, emotion was not the first option. He nodded and smiled. He was pleased; he had a proper mission now. But he knew better than Ruth that this was not a simple assignment. She was an excellent colleague. She knew everything she knew and never pretended she knew what she didn't. It helped that she knew a lot. She was uncharacteristically petite. This kind of assignment usually required more heft, but she was fearless. Fearless and brilliant was a combination he could work with. There were no fainting couches or therapists here. It pleased him that babysitter was not part of his brief.

Ruth was not Malay like Jamal. She was likely Chinese and Caucasian, but judging by the accent, American, not Chinese. He of course knew she was American, that wasn't a secret or exotic. She didn't say much about her family, which was odd. Her mother was a professor, her father a doctor. In his limited experience with Americans, he knew those who came to a place like this were not tourists or trust-fund babies. They were here because they knew they could do it. "It" in this case meant making sure this baby survived.

"You see? It's a boy."

"Yes, it's a boy."

"A boy," she said, as if the options were unlimited. "What's today?"

"Wednesday."

"Wednesday? Rabu?" she asked, practicing her limited Malay.

"Yes."

"Ok, so 'Rabu'?"

"Sounds good."

"Rabu it is. Welcome to the world, Rabu."

And just like that, Ruth was responsible for the first live birth of an orangutan in the wilds of Borneo in five years.

CHAPTER 12

It was an old song, and Ron thought about it almost every time, but somehow it never got old. "Here, as I'm floating in my tin can." Compared to other ships, especially the mother ship, The USS *Theodore Roosevelt*, his wasn't much more than a tin can. The *Roosevelt* and its twin, the USS *John Glenn*, were the most technologically advanced space stations in existence. The US, China, Europe in partnership with Japan, Russia and the United Nations all had stations in orbit.

They all had the same essential design: a double wheel with an axis connecting the circles. The old style of oblong vessels with massive solar panel wings was no longer possible since the debris of the Satellite War would tear apart anything so fragile. The wheels could withstand all but the largest piece of junk. The wheels also created its own gravity only half of earth's, but better than months in zero gravity. With a crew of 120, it had to be large enough to give everyone at least the illusion of privacy.

The *Roosevelt* covered the Northern Hemisphere, the *Glenn* covered the Southern in an abbreviated polar orbit. Rather than the traditional orbit where a satellite would cover the entire planet in 92 minutes, each station covered their half of the globe in 29 minutes. The *Roosevelt* ran a wave pattern of 70 degrees north, meaning most of Russia and Canada to 25 degrees north meaning all the US and almost all of China. The *Glenn* was on a shallower orbit since there was less land south of the equator, and because an array of satellites over Antarctica made it unnecessary for the ship to dip that close to the South Pole.

The two US stations were the largest. China was close behind; the mission as complicated and the crew as large, but since they had a long history of working in close quarters, the designers had no problem with reducing the size. Russia's was mostly for prestige, but Moscow was obsessed on spying and monitoring the climate. Europe and Japan were all about research and communications. The UN stations served all the nations that could not launch their own stations, providing them with research, and monitoring of weather and human phenomena, and communications. And all of them were obliged by treaty to perform one vital function away from the stations themselves. They had to clean up space junk.

The Satellite War destroyed virtually every satellite, space station and ship in space that day, except for, mercifully the vital geostationary satellites in the High Earth Orbit of 35,000 kilometers. Most destroyed satellites were in Low Earth Orbit 700 to 1,700 kilometers. The larger pieces pulled back into orbit and crashed into space stations and ships on their way through the thermosphere before burning up. The newly smashed vehicles then destroyed others in their orbit. Those pieces of the past were still orbiting the earth. Some larger chunks got drawn into the Earth's pull and burned up on re-entry but junk the size of a pin to that of a horse was still roaming the heavens, ready to smash anything to bits.

This was where Ron came in. He had the job embodying the ultimate contradiction: a boring job in space. His tin can was a low orbit garbage truck. Ugly, slow, designed for survival at the expense of everything else, including aesthetics. His ship was the Swiss Army Knife of space. Shaped like a rugby ball with four arms, two equipped with pinchers, two with magnets. It also had a sagging pouch like a worn-out kangaroo.

The ship's sole purpose was to make excursions from the *Roosevelt* and search for debris, collect it and return it to the station. Because of their size, the *Roosevelt* and *Glenn* had higher orbits, were closest to the debris field but slightly above the worst of it. They had the lion's share of the collection work.

The sweepers were periodically deployed to catch what they could. If the *Roosevelt* was geo-synchronist, meaning parked above a single spot of the Earth, then the sweepers could do their work and zip back to its stationary home base. But since the Roosevelt was in a sun-synchronist orbit, the sweepers and the space station were out of sight of each other for approximately 14 of the 29-minute orbit when the space station was on the other side of the Earth. The geo-synchronist communications satellites in High Earth Orbit kept them in radio contact, but for vital minutes of every orbit the tin cans were alone in space. Which was why the sweepers were deployed in pairs.

Once back in the ship, under the supervision of an officer who had a job no one ever said out loud, junk would get categorized and sorted. Ron's ship was the RV, Recovery Vehicle 3. Leadership didn't bother to name them, so pilots named them according to their whims. Ron's ship was Davy. At the moment, he was enjoying the RV's one perk, large windows. Since the sweepers went straight into debris fields, the designers felt eyeballing space was a useful complement to all the sensors on board thus they had unusually large windows. He found the emptiness of space relaxing and when the Earth floated into view; it felt like a religious experience. "God made two great lights: the greater light to govern the day and the lesser light to govern the night. He also made the stars. God set them in the expanse of the sky to give light on the earth to govern the day and the night, and to separate light from darkness. And God saw that it was good." And Ron agreed.

A pinging on his console interrupted prayer. Time for protocol.

"Bridge," he said into the radio, "I'm getting a heading of 00-45-7. Do you concur?"

The Roosevelt's helmsman, who was monitoring as much of space as was possible, replied, "Concur, heading 00-45-7. Bogie is possibly 100 clicks in front of you. Do you have visual?"

"Negative, but it's out there." Watching his panel and checking out his window, he saw nothing. If whatever it was, was 100 kilometers away, he would only see a speck of light. Then a sudden loud thud from outside the ship rattled Ron, not so much for its power, but for its invisibility. Several yellow lights started flashing. He manipulated some controls.

"RV 3, we're getting a yellow alert. What happened?"

"A bogie hit me, had to be pretty small. The sensors detected nothing. Readings show no damage." He manipulated one of the exterior cameras and brought the image onto one screen. "There, I see it, minor dent on the starboard side. No breach. But I can't see the bogie either. Should I try to find it?"

"Negative, focus on the original bogie, it's moving too fast, it may be out of range soon."

"Affirmative."

"Bridge, I have established visual contact. Do you see it?"

"Affirmative. Can't make it out. Does it look like anything to you?"

"No, and it's still moving away from me, still can't get a good fix on it."

"Don't take too long, you have a rendezvous with the Roosevelt on our next pass."

"Affirmative."

The bogie performed its zero-gravity dance as Ron

approached. Alternating between his window and monitors, he tried to get a fix on it. It was big for space junk. That almost always meant metal, so he readied the magnetic arms. He was hoping it would be too big for the claws. He had collected so many scraps of solar panels, tubes, air tanks, but no human remains. Thank God, he felt it was his turn for something big and interesting. Maybe an engine or a ridiculous hope an old-fashioned computer that somehow was still working.

"I see it. It's a generator. Can't tell whose. Maybe ours. Maybe from the '20s…"

"Roger that, I see it. The calculation on the weight is half a tonne."

"Agreed."

There was a pause Ron did not like.

"You're in danger of tanking. Weight of the bogie, your fuel supply, distance from the ship. You can't do it."

"Negative, I can do it." And as if to prove it, he pumped the boosters and extended the arms as far as they could go. The entire ship spasmed as the magnets caught the junk. "See," he said, trying not to sound too triumphant. "Yep, about half a tonne. Definitely going to slow me down."

"Negative. RV 6 has more fuel she will rendezvous with you. Pass it off to her, you can't handle the weight with the fuel you've got."

The professional pilot's smooth space jockey voice, poorly imitated by countless other pilots since the Gemini Program disappeared. "What? Come on, man, I've been picking up the most boring crap for months. This is the first time I've ever had anything that might be worth looking at. I want to bring it in."

"Negative, we can't risk you floating off. You can see it when we get it onboard."

"But…"

"Permission denied. Do I have to remind you the Captain monitors these transmissions?"

Without responding, Ron swung his ship around to face RV 6. That Kate was piloting it only made it worse.

CHAPTER 13

Mr. Lopez addressed a hall full of undergraduates. Since this was the University of New Mexico, the vast majority of the students were Hispanic, with a sprinkling of whites and Native Americans.

"Corn has been a staple of humans in this hemisphere for at least 10,000 years. It is not dramatic to say that without corn, we would not be here." Professor Lopez was conducting his weekly lecture. He liked these outings. He spent most of his time with graduates in seminars and research projects where a breakthrough if it were to happen would happen. These were the students he wanted, who wanted him. But these weekly lectures were a carnival show where everyone shouted, and the lights flashed. But it was out of this, cattle-call that Lopez could find the next round of hopefuls.

"They cultivated corn in the Valley of Oaxaca 10,000 years ago. Over the millennia, it crossed pollinated both naturally and through human intervention to produce what we estimate to be more than 1,000 variations by the time the Spanish landed in Mesoamerica. Yet by the beginning of the 21st century, 80% of all cultivated corn was only three varieties none of them resistant to climate change. A lack of water, increased heat, and pest mutations led to an inevitable crash in corn production.

"The question becomes what strains of corn can grow here, meaning the Southwest United States and northern Mexico now that 'our' corn has migrated north. In the Dakotas, the new Corn Belt, where corn competes with wheat for remaining water, the crops will ultimately die out. Wheat can and has moved north. But corn as we understand it cannot. GMO has proved to be a failure. The rigid structure of GMO makes it impossible to adapt to a changing climate. Therefore, we have to go back to our roots, both biologically and metaphorically, for the answers. We are working with hybrid species and species indigenous to Mexico but have fallen out of favor decades ago. Most of these indigenous strands come from Mexico, but don't tell the President or he may forbid you to eat it."

The students caught that. The professor was making a joke. A small, mirthless ripple of laughter followed.

"Many of these species fell out of favor because people no longer liked the taste. For those facing poverty, it is a luxury they cannot afford. These species do not apply themselves well for mass farming. Small family plots, but not on the scale needed to feed much of the hemisphere. It has been nearly impossible to find strains not infected by GMO. The few we have identified are not suitable for large-scale human consumption."

"If you continue in this field, you will be intimately, maybe even obsessively, involved in developing new species, hybrids, and strains that need to be blight resistant, able to survive on too little rain and too much heat. You will have to increase the size of the kernel while decreasing the size of the stalk and cob. This is no small matter, nor is it a matter for scientists alone. People throughout the hemisphere from the peasants of Oaxaca to, well, you are constantly experimenting. The next great breakthrough could even happen in someone's backyard. I have four hybrids planted in my yard. I'm letting nature cross-pollinate. The results may be a surprise to all of us."

CHAPTER 14

Dr. Simon Asanti woke up tired every morning. His first thought of the day always, "how many people died last night?" As the director of the Nigerian section of the World Health Organization, decisions ruled his day. Decisions about who lived, who got medicine and clean water, how much reliable formula was available to nursing mothers beyond help.

A native of Cameroon, Dr. Asanti knew more than any human should have to about misery. Like all of West Africa, climate change had pummeled Cameroon, which resulted in a rise in sea-level, loss of fresh water and reliable growing seasons, and inevitable social unrest. But nothing prepared him for Lagos.

The UN House in Lagos was the largest in Africa. There had been raging debates over whether they should merge all UN agencies to increase efficiency, which would also increase its value as a target or keep them separate to produce the opposite results. The latter option, less tempting and harder to defend. They ultimately compromised but leaned toward consolidation. A single UN House placed within a compound in the traditional African construction. There was a central building and outlaying support buildings in the classic European and North American fort design. The perimeter was not a uniformed rectangular wall but rather an octagon with a protrusion at each angle. Each protrusion was an entry for different purposes: health, food, refugees, security, etc. That way there would never be a critical mass of civilians milling around one entrance, inviting a suicide bomber or mortar attack. Should anyone try to storm one entrance, they could seal it off, and protect the rest of the compound. Such were the lives of people trying to save lives.

Lagos had suffered terribly from climate change. The fragile combination of low laying lands interlaced with waterways was always under stress as the population of the city grew. But with increased storms, rising sea levels and pollution from multiple sources, it not only lost land but lost its natural buffers from the ocean. As a result, those islands and small bodies of water: Badagry Creek, Snake Island, Tarkwa Bay vanished, as did the eastern neighborhoods wedged between the Atlantic and Lagos Lagoon. Without its natural barriers from the ocean, the Lagoon got pummeled by saltwater washing in from the Atlantic. Pollution increased and by 2052, Lagos Lagoon was a dead zone. The city itself suffered grievously: besides the ecological upending caused by the loss of shoreline and the Lagos Lagoon, poverty increased as temperatures increased, old diseases resurfaced, and new diseases found breeding places in the fetid soup of one of the world's largest, and poorest cities.

This was where Dr. Asanti woke up every morning.

CHAPTER 15

George Cranston Sr. was a wonderful old man. A lifetime in politics made him an expert in reading people. He could make the most cynical, smile. The most insecure, relax. And the most pompous, accept him. He was the man you wanted him to be. He was also a cobra in a very expensive suit. When he said, "I am your friend," he meant "I won't hurt you." That made him a fixture in Washington for five decades, but someone who never held elective office. His son went further, largely because his dad knew where they buried the dead bodies. He often put them there. Yet, he was backing the losing team. He could have switched sides, Ailes would have given him anything he wanted, but he remained a leader of a dying party.

Everything everyone needed to know about US society was that in 1960 the richest metropolitan area was Detroit, in 2000 it was Washington. In 2050, it was still Washington, only more so. Government was business. The citizens would rail against it as they cashed the checks. For decades, an entire class of professional grew in Washington who got rich attacking Washington. If they ever succeeded, they would not have known what to do. It would have been as if a turtle constantly complained about its shell, and then the shell magically disappeared. The inevitable result was that the turtle would die. Government could rob industry, but industry could not rob government. Industry could own government, but only as long as they pretended it didn't. This was why George Cranston Sr. survived and George Cranston Jr. wasn't a laughingstock.

This was also why the Cranston family had an extremely lovely and permanent home in Washington. Georgetown. It was always an elite neighborhood, but since it was on a cliff and not the lowlands made it even more special. George Jr. could not live in Washington his entire life, he had to be part of the great American landscape. So the family set up residence in California, George attended college there, had a few appointments overseas and ran for Senate. He had to be a senator from California. A senator from the District was the worst job in politics but one with the toughest competition. So this Georgetown house way the center of the Cranston solar system while the son had to pretend it wasn't.

These days the house was also the unofficial campaign headquarters. There was the party headquarters, but this was where they made the essential decisions. Partly because the HQ had to be near the Senator and partly because it was much easier to secure a house than an office building. As Cranston's 360, his personal security expert Sean swept the house regularly, mixing frequencies for communications, setting up dummy routers and planting booby traps for spies. It was a safe place.

The old man's library was the favorite room. Antique books and the best computers shared space with mementoes of past and current glories. This evening's council was the usual team: the two Cranstons, Nancy, Sean, Mei Rosen and Maggie O'Malley, Cranston's campaign manager. O'Malley should have been a Cranston. She shared the love of the hunt and the kill. She was lean, not lean as in skinny, but lean as in disciplined. Her film star face helped her move through this world. Rosen, the chief legal advisor, was younger than O'Malley. Like Lilly, she was an Expendable, but unlike Lilly, she embraced the rage that propelled her career. There was a pattern among the people who worked for the Cranstons.

They were waiting. On the main screen in the room, Lilly's interview was running, a clear sign for whom they were waiting for. The door opened and Lilly walked in, followed by Elena. Everyone acknowledged everyone, but only Elena and Sean touched a gentle, chaste hug.

"Oh, for God's sake, you two," the king of the house roared, "You know what you want to do. Go ahead." The pair shared the romantic kiss they wanted. Nobody teased, nobody smiled. Now the meeting could begin.

Cranston leapt in. "Didn't any of the coaching take hold?" he said to Lilly, "They're provoking you. Ultimately, it doesn't matter what you say, they're make it fit their narrative. But for God sakes, don't make it easy for them!"

"I'm sorry. I was trying to talk about policy, not my personal life."

It was Maggie's turn. "You're a candidate for vice president of the United States, you don't have a personal life."

Volley back to Cranston. "No one will listen to you to if you concede any of their points, accept any of their premises, start sentences with 'but' or 'however.' You must prove from the first impression you can be in charge."

"Stick to your strong suit you're not a professional politician," Maggie said, "Look for the solutions in the certainties of science..."

Mei added, "I still don't like 'certainties' too fundamentalist."

"Good alliteration, though," said George Sr.

Maggie countered. "No one can get any traction with the idea that she's a fundamentalist."

Cranston added, "A key piece of our constituency is comfortable with science. They see it as part of the solution, not part of the problem. The Doctrinists are incapable of co-opting that. That's her one strength." He could have said "one of her strengths," he could have said "Lilly," and not "her," but he didn't.

There was an uncomfortable silence. "Team Cranston" was out gunning "Team McDowell" while virtually ignoring the fact that McDowell was sitting in front of them. Everyone also notices that Lilly wasn't defending herself.

More out of boredom with a too-easy fight than pity for the victim, Maggie changed the subject.

"Let's try a few debate questions: 'Dr. McDowell. There is a school of thought the world is approaching a second tipping point. Do you agree and if so, can we counter it?'"

"There is ample evidence that a large section of the Smith Glacier in Antarctica is in danger of sliding off the shelf as did the Greenland ice sheet. The deniers were wrong then, and they are wrong now. We failed to prepare for the first one, and we are just now recovering from that mistake. The human race cannot afford another such mistake, and we cannot rely on the incumbent party to address it properly."

"Good, sharp and to the point. And reminds everyone the Doctrinists screwed it up royally the first time. 'Incumbent party' has tested well reminds people that Hayden is a continuation of Ailes." And then without missing a beat, "Dr. McDowell. What about the Iranian troop movements are they simple self-defense or a provocation?"

This startled the logical professor. "I thought we were talking about climate issues."

There are groans around the room, Cranston didn't care that everyone knew that his groan was the loudest.

Maggie dropped her words like a bullet. "You must think on your feet. These are not polite people. They will not play by anything you think of as rules."

"Never mind this now," Cranston interrupted, desperately searching for a topic on which Lilly could focus, "We need to talk about the Chinese Device. You had your briefing? So what do you think?"

"There's really not enough data here. They couched the briefing in equivocations and admittedly unsubstantiated theories..."

"What do you think *politically*? If word gets out during the campaign and it will if it suits Ailes' purposes how will that affect people's views of us? Hayden will play it against us. Do we have a chance of swatting it back?"

"Again, it depends on what it is."

"We may never know what it is. What's important is what people think it is."

"Then they will think it's a weapon. It doesn't matter what it is or what Hayden and Ailes say it is, the public will always react in fear first. They will see a weapon and it will hurt us."

At least she understands that much, Cranston struggled not to say out loud. Before anyone could say anything else, a three-note chime sounded. Everyone looked around to see where it was coming from.

"That's me," Sean said, "Those hackers are becoming more aggressive. I wanted some kind of early warning system. I noticed that before a hack, a distinct pulse precedes it. The chime sounds when it detects a pulse." He picked up the console and with a few strokes the image of Lilly disappeared from the screen and replaced by an ordinary transmission like a soap opera.

Mei shrugged. "So, what's the big deal?"

For once, Sean didn't have a suitable answer. "Nothing. It's what's supposed to be on. Makes little sense, the pulse was there." The show ran as he checked his data. Someone's missing brother was actually the son of the father of someone and then: "Sid."

In a voice not belonging to the actor and completely out of context, the word "Sid" popped out of his mouth. A moment later, it happened again with a different actor. Suddenly the room was interested in the soap opera.

"Did he just say 'Sid'?" George Sr. asked.

His son answered. "That's what it sounded like to me. Try a different station."

Sean complied and pulled up O'Brien's show.

"Must you," Maggie muttered.

"It was easy." Sean tried to make it sound like an apology, but his twitchy anticipation gave the game away.

This was the self-proclaimed "America's Network" and was too easy to find. It was unofficially the default setting for all channels. The government didn't mandate that, of course, that would violate the First Amendment. It was just decided by the market that the default channel should have the most traffic. And coincidentally...

O'Brien was the star: five minutes at the top of the hour through most of the afternoon and a full hour every evening. He was, of course, the voice of the average American. "General Hayden's bravery under fire is so self-evident that even the most – SID – hater should get down on his knees and thank the Doctrinists for – SID – protecting the homeland..."

"This is live, isn't it?" Cranston asked.

"Yes, he's the only one allowed to broadcast live," Maggie answered.

"They haven't noticed?"

"Maybe no one in the studio is listening. After all these years, O'Brien must be background noise to them."

"Cranston and his foreign partner – SID – will not defend

us – SID –." O'Brien became visibly distracted. "Apparently, we're having some audio issues. We're going to run a recording of General Hayden's speech yesterday – SID – to the Christian Council of Washington." His nostrils flared. "Now."

The picture was now of Hayden giving a speech, but with no audio. Every few seconds, the same voice said "SID" as the letters "S-I-D" flashed over Hayden's face.

"I'd be enjoying this if it wasn't so scary," Mei said.

Sean was enjoying this. "This is the longest transmission yet. Unless they've developed extraordinary cloaking, then tracking them should be possible." But just then the screen went black. Everyone looked at Sean.

"It wasn't me. I wanted it to continue. The studio pulled its own plug."

"And that was the hackers?" asked George Sr.

"Absolutely."

George Sr., whose job it was to know the past, said, "Sid? Is that supposed to mean something?"

Maggie, whose job it was to anticipate the future, answered, "It does now."

CHAPTER 16

It had been a week since Cranston's first briefing about the mystery in China. Every day his security briefing had nothing new. When asked, the robotic reply was, "Nothing today, sir." Finally, Rogers concluded his briefing, "Two officials will brief you this afternoon at 1300 to give you an update on the Chinese Device."

"Chinese Device'? Is that what you're calling it?"

"That's what everyone is calling it."

"Everyone?" He wanted Rogers to think he had let something slip. "Whose everyone?"

"My superiors," he said, hoping he had caught himself.

"Oh, thanks. Looking forward to it."

CHAPTER 17

The funeral for a general is always a solemn affair. Honor guard, a recorded 21-gun salute. But for anyone paying attention and few were, they would have noted an odd feature of this occasion. He was not being buried in Arlington as would be normal for a four-star Air Force general. Instead, his final resting place was the military section of a small cemetery within view of the Air Force Academy. Officially, it was his request. There was also no eulogy. Also, officially at his request. The final oddity was the small number of mourners, mostly elderly men. Veterans, but only one of them was in uniform: an Air Force general. There were also two younger men, both in their later 30s, also in uniform. Both were captains: Isaac "Ike" McClellan and Peter Reilly.

The funeral ended. Most of the mourners shook Ike's hand, acknowledged Peter and moved on with barely a word. The captains were walking away when one of the last mourners caught up with them.

"Captain McClellan, my name is Martin Guerre, I was your father's lawyer. Do you remember me?"

"No, sir, I'm sorry, I don't."

"Didn't think you would, it's been at least ten years. I'm very sorry about your father, he was a fine man."

"Thank you."

"As you probably know, the reading of the will is on Thursday, but your father left me some very specific instructions." With that, he reached into his pocket and took out a small, sealed plastic box. It was locked and sealed shut. "His instructions were that I personally hand this to you upon his death, regardless of his will or the circumstances of his death."

"The circumstances of his death?"

"I didn't fully understand that either, but those were his words. The most important thing for him was that you were to get this as soon as possible."

Ike looked at the box warily, but then realized that an old man with something in his out-stretched hand was not normal. So he took. "Why didn't he give it to be personally? I saw him less than one month ago."

"I don't know, and even if I did, I would not be at liberty to say. I represent his interests. Your father's instructions were quite specific. Here's the key."

"Thank you."

"You're welcome. See you on Thursday, then?"

"Umm, oh, yes, thank you."

Guerre left with a nod to the two captains, even though he had barely acknowledged Peter standing next to Ike. Peter mirrored the attitude by not moving or speaking the entire time Guerre was in front of them.

"Well?" Ike asked his friend.

"Well, what? Are you going to open it?"

Ike studied the box and key, looked up and noticed the lone remaining mourner. The general was walking towards them. He pocketed his new possessions.

"I think opening it in private is a better idea."

As the superior officer approached, the captains snapped to attention. The general returned their salutes rather casually and offered them his hand. The pair noticed that the general like themselves had gold Christian crosses on their lapels.

"Captains. At ease, please, not here, not today. I'm General

Adams. I had the honor of serving with your father. Captain McClellan, I am very sorry about your father. He was a fine Christian patriot, and he deserved more respect from his country." Looking back at the lonely graveside, he said, "Look at that, when was the last time a four-star general did not receive a live 21-gun salute at his funeral? Never mind the President, did the Secretary of Defense at least write you a condolence letter?"

"Yes, sir."

"A formality, right?"

"Yes, sir."

"The president is a fine man, but even he has had to knuckle under to some of these people. He has to give them something. They revile your father, even in death."

"Frankly, General, I don't really care."

The general smiled a tight, wintry smile. "Nor should you. You come from the finest stock this nation has ever produced. Humble yourself to no one but God."

"I try, sir, that is what Father always said."

"He was always right, always." He couldn't help but glance at the pocket containing the box. "This is a time of mourning and celebration. Your father is at this hour with the Lord. There will be a day soon, I am sure, when I will see you both of you again. God speed."

"Thank you, sir."

Adams turned and left, not glancing back at the grave.

CHAPTER 18

Katsina endured. Once an important city of the Sahel, it was now trying to beat back the Sahara. Like slow motion lava, the sands of the great desert marched south, insatiable, growing stronger with every year of increased heat, stronger winds and less rain. Ripping out the forests to the south and the ravenous Sahara to the north, the fragile strip of green around Katsina finally disappeared.

But the city didn't. It wasn't the vibrant trade hub when Timbuktu was one of the great cities of Africa, but the people dug their roots deep down, past the sand, past the vanished water table, past whatever there was down there and grabbed on. There was nothing there except rock that they could cling to. It anchored them. That was all they asked for.

The population had dropped by half over three decades, so housing was the only thing Katsina had in abundance. Like most cities in similar situations, they abandoned the neighborhoods first, while the population continually contracted until they were in a tight core that was safer and offered a better chance at reaching what services remained.

Nearly all efforts had gone into preservation, not trying to build anything new unless they were more energy efficient housing to keep people from baking to death. The most obvious exception was a distinctly un-African building. Built at the northern edge of the city as if it was daring the Sahara to come and get it.

UN Biogeological Station A4. It was an inter-locking series of buildings: greenhouses, low towers with solar panels, and geodesic domes housing plants for extracting water and sheltering humans. Most sections covered with the best "smart" glass available, solar panels, condensation catchments, and plain old windows. They automatically adjusted during the waxing and waning of the sun so that by high noon, they were nearly opaque. They were strong enough to withstand the sandblasting of the most murderous Sahara storms.

In one greenhouse, Dr. Theo van Bissem was examining small plants just barely taller than shoots. They were in trays at waist levels, but Theo was so tall that he still had to stoop and swat to get a decent look at the little green things. Thin and in his 30s, he was clean shaved with a short haircut. Like most people in this line of work, short hair was less about style and more about reducing the parts of the body that could trap sand. He alternated his attention between the plants themselves and images on his hand-held computer. He wasn't smiling, but then again, he never did. He barely looked up when Robert Nyong entered the chambers. Theo heard the click of the hydraulic door he knew whom he had called so he didn't bother looking up.

"Weather?"

"Not today, not the next three days, maybe next week. The station isn't optimistic," Robert said, checking his computer.

"Can they hold out that long?"

"Some will but the majority are already weak. Theo, I don't think the station will survive." The studious Nigerian, although ten years younger than the boss, used Theo's first name freely. Formality was a waste of time. So long as everyone did their jobs, the boss would have answered to "hey, you."

"Perhaps. I suspect we can probably figure out what killed them. Did they bury the dead?"

"No, burnt, the high-density incinerator, Raj didn't want

contagions to escape if that is really what caused the die out." Theo flashed a sideways eye that meant Robert better follow with the right next sentence. "Samples for the roots, stem and leaves of each preserved and quarantined." Theo looked back down, that was the right sentence. "Of course, the burning is another reason to get out there as soon as possible. The burning chewed through too much power. They're not regenerating fast enough."

Holding up one of the tentative plants, Theo said, "These are the best we've got. I would have preferred them to be older, but they're exhibiting several positive resistance strains. I'm going to go out with the replacement crew. I want to see for myself."

"Right. But isn't that EuroNet crew coming next week?"

"Ten days. I'll be back by then," he said as he gently replaced the plant and ever so gently touched the tiny field of rich soil. "Unless I stay there."

CHAPTER 19

The scene could not have been more formal than if it were an 18th century oil painting. Senator Cranston was sitting at his desk with Sean standing behind him to the boss' right. Standing in front of the desk were three very proper gentlemen one in an army uniform and the other two in perfect suits with Nancy standing back as an assistant should. Army General Claussen and Secret Service Deputy Director Steinberg and Rogers. With all that firepower, Rogers was clearly unnecessary. I wonder if they think I don't know he's here to read my body language, Cranston thought. At the moment, there was no body language to read. They all stood frozen. The general hated it, but he was in the office of a US senator, so he had no choice but to wait.

"Gentlemen, please sit," Cranston said after a too-deliberate pause. "Thank you, Nancy." She left silently. Steinberg looked back slightly to be sure that was what she was doing. The three sat down as formally as possible, stiff, erect, with their feet planted firmly on the floor as if they were ready to bolt at any moment, something they dearly wished they could do.

Finally, Claussen was as comfortable as he was going to be. "Senator are you ready for the briefing?" said the general.

"Yes, General."

"All transmission devices off? Have you scanned the office?"

"Yes, sir. I checked everything ten minutes ago," Sean answered.

"No offense, sir, but this is protocol. Rogers." The agent responded by taking out a scanner and turning it on. A red light went on. "There's a transmitter in here." If the men could have been more uncomfortable, then this did it. "Oh," Rogers added, "It's my phone." He reached into his pocket and the scanner's light switched from red to green. Sean noted he never actually saw a phone.

The general took a thin flat screen monitor out of his metal attaché case, turned it on, and handed it over to Cranston. Doing so required the general to rise slightly from his chair. Cranston had to get up from his chair and reach over the desk to receive it. Neither Rogers on one side nor Sean on the other made any attempt to help, to touch the computer. Cranston examined the image for a few moments, his first look at the Chinese Device. He placed it on his desk and took out a pair of reading glasses. After a few more moments he said, "So this is the Chinese Device? Obviously, I'm not an expert on any of this, so why don't you tell me what I'm looking at." He picked up the monitor and showed it to Sean, who looked at it without touching it.

"First of all, I am compelled to remind you that this briefing is being conducted under section ten of the Official Secrets Act. You may receive this security briefing, but we prohibit you from making copies or notes from this and you may not discuss this with anyone lacking the proper security status. We will take this monitor with us when we leave."

"Understood."

"We now believe the Chinese Device is a prototype for a large machine. To the left of the schematic, you will see it is incomplete. Based on the analysis of the complete parts of the schematic, we believe the missing section is the power source."

"What about the big question I don't have to be an expert to ask: is it a weapon?"

"We place it at a 75% probability that it has a military function."

"Nice parsing of words. I said 'weapon,' you said, 'military function.'"

"It could have a military function but not specifically a weapon."

"You're backtracking from the government's original position."

"The government does not have an official position. I am relaying to you the best information the United States security services can provide. How anyone interprets that information is beyond my responsibilities."

Sean thought this was an appropriate moment to join the conversation. "A popular rumor is that it is a concentrated particle beam, something that could shoot down our missiles and aircraft."

"Rumors, exactly. That is a workable hypothesis, but it is one of many...."

"And this appendage, could that be anything but a cannon?"

"Yes, it could be a telescope, but that's highly unlikely given what else we know about the Device. It could be a sensor."

"Which could have a military, commercial or scientific explanation."

"Exactly."

Cranston took back the reins. "I'm the last person to give the Chinese the benefit of a doubt and I understand you would be derelict in your duties if you did not consider the possibility of a grave threat to the United States, but how much attention did we give to the idea that it has a benign, reasonable purpose?"

"Yes, of course. While the schematic could be open to various interpretations, we also factor in the Chinese behavior which contradicts innocent scientific or commercial activities."

"And when exactly have the Chinese been innocent of anything? They're secretive about everything, commercial secrets can be as vital as military ones."

"I understand you have to make political calculations, but again that's not my brief."

There is an awkward silence. Cranston and Sean continued to look at the schematic. The general continued to say nothing, and Rogers continued to stand.

Finally, Cranston broke the stalemate. "That's it?"

"We have fulfilled our obligations under the law. The monitor, please."

Cranston gave it to Claussen, who turned in off and place it back in his attaché. After exchanging formal handshakes, Sean escorted them to the door. Cranston sat at his desk, contemplating the ceiling.

As the visitors made their way out of the Senate office building, General Claussen turned to the still silent Rogers. "Well? What do you think?"

Rogers thought about what he didn't want to say and then said, "He was more formal than usual, but your rank could account for that. No unusual ticks or movements."

"What did he mean about being the last person to give the Chinese the benefit of the doubt?"

"His mother was on the *Orion*."

"Really? But he has a Chinese assistant and Chinese running mate."

"Chinese-*American*," Rogers corrected in the most subservient manner possible, "He focuses intently on the individual. It's an important element in his profile."

Meanwhile, in Cranston's office, the senator was sitting while

Sean turned on the computers. He then pushed away from the desk, giving Sean access to the desk drawers. Sean opened the center draw and took out a nearly transparent tablet.

"Did it work?"

Smiling, he looked up to his boss. "Yes, sir." He handed the tablet to Cranston and went over to a side door. Opening it, he escorted Lilly and Worth into the room. Worth was in his forties, walking like Claussen but wearing civilian clothes. As the saying went, "Once a Marine..."

Cranston rose. "Lilly, thank you. Everyone, have a seat." They did as Sean projected the contents of the tablet onto the larger screen. It was the schematic for the Chinese Device.

"How was the briefing?" Lilly asked.

"In a word, lies," Sean responded.

It was Worth's turn. "What odds do they give that it's a weapon?"

"'75% probability that it has a military function.'"

"Their words?"

"Yep."

Lilly and Worth, her 360, studied the image intently for several minutes. Cranston and Sean could barely restrain their impatience.

"Why didn't their scan pick it up the copying?" Lilly asked Sean.

"Extremely low-level frequency. Less than a watch gives off. The download only works a short distance and must do it slowly. That's why the monitor had to stay on the desk as long as possible. Also, very fortunate we have a wood desk. If we had switched it, Rogers would have noticed."

"Do you believe the scale is accurate?" Lilly asked.

"Yes. Which means what we are looking at is about 70 meters long."

"On what do they base the premise that the missing section represents one third of the size?"

"We don't know."

"So, they could be guessing," said Worth.

"Or throwing us a curve ball. But that one-third number is out there."

The technical parsing was important, Cranston knew, but he needed the big picture, so he finally spoke. "How important is that?"

"There is no apparent power source. So, the assumption is that the missing piece is the power source. If only one third is missing meaning 30 meters, or so then that's enough for a tradition power source plus some auxiliary machinery. If there is more missing..."

"... Say, that what we are seeing is really only half of the Device..." Worth added.

"... Then it could be an extremely large power source, or a traditional power source plus one or more other major features."

"Meaning we are flaying, around even more than we know," Sean said.

"Exactly."

"Alright, enough," said the boss, "Let's focus on what we can see. So that, what? Appendage? A cannon?"

Worth answered. "Without knowing the thickness of the tube, it's hard to tell. If it's a cannon, it would have to be thick enough to withstand the pressure and heat of the projectile."

"A particle beam?" Sean suggested.

"Possibly, then thickness would be less of a concern."

Lilly interrupted the dialogue with a simple firmness that disguised the impact of what she was saying. "That appendage is not a cannon nor beam. It's not designed to be a weapon."

Everyone looked at her, startled and impressed. Cranston's low opinion of her did not extend to the belief that she babbled nonsense. "That's the first unequivocal sentence I've heard all day. Why do you say that?"

Pointing to a blockish section near the base, she asked Worth, "Doesn't it make sense that this is a variant converter?"

"Yes."

"Converters are a universal size. So, extrapolate the size of the device from the converter. The cylinder is 40 meters long and one meter in diameter."

"No projectile of any military value is going to be that wide."

"And it's too wide for a particle beam."

"The Pentagon has to know that," Sean interjected.

Cranston was displaying the twitch the others had learned to avoid. "Of course, they know. Ailes is feeding us a steaming pile of it. Hayden bases his campaign on the best intelligence, and we get this dog-and-pony show. What's the bottom line?"

Worth was confident. "70 percent probability that it's not a weapon."

Lilly added, "70 percent probability that it's not a weapon."

"Bastards," the presidential candidate said.

"We have to be careful here," said Sean, "We're not supposed to analyze the schematic so thoroughly."

"So, we have to base our strategy on a truth we're not supposed to know."

"And that we know is treason," said his aide as he deleted the schematic from the screen.

CHAPTER 20

arbury Point was dead during the day, but alive at night with the dying. The point was a part of Washington's maritime and industrial history, the jut of land on the east bank of the Potomac, downriver from the District. For decades, it had been an isolated storage site for the oils, metals, and chemicals that drove industrialization but poisoned everything around them. Finally abandoned, it just sat there, weighed down by its faded past and the toxic and heavy metals that had settled into the soil. First Washington real estate sky-rocketed, then it started disappearing, so anything that was more or less dry was desirable. That included the toxic Marbury Point. First it was the artsy types, no children and no food but magically the lead and mercury in the water and soil evaporated then they built housing. That boom lasted only a few years before the tidal surges started pounding the buildings and storage tanks. By 2052, the new rot had set in. The kids who didn't care took over the hulks of the massive tanks for parties and concerts. Ear-splitting tonal music, drugs, some acts that looked like sex, and the occasional self-flagellation and bloodletting kept them fueled until the daylight bored them to bed.

Washington was proof that climate change has a sense of humor. Rising sea levels reclaimed the land the city had taken away. In the 1880s, massive reclamation projects took from the river what became the western end of the Mall, the Tidal Basin the name should have been a warning and the East and West Potomac Parks. Now all of that except the Mall was once again part of the riverbed. Further away from monumental Washington, the swamp was the least of the worries. The land was too low and there was too much of it to protect. Floodgates where the Potomac met the Chesapeake Bay slowed the water down, but it was not enough. The airport named after a president who failed had to be moved inland. The Marines had to retreat from Quantico. The fancy marinas drowned.

The denizens of the Point were young enough to know only this world, but old enough to know what their world could have been. The younger generation always rebels, usually with reason, against the elder generation, but no generation had more obvious reasons to heap contempt upon their elders.

Statisticians sliced and diced the generations. The Greatest Generation that fought through the Great Depression of the 20th century and World War II was followed by the Baby Boomers that great demographic bulge that defined the rest of the 20th century and a huge chunk of the 21st. They just would not let go. Then the names got boring: Generation X, Generation Y, as if they could not bother to come up with complete words. But then someone rebranded Gen Y the Millennials, for those born in the last two decades of the old millennium. As kids they could see what was happening, but there was nothing they could do about it. It was like watching a rockslide and wondering, in desperation, if they could stand together and hold back the exact right rock to stop it.

The next generation was the one that really got screwed. They grew as sea levels and global temperatures rose. Born after 1997, it was hard to find an appropriate name. After Generations X and Y, Z was logical, except there was an uncomfortable finality to that. But Z stuck, helped by the nickname "Zoomers." The next generation could have been called the shit-out-of-luck generation. Alpha and Omega fought it out.

Some took a page from F. Scott Fitzgerald: Generation Lost. The name matched the new realities: birth rates were as low as they had been at the worst of the Depression and World War II; prenatal and infant mortality rose at a heart-breaking rate as the most vulnerable could not adapt to new threats of diseases; insects and the lack of food and water where they had once been sufficient. In a decade, international efforts that succeeded at the beginning of the century in reducing infant mortality and poverty and improving access to medical care and clean water disappeared with the ice caps, shriveled like the crops when the monsoon failed to arrive. The Dead Babies Generation was too morbid even for those days, so the Lost Generation won the day.

Over the decades, the slogans of the young changed, like the seven stages of grief, except they were nowhere close to acceptance. It appeared it took everything to get to anger and bargaining, so depression was as far as anyone could get. "Working through" was a joke.

First it was the armor of irony:

YOU DROWNED SANTA CLAUS
DID YOU ENJOY YOUR HUMMERS?
I MISS FISH

Then the anger and the threats:

WATER IS NOT FOR PROFIT
WHEN DID YOU KNOW MONEY WASN'T ENOUGH?
DO YOU THINK MARS WILL SAVE YOU?
YOU DRANK OUR FUTURE - WAIT UNTIL YOU ARE OLD
YOU WILL NEVER EAT STEAK AGAIN

As the decades progressed, revenge took over:

NO FOOD NO MERCY
THE MOON IS NOT FAR ENOUGH
BEG AND WE MAY NOT KILL YOU
BEG AND WE MAY NOT EAT YOU

The most popular was the simplest. Two words. They were everywhere, physical and virtual graffiti, songs and movies, hacks on phones and computers, chants at public events, clothing, even on their bodies. It was a popular tattoo. Some even had it inked – scarred – into their foreheads so anyone looking at them would see it. Turning away was impossible:

YOU KNEW

This world was awash in drugs. So many anxious people needed so many drugs. The drugs from nature, marijuana, and cocaine lost their influence as the vanishing arable land got used for food, no matter how inefficient. Even tobacco had to surrender to the need for soybeans and corn. Only heroin from the poppies of central Asia continued production. Its only agricultural competition was cotton, and that needed more water than existed. Addiction, like nature, abhors a vacuum, so a boom industry grew in creating drugs in the lab. And the subsequent business of making as many of them legal as possible. There were designer drugs for the elites and the absolute scraps for the poor that completely rotted one vital organ or more. Reversing the trend of the 20th century, generations in the 21st saw a steady decline in median age. In the countries most devastated by climate change, the main causes of death remained hunger, disease and war. In the richer countries still somewhat protected from the worst, generational depression, low birth rates, increased birth defects and suicide took a steady toll.

That night at Point was especially riotous. A new batch of a favorite drug, *Troynoy Iks*, Triple X in Russian, or *Iks* had arrived. The rumor was that it was a modified formula. Demand was high and no one knew if it was really Russian, but the name had just the right shading of mystery and misery to incite the target audience. There was the usual amount of vomiting and concussions. But then a 23-year-old had a stroke. And then another.

The police arrived and unlike the old days of speakeasies when patrons would flee, this crowd was too far gone or bored to run. Rounding them up was like collecting dead kittens. One veteran collared a clearly underage girl who was snarling at her fingernails. As usual, she had lost her identity card.

"Name," the cop started the routine.

"Slasher."

"Real name."

"Vik."

"*Last* name."

"Cranston."

CHAPTER 21

An angel donor was financing Mr. Lopez's work. If it were up to the university, his research would have shut down years ago. While the research was useful, Lopez was not. Corporations made enormous endowments to ensure research stuck to the approved avenues of chemical and genetically modified solutions. Only a few universities mostly in California and Georgia had agricultural departments dedicated to finding organic solutions to the impact of climate change on crops. In addition, while most non-chemical research centered on breeding new varieties, Mr. Lopez was moving the opposite direction. He wasn't the only one working on reverse genetics, trying to breed out centuries of "impurities" and resurrect the original corn, but he was the most vocal about it. At the University of New Mexico, Lopez was alone. He was not the most popular member of the faculty.

Whenever someone knocked on his door, it was always a student. Eager, inquisitive, they had to know the answer. So, when the opened door revealed the Dean, Mr. Lopez was thoroughly surprised.

"Carlos, doing well?" the Dean asked.

The Dean was never casual, so Mr. Lopez' answer wasn't either. "Yes, why?"

"We've known each other for a long time, so I feel I really should warn you about things that are being said about you."

"'Being said.' How conveniently passive. What is 'being said'? And I suppose I shouldn't ask by whom?"

"You're using your position in this university to criticize the president's immigration policies."

"No, I am using my position in this university to teach about corn."

"You didn't say that the president would forbid the eating of Mexican corn? We're supposed to pretend 'corn' doesn't mean… something else?"

"That doesn't sound like a joke to you?"

"And what about you talking about Aztlan? Was that a joke, too?"

"Aztlan? I never said Aztlan."

"If not, what did you say?"

"Nothing like that. Oh wait, I mentioned Mesoamerica that's hardly the same thing. Mesoamerica is an archeological term. You see what is happening here, right? Everyone knows that 'Aztlan' is code for a greater Mexico taking back Texas and the Southwest. I never used the word, I don't use the word, I don't believe it. Someone is stirring the pot."

"Be that as it may. Remember, there's an election coming up and everyone knows who your daughter works for. Stick to corn and forget about the jokes."

CHAPTER 22

The Galma satellite station, deep in the desert of Niger, looked much like its parent station in Katsina, only smaller. No one had ever taken a poll. This was likely to be the most isolated, god-forsaken, brutalized building on the planet. Theo's small, short-range airship, a sand-hugger hovered over the landing port as the roof slid away, closing immediately when Theo was safely inside. The less sand that got in, the better.

Theo stepped out, followed by two assistants carrying two trays of shoots. The agent-in-charge of Galma, Raj Gupta, was waiting for them on the other side of the airlock.

Without hesitation, Theo reached out with his left hand to shake hands with Raj. Theo had known Raj for several years he easily overcame the impulse to shake with his right. Raj never shook with his right hand he didn't have one. He was born with his right arm stopping just at the elbow.

"I'm glad you finally made it," Raj said. The "finally" would have bothered Theo if he cared what anyone thought of him.

"Anything left?"

"Next to nothing. Do you think these will work better?"

"Perhaps. If it's something in the soil, perhaps. They've proven to be the most resistant strain. But if it's a microbe, not likely. Each try is marked for its particular resistance. If it's something in the soil, we should be able to pinpoint it according to the survivors. If it's a microbe, then these aren't going to make it either. Any progress on that?"

"No evidence of a microbe, at least a new microbe. The

good news is that we may have simply underestimated the acidity of the soil. If we're right, these saplings will do better once we finish treating the soil."

Theo, Raj, and the assistants arrived in the nursery. Raj motioned to a side table as the spot to place the saplings, while Theo turned immediately to the plants embedded in the nursery. With a look of disgust, Theo dropped to his stomach and examined the leaves and stem, even the soil, as if his fingers could detect something the microscopic tests missed. The plants were in terrible shape. Half a meter tall which was excellent for their age but the leaves were twisted, drained of all color.

"Do you really believe all this can be attributed to acidity?"

"It's a theory. Do you have any new ideas?"

"Did you test for radiation?"

"Radiation? There's some low-level radiation from the naturally occurring minerals, but nothing we haven't accounted for."

"I don't mean natural radiation, man-made radiation. In your report, you indicated some saplings looked burnt. That's this batch?"

"Yes."

"Did this soil come from the east of Galma?"

"Yes, how did you know?"

"An educated guess. Give me a sample of one of the burnt saplings so I can run my own tests."

Raj had learned not to be offended. "I don't know what you're driving at. There were never any nuclear power plants here. Where would the radiation come from?"

"Stupid humans."

CHAPTER 23

Dr. Asanti stared into the microscope. He always moved slowly. His staff never knew if it was simply his nature or if the permanent exhaustion made him that way.

To an untrained eye, what he was looking at was quite beautiful. A gentle swarm of cute little bumpy things sliding against each other, always moving, always bumping, but never hurting each other. A few of the bumpy things looked like deflating balloons, other looked like squished stars. The atomic microscope gave them bright colors red, gold, and pink. A microscopic playground. Dr. Asanti's eye was not untrained.

"From where?"

"A clinic in Mawere.

"Symptoms include rash, headache, swelling joints and what else?" He knew where this was going.

"Bloodshot eyes, blood in the urine, bleeding gums."

"In other words, blood."

"Yes, sir." The nurse knew the answer already. "Is it mutating?"

"Yes," he sighed.

CHAPTER 24

Despite decades of efforts to revive the orangutan population in the wild, the efforts of scientists and conservationists, including Ruth, to tip the ratio of orangutans born in captive and in the wild in favor of the wild continually failed. Even when carefully monitored families like Rabu's were counted as "in the wild" there were still three captive births to every wild birth. Even under the best of circumstances, it would have been a slow process. Orangutans only gave birth every six to nine years, almost always a single baby, and offspring stayed with the mother for up to four years. They didn't breed like rabbits. The orangutan survival networks tried to mate a captive with a wild. Ideally the female would be the wild partner, but statistics and individual apes' preferences made this mostly impossible. Apes aren't stupid, they mated with whom they wanted without basing it on a computer model. So Rabu's parents were both born in captivity and gradually reintroduced into the wild, with mixed results. Orangutans were the only fully arboreal ape, living its entire life in the tree-tops, rarely dropping to the ground. They roamed widely through the jungle, nesting every night in a different tree, giving birth and nursing in the trees. The arboreal life was so total that it was possible for a five-year-old to have never touched the ground.

That was no longer the norm. Captive apes couldn't roam the trees, so every generation lost a bit of the natural impulse. They still nested in trees or artificial perches, but reality forced them to live on the ground. This was one of the reasons for trying to mate wilds and captives to get the captives to relearn the arboreal life. The captives had been coming out of the trees since the wide-ranging areas were not possible, the hope was the wild would teach the captive to go back to the trees, especially the females since giving birth and nurturing the young in the tree-tops was the natural order. Neither of Rabu's parents had experience in the trees. They were re-learning, an occasional wild orangutan would pass through their territory, they would follow suit, but would return to their nest on the ground. The Reserve tried to encourage them but there were no way humans could move across the tree-tops as easily as an orangutan so they couldn't demonstrate what they meant.

The other nature instinct that was lost was that the male usually left the female shortly after the birth of their baby. But Kai, Rabu's father, wasn't doing that. On the one hand, Ruth felt relieved because she liked to see the family together, but on the other, her whole purpose in life was to create space for the apes to return to their natural state. The scientist had to keep fighting the romantic.

One future event Ruth was most anxious about was when Rabu would leave his mother. In the wild, that usually happened around age five or six. Without other orangutans as role models and this being Nurul's first baby, would instinct triumph?

Over the decades, starting with Goodall, primatologists worked to develop a common language with other primates. Chimps, bonobos and gorillas were receptive. Baboons not so much. In general, monkeys never sat still long enough for a conversation. Fortunately, orangutans were more like the chimps. Since orangutans were exclusive to Borneo, the research and conversation work was intense. One of the largest primate centers in the world was at Tanjung Puting on the southern end of Borneo with 22 satellite stations around the island. Ruth's station was small she was the only scientist, she had one trainee, Jamal and his security team, and domestic help. Ten people in all. Like all the satellite stations, she was responsible for a small area of the rain forest and any orangutans living there or passing through. There were unobtrusive cameras and sensors implanted at key locations.

Ruth was now the center of quiet celebration with the birth of Rabu. Live births had been increasing as the apes learned to adapt and preservation efforts had begun to stop the slide. But the celebration was very quiet at headquarters. The government and the UN knew there had been a birth but not exactly where. Announcing the birth of an orangutan would have been like flying a huge flag saying, "Come steal me." Thus, most of the world did not know the orangutan population had increased by one.

Besides the obvious reason for excitement, Ruth could barely contain her eagerness to begin to teach Rabu language. She had never done it before in the wild. Through generations of trial-and-error, scientists had developed a solid vocabulary and training method. Generally, apes had a sign vocabulary of nearly 100 words, mostly practical needs like "food" and "play." It was more advanced for the African apes.

What progress had been made in Borneo had mostly been wiped out with the apes themselves in the '30s. There were tantalizing hints that language skills were being passed from parent to child without any human intervention. That progress was lost, and efforts had to begin from scratch in the '40s. The average lifespan of an orangutan was 45 years and females did not give birth until 17 therefore it would take at least 50 years to study the impact over three generations.

Ruth had practiced in controlled settings, focusing on words like "hungry," "thirsty," "water," "food," "sleep," and her favorite: "hug." Babies hug. Period. If the species has arms, the babies hug. Chimps famously kissed. As much as she loved her neighbors, Ruth just could not wrap her brain around kissing an orangutan. So lots of hugs. Not too much effort was put into adjectives, only the essential ones: "happy," "sad," "good," "bad," "clean," "dirty." Ruth had inherited a rich history with the orangutans. Several generations of great apes had learned the sign language. Ruth was very jealous of the team who first realized the apes were passing the language on to the next generation.

Last year, on her first visit to the family, Ruth brought gifts. This was what the orangutans expected. "Gift" and "food" were comfortable words with a stranger. Kai signed to Ruth: "Where Karen?" Ruth gasped and teared up. Damn, she thought, I should have anticipated that. The truth was in words the team chose not to teach the orangutans. Finally, Ruth said and signed, "Home." Kai signed, "Hug."

Today was Ruth's first visit to the family since Rabu's birth. Approaching the apes especially new parents required a fine line between stealth and familiarity. Too quiet and they might consider it an ambush, too loud and they might run away before realizing who was approaching. One practice was to carry a small can of pebbles. They would hear the noise but since it wasn't a natural sound, they didn't immediately assume danger. Ruth thought to try whistling. It seemed to work not so certain that she would write it up in a journal but enough for her to feel she was truly communicating. She walked through the underbrush whistling Mozart (she had no idea if they cared about the distinctions within music but it was fun to experiment) and carrying a small bag of gifts meaning food. It was important that the scientists not coddle the apes, but this was a special occasion. Ruth knew exactly where the family was, so she kept an eye out for movement as she approached. Kai came out of the brush and growled a bit before seeing that it was Ruth. He let her pass and approach the nest. Rabu was still a weak little bag of hair in his mother's arms but was beginning to turn his head and grasp. Ruth sat down in front of the family and gave the parents the fruit.

Ruth spoke in her mixture of words and signs. She spoke in full sentences although everyone assumed the apes only processed the keywords.

"May I hug the baby?"

"hug – baby"

Ruth almost wept for joy when Nurul handed over her precious little one.

"Congratulations. We are all very happy for you. I have a gift for your baby."

"Happy – you – gift – baby."

She took out a small tracking bracelet similar to the ones the parents had been wearing for years showed it to Nurul and Kai and attached it to Rabu's ankle.

"This way I can always help you if you need me."

"I – help – need – me."

Rabu picked at the bracelet, tapped it, rubbed it, and then tried to eat it.

CHAPTER 25

From the street, you could not see much beyond the seawalls. But from the restaurant atop the World Trade Center, ghosts of the past were visible in every direction. The seawall had been built on the west side of West Street, meaning all the construction of the late 1990s to 2010s were now on the wrong side of history. Since it wasn't a sudden loss, the high-rises for the most part had been carefully dismantled so that the materials could be used elsewhere. Massive pumps under the World Trade Center and other key downtown locations had been built to protect the heart of the neighborhood from the ever-increasing tidal surges and hurricane-inspired flooding. New Yorkers could be called and were called a lot of things, but "foolish" was never one of them.

There was still the human insistence on disconnection that allowed New York to develop the waterfront while figuring out how to deal with losing it. Earlier than most US cities, New York began preparing early, and it showed. The combination of foresight, billions of dollars and a granite bedrock helped Manhattan push back against the first stages of sea level rise as opposed to the Miami real estate crash which was not only a literal crash but also both sudden and foreseen. The seawalls extended to 14th Street, which was enough for these decades while the next generation of walls were planned.

From the restaurant, the changes to Brooklyn were also apparent. The heights of Brooklyn Heights had protected that neighborhood, but the historic waterfront the land of Fulton and Whitman was abandoned. The sandy south of

Coney Island, Brighton Beach and Sea Gate were early losses. Fantastic amounts of money had poured into developments in Red Hook and Dumbo, so seawalls were built to offer some protection. But the city was resolved to the fact that in 30-40 years, these walls would not be enough, and Brooklyn would have to retreat further, abandoning Red Hook and Dumbo as she had done with Coney Island and Brighton Beach.

Walls would protect Liberty Island and Ellis Island at all costs. But Governors' Island has essentially been abandoned to the rising sea level. The first seawalls had already been breached, so the city decided it was better to use its resources to protect the boroughs and left the island to the mercies of nature. Every year, more of the island was pummeled by storms while the lack of human activity meant the buildings continued to disappear under the wild growth. One consolation was that migrating, and sea birds found a new safe roost.

The view from the restaurant was also created by some people eating there. Either by creating the protections or creating the need for the protection, there was hardly a more elite gathering in the city. It was the kind of place where Ailes' chief of staff could eat without turning any heads.

He sliced into his medium rare steak. His companion had ordered the lamb. The Chief poured more wine into his companion's glass. They had known each other for decades, nearly always in opposition. But this was a 30-year-old bottle of French wine.

"It's going to be an interesting election we all know that. Frankly, Hayden isn't our strongest candidate, but we haven't had a military man for a while good visuals. Election Day shouldn't be too much drama, but the next month could be interesting."

"How so?" asked the companion George Cranston Sr.

"You've heard rumors about something new, a wild card."

"Rumors, yes."

"And only rumors, of course. The senator wouldn't violate the Official Secrets Act by telling even his father something from the Daily Security Briefing."

"Of course not, it's only rumors."

"Well, it's not. The Chinese are building something massive in Zhidoi. We're calling it the Chinese Device. I think it's safe to say that it'll be more than rumors in time for the election. It will be an election issue. And with you guys having a running mate of McDowell's... ethnicity can't help you."

"Really? I would have thought the opposite, having a vice president familiar with the Chinese would work to our advantage."

"Familiar is not the word that will be used. Look, let's cut to the chase. One old war horse to another. Make it easy on yourselves, go through the motions, accept defeat gracefully. We're building back up nicely the pie is growing. Soon there will be bigger pieces for everyone. And I mean everyone. Only the Chinese are even trying to rebuild their military to any serious extent. Space and the moon are off limits, no one will ever match our navy. Neither one of us are stupid enough to challenge the other on land. That leaves missiles and the air force."

"Which is where the Chinese Device comes in?"

"That's my hunch. Anti-missile, some sort of disruptor against aircraft or even spacecraft on re-entry. The American people are going to want a President who can address those new threats. That's our guy."

"So we roll over and play dead? You expect that of me and my boy?"

"Not play dead, play ball. We'll take good care of George, and McDowell too if you wish."

"Doesn't sound very democratic."

"Democracy evolves. Read the Constitution. You must have noticed that by now," the Chief said as he stabbed his last bite of steak.

CHAPTER 26

The Prairie Grass Evangelical Church was a standout among the mega-churches of America. First, it really was in the prairie. They built most such churches in car-friendly suburbs, but decades earlier, the elders of this church moved back to God's creation in the Great Plains. It was low to the ground, hugging the prairie, the walls and roof the colors of the soil and grass. "The feet of the Lord touched the earth, so should ours," the elders of the church told the architect. Only the steeple soared above the grasses. Except for the cross, solar cells coated the steeple. There was little wood, of course, but the steel and polymers were coated to create the illusion of wood. It was the kind of church Frank Lloyd Wright would have built if he had been religious.

They had also placed most of the parking underground so that the prairie not pavement would surround the church. They paid for a spur from the monorail, laid a photovacular roadbed, and in the long tradition of churches, organized a fleet of buses to bring the poor and elderly congregants to the church. They sprayed brown water over the grounds on Saturday night so the grasses would look as fresh as possible. A windmill at the far end of the grounds pumped water and supplemented the solar panels. The Prairie Grass Evangelical Church was completely self-sufficient.

Freed of his cubicle, Mr. Anderson smiled and sang along loudly with his off-key pitch, taking comfort from that fact that Mrs. Anderson's beautiful voice would balance the scales. Pastor Tshua "Harry" Hang led the congregation in the hymn

"His Eye is on the Sparrow." The pastor was a third-generation Hmong; the Lutherans resettled his grandparents after they escaped from Laos. Tshua meant "to have compassion" in his ancestral language. He was very proud of that but decided years ago that Harry was easier for public consumption.

The hymn ended.

"Pray for our brothers and sisters
In distant lands, selflessly working/
They are the children of the Beatitudes!
Blessed are Peacemakers!"
The congregation made a joyful noise. "Praise the Lord!"
"Blessed are the meek!"
"Praise the Lord!"
"They are seeding the earth with God's bounty! They are curing the sick and comforting the dying!"
"Praise the Lord!"
"I tell you the Truth, whatever you do for one of the least of these brothers of mine, you do for Me."
"Praise the Lord!"
"Amen!"
"Walk with the Lord and glory in His goodness and protect His creation!"
"Amen!"
"Amen!"
The service ended, and most of the congregants filed out. Some remained to continue praying, a few wept silently. Mr. and Mrs. Anderson separately slightly from the flow and soon found themselves in private conversations.

"Everything going well?" Mr. Wentzler asked Mr. Anderson.

"I suppose. Had a really annoying case the other day, a mechanic wanting to do farm work. When I told him that would not happen, he switched to wind farm maintenance. I cut him off entirely."

"Was it a close call?"

"Not at all, wholly unqualified and was most likely hiding exposure to Texas Cholera." Mr. Wentzler recoiled a bit. Mr. Anderson made a mental note not to share so much.

"So if you were justified, what's the problem?"

"I told him that waiting list for the wind farms was full…"

"That's true."

"I know. But why can't we build more wind farms? There's room. The buffalo migration isn't affected. I don't know about bird migration, but a lot of those species are already gone. So why not?"

Mr. Wentzler made the sideways glance of someone practiced at speaking his mind, even at church. "Not under this administration. More wind farms, more energy, more energy, fewer strategically timed brownouts. Election's coming, have to keep people off balance."

"'Promise of a better tomorrow' cutting close to the political muscle. They all promise a better tomorrow, after wrecking yesterday."

"But only one can deliver it."

Mrs. Anderson noticed an elderly woman standing just to the side. Even here, the elderly tried not to be too obvious. She approached the younger woman cautiously. "Excuse me, is it correct that you raise mousers and rent them out?"

"Yes, ma'am. I've trained three of them. I hire them out by the night."

"Do you accept payment by barter?"

"I prefer it. What's your offer?"

"I'm very good in the kitchen, especially baking."

"Bake? You bake pies?"

"Oh yes. Apple, cherry, peach when I can. Rhubarb."

"An apple pie for Thanksgiving and one for Christmas. And two cherry pies when you can next year. How's that?"

"Fine. Thank you. It'll take a bit to get enough apples, but I'm sure I can do it in time. How soon can you come?"

"Tonight, if you wish. Do you know how many mice you're talking about?"

"At least two. Which of course means there could be a nest."

"If the nest is nearby, Arnold will find it."

"Is one night enough?"

"Usually, never more than two."

"Then, yes, please. Come tonight."

"I would discourage you from using the kitchen tonight. You have no pets or other animals? No small children?"

"No. Is that important?"

"Vital."

CHAPTER 27

The Cranston brain trust was meeting in the townhouse: the candidate, George Sr., Maggie, Sean, Mei and Nancy. The father had center stage. "We start from the assumption that Ailes doesn't really expect us to roll over," completing his briefing about the lunch in New York. "So, they are afraid of something, something we don't know about but could threaten them. Political? Do we have the votes to win? Foreign? He's probably right that the Chinese Device plays into Hayden's hands, and we can be sure knowledge about the device will turn up at a convenient moment. What have we got that we don't know we have?"

The candidate replied. "One possibility is that a second tipping point is just beginning to sink in with the public. Hayden will insist that the Doctrinists are best positioned to keep America strong. We can keep linking the 'tipping point' and the 'Doctrinists' but that's not an association they'll like, given their performance with the first tipping point. There may be something bad on the horizon we don't know about."

"That's not enough," Maggie said, "Even without a second tipping point, the Doctrinists lose on the environmental front, but they always lose on the environmental front and still win. Besides, what kind of environmental catastrophe could they possibly know about that no one else knows. There's got to be more."

Sean played to his strength. "Maybe they're afraid of SID. It's a force they can't control. Despite their rhetoric, they're likely convinced we're not behind SID. So, we're not SID and they're not SID. Who is SID? They could be afraid that SID will disrupt the election."

"Or prevent Ailes from disrupting the election. It's the uncertainly that's driving them nuts," said Maggie, somewhat relishing the thought.

"Shouldn't SID be driving us nuts?" asked the senator, "What if SID is an elaborate feign by the Doctrinists, that they really can control SID when it counts the most on Election Day."

"They don't need SID to screw around with the election," Mei said, "They have the federal government for that. We know our votes are going to disappear, we're going to counter it as best we can, but we're no match for them. It's a basic consideration of our strategy."

"Ok, focus. First, politics. Can we win a fair fight..." Cutting off the instinctive protests, he added, "I know it's not a fair fight, but let's look at all the variables. Maggie."

Maggie clicked on her computer. There was a large screen at one end of the room, and it suddenly brought up a map of the United States. A visitor from the 20th century would have recognized it: the same 50 states, the same internal borders. However, the map showed changes in the coastline: Cape Cod, May and Hatteras, gone. As were the Florida Keys, the Outer Banks, Mississippi Delta, and much of the Texas Gulf Coast. The southern California coastline retreated. San Francisco Bay and Puget Sound appear much larger and the smaller islands of Alaska and Hawaii, also gone.

Maggie clicked again, and the map became an electoral map, showing all the congressional districts. "Okay, 420 congressional districts; 420 electoral votes; 212 needed to win. We've got most of the coastal vote, but Ailes is right, Gulf coast votes don't count for much. A lot of them don't vote, and some have been in camps for almost 20 years now. Every storm or outbreak shifts the population more, so it's easier to stop people trying to vote. Those who do vote can have their votes disappear. It's a phantom victory with a phantom constituency. Still, what votes there are, are ours."

She shifted the focus of the map. "With those congressional districts all along the Pacific coast, all of Hawaii and most of Alaska, the Northeast down to North Carolina, nearly all of Florida and the Gulf Coast turn green. That should be 92 districts, but realistically call it 80. Working inland, we can hold many of the interior districts of California, Oregon and Washington, some of the interior of Texas and Louisiana districts." She turned these districts green. "New Jersey and Delaware such as they are ours." More green. "In New England, New York, Pennsylvania and Maryland, we lose ground the further inland we go. The Mountain, Plains and Great Lake states are mostly the Doctrinists." Now some districts are purple. "They've been pumping up energy and agricultural programs across the region..."

"Programs we started..." George Sr. said.

"Which is no longer a part of the official history," his son added.

Maggie continued. "The bright spots are some urban and high-tech districts that will probably go for us. The Doctrinists have poured a lot of money into these towns but say what you will about Lilly she is helping us in these districts. They don't care about race and they like the way Lilly talks about science as salvation." A few green islands appear within the purple sea large cities and towns famous for their universities including Chicago, Omaha, Huntsville, Raleigh, Denver and Minneapolis/St. Paul. "We've been concentrating on these from the start. Highly educated, motivated voters.

People who won't let their votes disappear. We pull them into our column, expand outward into their satellite towns, hold our own on the Atlantic and Pacific coasts, and we're within reach. If, *if*, we can get a decent turnout on the Gulf and the poorest districts *and* have those votes counted, I put us at 204 votes. We expand to just a few satellite districts and we win. But we know the Doctrinists can easily manipulate the Gulf vote and a few isolated interior districts, and we fall short by as much as 20 votes."

Everyone silently made their own calculations. George Sr. was the first to speak. "Chicago goes from four to six votes. Omaha goes from one to two. Chapel Hill goes from one to two. Minneapolis goes from three to four. Huntsville goes from one to two. Denver goes from three to four. We win a fair election."

"Irrelevant," Mei countered, "How do we win a crooked election?"

CHAPTER 28

Mrs. Anderson arrived at the house just after sunset, holding an animal carrier and a small backpack. It was a simple suburban home, with a prairie grass lawn and a few trees. There was also a large decaying stump of some grand tree, maybe a cottonwood that had not survived. It must have provided magnificent shade and comfort when Mrs. Ullman was young.

The house was modest and clean. A few photos and knick-knacks from a vanished life sat on shelves and covered the walls. Mrs. Anderson opened the carrying case, and the cat sauntered out on giant cat paws, like a soldier anticipating an ambush and knowing he would win. Mrs. Ullman stood by in awe. She had heard of such creatures but had never seen one. It was a feline of pure hunter descent, the claws, eyes and mouth of a predator. What was so remarkable was that its head was larger, and legs were longer while the body was thick and strong. As if they had crossed a cheetah with a bobcat. It was power and speed in a single animal. Mrs. Anderson obviously knew what she was doing.

"Arnold, stay."

The cat obeyed. A cat, obeyed?

Arnold's claws extended, his head slowly turned side to side, a menacing hiss poured from his clenched mouth. She snapped her fingers. "Arnold, come." The beast followed as the women ambled through the house, stopping in the kitchen. Arnold was unimpressed until he got to a door near the back of the kitchen. Arnold's claws fully extended now, and his back hunched.

"What's this? The basement door?"

"Yes."

She opened it and Arnold immediately disappeared down the stairs.

"We start, here. Prop this door open but remember to keep all other doors and windows closed. We trained Arnold not to leave a house, but it's always possible he'll forget his training if he's in pursuit. If it doesn't look like he finished the job tomorrow, then we'll try a second night and let him out in the yard. That can be risky, but it shouldn't be necessary."

"Is it likely to be... messy?"

"Sometimes, depends on the size and number of the mice he catches. Not to be indelicate, but usually he swallows them whole. If there are too many or are too big, he may leave... remnants. I'll clean them up, that's part of the service."

"Thank you." They returned to the living room and sat quietly for a few moments. "If you don't mind me asking, how did you get involved in this work?"

"I grew up on a farm, had cats and dogs. During the '30s we all had to do whatever it took to survive I took to breeding mousers easily. I always liked cats. One day we traded for a mouser. I bred it with a big, mean stray we had caught. Arnold's great grandparents were the result. The need for mousers isn't as great as it used to be, praise God, but I still keep busy."

Mrs. Anderson left. Mrs. Ullman went to her room with a pot of tea and some sandwiches. She told herself she would be very comfortable this night.

She stayed in her room all night. She couldn't help herself and listened. She heard nothing. "Of course, I can't hear. It's a cat. That's the point." And then she heard the shrieks. The first shriek of the hunter, a very un-cat-like guttural explosion, more like a motorboat revving up. The second shriek was death. She got up, checked to be sure she locked her door, took a sleeping pill and went to bed.

CHAPTER 29

The two women of different generations, the mentor and the student, were walking along Central Park West. They appeared to be strolling, but there was a specific destination. The Museum of Natural History in New York was Lilly's home. Ever since she was old enough to read, she dashed to the stone bench engraved with "SCIENTIST." It was where they now sat. Looking across Central Park West towards the park, she always meditated on how much had changed. Especially the trees.

When she was young, the elms, maples, tulip trees, ash and linden (no monoculture nonsense here) looked like the tallest trees in the world to her. As she aged and New York got hotter, introducing fungi and insects northern hardwoods should never have to face.

Every year a few more trees lost their leaves, and had their bark corroded and splintered until they finally died. By the time she was in her 30s, many of the trees she had known as a child were no more. They attempted to plant hybrids and subtropical species, but it was a lost cause. It had only been in the last decade that new hybrids took hold. The trees were healthy but still young and vulnerable. Elena so wanted to know what Lilly was thinking when she looked across the park and the decades.

"My parents took me here several times a year. It was one of my favorite places in the city," she said, knowing what Elena was thinking but exercising her prerogative of not answering.

They were comfortably alone. Washington had decided she didn't merit a Secret Service detail.

"Well, for someone raised in Brooklyn, you had that advantage over me. I didn't see it until a family vacation when I was, maybe 15."

"Couldn't get enough of this place."

"The dinosaurs?"

"Of course, what child do they not fascinate? But also, the dioramas of all those exotic animals, the Blue Whale suspended over our heads, even the non-exotic forests scenes drew me. I'm a city kid. Even a beaver dam was wondrous. Of course, by the time I was able to fully grasp what 'the natural world,' meant the losses were already accelerating. The museum started running a kind of 'doomsday clock' on species and habitat loss. They never called it 'doomsday clock' it was a media nickname, but that didn't stop the usual suspects from screaming fear-monger, America-hating or whatever. The museum never backed down. I guess that's when I went into science."

"One of these days, I'm going to ask you to tell me the whole story."

"Fine, but you'll never get the whole story."

"I know you don't like to do that in public, because all the Expendable stuff gets raised. But there have to be amazing stories from Columbia, about your..." The casualness of the setting tripped up Elena.

"My parents?"

Oh, no. "Expendables" and "parents" in the same minute. This would not end well for Elena. The casualness of the setting tripped her up. She looked around desperately. It wasn't easy to cross Lilly, but she had done it. Mercifully, she saw what she had hoped for. "There he is." Lilly looked up as Worth walked up the stairs. He was carrying a water bottle and nothing else. He shook hands with Lilly and shared an affectionate peck on the cheek with Elena.

"Thank you, Elena," Lilly said while keeping her eyes on Worth.

"Oh, yes, ma'am. I'll be at the office." Leaving was a relief. Worth took her place on the bench and placed the water bottle between them.

"Have you got anything?" Lilly asked her 360. Worth slowly pulled a small cylinder out of his pocket. "That's not very large," she noted.

"It disrupts attempts at eavesdropping for a five-meter radius. That's enough for here. A more powerful device has too distinctive a signal. Anyone monitoring this signal would get the same reading you'd get from a thousand off-the-shelf privatizers."

"The White House hasn't leaked nothing yet. What do you suppose they are waiting for?"

"Maybe they want more data, waiting for a more politically expeditious moment, maybe they won't use a state secret for political advantage..." Even Lilly couldn't give the benefit of a doubt on that one. "... I suppose that's not likely."

"I've been thinking more about this, doing a bit of research. When you first saw it, did you think 'telescope'?"

"Of course, it's a classic shape. But no one has built an earth-based telescope of that size in decades. They can't compete with the space-and-Moon-based telescopes. And even if it was, why would the Chinese make such a big deal about hiding it? No, I dismissed that notion out of hand."

"So did I, for the same reasons. But what if it's not *a* telescope but that it *telescopes*?"

"Meaning that it extends. That's certainly possible, but that makes it even more unlikely to be a weapon. Each section of the cylinder has to be even thinner that the whole. The thinnest metal would never withstand a firing of any military value. That only works if they have a new alloy. There are several promising ores being found on the Moon. But it's impossible for China to have gotten enough ore and successfully developed a new alloy *and* applied it in such a practical manner in so short a time."

"So, we still maintain that's not likely to be a weapon. But what if whatever comes out of it is not a weapon? There have been plenty of attempts over the decades to reduce global pollution by firing sulfur or other aerosols into the atmosphere. What if the Chinese Device is a variation on an old idea?"

"Hardly worthy of so much secrecy," Worth argued.

"They are very secretive. We might decide that they would brag about such an experiment, but they don't think that way. Their instinct is for secrecy."

"It's a possibility."

"We could change our perspective again. What if nothing comes out of the appendage; what if something comes in?"

"A sensor? You're running out of hands."

"Possibly. On both counts."

"Sensing what? Zhidoi has high pollution, you don't need a super-secret sensor to figure that out."

"Radiation?"

"What kind? We can already detect every known radiation. Unless they are planning to create a new radiation and want their own detector. In which case, we're not looking at a weapon itself but an auxiliary to a weapon."

"Careful, you're getting into O'Brien territory there creating facts that fit your prejudices. We don't know what the Chinese Device is and you're creating another secret weapon where there's zero evidence that it exists."

"I recreated the schematic from your, mine and Sean's notes and gave it, and one small piece of research to interns and staffers in Washington, and Chapel Hill. They do not understand how it fits into the bigger picture, and just as importantly, no one spying would know unless they knew what everyone was doing. I don't see too much that helps us. That big picture is on the data chip taped to the bottom of the water bottle. Probably best to transport it by hand to Sean as soon as possible."

"Fine. Elena is going back to Washington tonight."

The meeting was over. They didn't know what they had told anyone else.

CHAPTER 30

Mrs. Anderson arrived the next morning at dawn. Mrs. Ullman wasn't sure how long she had been buzzing, she was still groggy from the pill. She cautiously opened her bedroom door, looked around especially on the floor saw nothing unusual, and proceeded downstairs. Mrs. Anderson came in with a case of cleaning products.

"Everything alright?"

"It was noisy for a while. I had no idea they could scream like that."

"Sorry, I should have warned you. Are there any remnants?"

"I haven't looked."

Entering the living room, they noticed some smaller pieces of furniture had moved. There were a few blotches of blood on the carpet.

With the familiar snap of the fingers, Mrs. Anderson said, "Arnold, come."

Arnold slowly emerged from his portable cave, kicking animal bits ahead of him. He hunched over the prize, guarding remnants of his prey. Some piece of a tail, some bloody fur, two heads the size of Mrs. Ullman's fist. They were rats, of course. They both knew they were talking about rats. "Mice" is a gentler word, little furry things out in the field, nibbling cutely on the grass. These were rats, with all the history of disease and ugliness trailing behind the word like the plague.

Mrs. Anderson scooped up the ugly bits with pinchers and deposited them in a plastic bag. She sprayed what was probably disinfectant on the carpet and turned to Mrs. Ullman,

"I'll let that set and clean it up soon." What "it" was, the two women wordlessly decided that part of the conversation was over. She snapped again. "Arnold, more." Arnold strode with the confidence of a professional who knows he has done his job well towards the open cellar door. He let the humans catch up, and then he bounded down the stairs. He led Mrs. Anderson to a dark corner. Directing the flashlight on the spot, she took out the pinchers and plastic bag. She pulled something out of the darkness and dropped it in the bag. Then she sprayed the spot.

"There was a nest," she remarked. Mrs. Ullman didn't press for details.

Back upstairs, Mrs. Anderson checked around the kitchen and the rest of the ground floor, occasionally scrubbing or spraying a particular spot. Mrs. Ullman chose not to follow and waited in the living room with Arnold plopped down in front of his carrier.

Mrs. Anderson took out a ball of something and rolled it towards Arnold. Suddenly, the killer was a kitty and batted the ball around a bit before eating it.

"Trout, catnip, and some herbs," Mrs. Anderson answered the unasked question, "It cleans the palate, so to speak."

Without prompting, Arnold walked into his carrier and laid down. Mrs. Anderson snapped the door shut.

"I don't think we will have to come back tonight."

CHAPTER 31

Sanjeet Chaudhry swam deep among the fish, turtles and sea lions. No scuba gear, only fins, a mask and snorkel. As much as a seal as a man, he languidly crisscrossed the sea, deeper and longer than a human should. As the director of the Galapagos Islands' Darwin Recovery Station, he knew full well what was down there or more to the point, what was not down there, but this was always a good excuse for getting away from the computers.

Although isolated from the continents and subject of intensive conservation efforts, the Galapagos were still islands and subject to the global changes in oceans and the atmosphere. The changing ocean currents and the increase in El Niño conditions of warmer and wetter storms had a daily impact on the millennia-old balance on the islands. The coral reefs had not been subjected to the same abuse as those closer to industry and shipping, but they were suffering the same fate of bleaching and starvation.

The combination of traditional El Niños and accelerating climate change made the islands much wetter and warmer that in the past. The wet season was longer and wetter while the cool season needed by the coral reefs, fish, and some land animals like tortoises to replenish their food supply and aid in reproduction shortened. Coral reefs lost nutrients and were subject to warmer and more acidic water, meaning they died and the sea life dependent on the reefs also declined. Some years the weather was so wet, the eggs of tortoises and iguanas in effect drowned. Bird nests disintegrated. Several species of cacti became too waterlogged to survive.

He swam clear of the wave generators. The generators converted wave action into electricity and desalinated water, enough of both to take care of all the islands' needs. This wasn't the best place for such generators, they worked best near the coastlines of continents where the seabed was not so deep, and the tidal actions were stronger. Placing them at the Galapagos was not a unanimous decision: the sharp drop-off of the ocean floor meant they had to be so close to land that they might interfere with sea creatures. But solar wasn't providing enough and wind turbines most definitely caused problems for birds. The desalination aspect was the deciding factor: everyone needed water.

Still officially a possession of Ecuador, the central government swallowed its nationalist pride and agreed to share maintenance of the islands with an international consortium of nations, scientific institutions and the UN. On its own, Ecuador controlled human population, invasive species, logging and overfishing, but alone it could not deal with the rapid deterioration of this gem of the oceans. There were dozens of tiny islands in the archipelago, some only pebbles in the ocean. Saving them was impossible, so scientists tried to resettle as many animals as possible to other islands, leaving these pebbles to their fate.

As always, the greatest threat were humans. People had lived on the islands for more than two hundred years. Population growth and the damage that accompanied that destroyed plants and animals. Over-fishing depleted the stocks around the islands. Foreign species overran the indigenous. Fortunately, there was no repeat of what sailors and pigs did to the dodo, but it got close. As climate change continued to weaken the islands, they addressed the most aggressive invasive species. The most controversial decision was to depopulate the islands. Fortunately, there was no such person as an indigenous Galapagonian, so there was no Trial of Tears. From a peak of some 25,000 people in 2010, by 2052 only 5,000 humans called the Galapagos home. That didn't include the hundreds of foreigners working on various conservation, adaptation and educational projects. But these projects now employed hundreds of those 5,000. Humans retreated to just three of the islands Santa Cruz, Isabela and San Cristobal. There were a few small fishing villages on the outer islands to accommodate seasonal work, but no one lived there permanently.

In the 2030s, science bested fishing as the second major employer. Number one was the tourist industry. But tourism, no matter how "eco" was also curtailed. The size and number of ships and planes allowed to come steadily decreased over the years. Eco-tourism was the major source of income for the economy, especially after the fishing stocks collapsed, but with fewer people to support, the need for tourist money decreased. The human footprint on the islands had decreased dramatically, but it was too late. All the efforts on the Galapagos centered on one question: how long can we delay the collapse?

Sanjeet Chaudhry knew all of this. As chief of the Darwin Recovery Station for the last ten years, he was a part of that living history. But he wasn't thinking about all of that so much. Finally, nature made its ultimate demand, and he surfaced, gasping not only for air but out of sorrow. Despite all the scientific gear loaded into the boat, he had used none of it. As he lifted himself into his boat, all he thought about was that the waters had died a little more.

CHAPTER 32

As sea-levels rose, the great coastal cities had three choices: build seawalls and other protective barriers, move the city inland, or abandon the city. Rich cities including New York and Singapore built seawalls; others moved inland; some cities, including Miami, New Orleans and Accra because of a combination of geography and weather were abandoned.

Shanghai has special problems. It was at sea level and the coast had been developed up with billions of dollars' worth of high rises, the Yangtze River was bloated, the surrounding land around it riddled with smaller rivers, lakes and wetlands that became saturated with salt water both from the rising sea level and salination of the aquifer. The city was being hit from the front, back and underground. The first line of defense had been the same as any city seawalls, breakers and artificial dunes built out to create buffers between the rising sea and the gold-plated real estate. They performed triage.

Changxingxiang and the smaller islands were abandoned. When that proved to be a stop-gap solution, Shanghai both pushed inland and eliminated some of that land. The inland cities of Suzhou and Huzhou were now part of "Shanghai" while the network of tiny lakes around Taihu and Yangcheng Lakes and the Baixian were expanded with canals built to control the aggressive water. They sacrificed huge chunks of land to protect the rear flank of the city. Everything was secondary to maintaining the history, the pride, and the money of Shanghai.

Shanghai also looked to Tokyo for solutions. Understanding what was coming before coal-addicted China did, Japan planned a strategy to build out into the water. In effect, the idea was not to run from the water but to adapt to it. Unlike Shanghai and – for a time before it became impossible – Miami, rather than bulking up its rear guard, Tokyo reinvented the harbor. The city had been creating new land in the harbor for decades, so it wasn't much of a stretch. The difference was that the new islands were hexagonal, so they would be both resistant to killer waves and be able to channel and thus weaken the waves before they hit the rest of the city. They were both pawns and knights.

Building high remained an obsession worldwide, and that included Shanghai. Not all the skyscrapers from the beginning of the 21st century survived. It wasn't the sky that was the problem, but the shifting land now more like a giant sponge upon which they built them. New construction inland had strict height limits. Some of those restrictions had nothing to do with climate change. They forbade consulates and other buildings belonging to foreign governments to be taller than ten stories, which meant there were many massive towers around from which the government could look down on their guests. Walls and roofs were thick and embedded with alloys and polymers designed to scramble a variety of spying methods, including self-contained bubbles of spy-proof accommodations for particularly sensitive discussion. At the moment, one of those bubbles was being used by two diplomats: Harry Cheng, the first minister, and Erica Mosel, a science attaché.

Cheng began the briefing. "This is a follow up from the last report on the Chinese Device. One of our better-known drunks let something slip last night at a reception in Beijing. We know a German heard it, maybe a Russian. Our people stand pat in Beijing, with luck they will move their people from Beijing while we move in from Shanghai. The Chinese will figure one of us doesn't know what they are doing but won't know which one for a while."

"What's stopping them from stopping all of us?"

"On what grounds? It's a not a closed city. That's why you were selected for this, your cover is seismology a dozen obvious reasons for visiting the Tanglha Mountains."

"Is our man there still alive?"

"Bio-readings say yes. He could be in a coma. Too bad for him, but a break for us. There's no sign that the Chinese have figured out who he works for."

"Am I going to be the only American on the scene?"

"The only one of us. There are a few civilian medical and agricultural personnel there, anyway. It's be easy to steer clear of them."

Tall, blonde, and Germanic, Mosel did not scream "blend in" in China. She used her uniqueness to play the counter-intuitive card "Her? She's a spy? Are you joking?" Combined with a gift for languages, being a quick study, and knowing some science, Cheng decided she was right for the job. It wasn't exactly as if the Chinese weren't already watching to see which country was giving off signals it had been on the receiving end of that transmission. "What exactly am I supposed to find out?"

"Unusual movements of industrial or military convoys. The *Roosevelt* will check for any spikes in heat, radiation or energy from the device. It might catch large convoys, but that's not likely. I'll coordinate with you to see if the readings from space match any observations you make."

"Radiation?" That was one word feared in all languages.

"Just a possibility. Nothing shows any radioactive component to the device."

"How close can I get to the plant?"

"Nowhere close for the moment. We have a couple of locals eyeballing it, but they're getting nervous so they may disappear any day. We can't risk giving them any sensitive equipment, so that's your job. They have a dead drop; you never contact them everything passes through me."

CHAPTER 33

Peter's office was a mass of computers and consoles, ranging from antique 1980s to the cutting edge. Not only was he a 360, but he was a military 360, meaning he access to more gadgets than most people would want or need. Ike walked in and handed him a relic from the beginning of the century with a USB stick.

"Do you know what this is?" he asked Peter.

"Sure," Peter answered, "It's a type of data storage devise. Went out of use about 20 years ago. Is this what was in that box from your father?"

"Yes."

"What's on it?"

"That's what I want you to tell me. The technology is too old for my computer."

Peter examined the drive and checked for the proper plug. "This should be it." He plugged it in, touched a few keys and a menu of eight files appeared on the screen.

"What are we looking at?"

"Data files. Eight files roughly the same size. Any idea what's on them?"

"No."

"Ok, only one way to find out." He tapped on the first file. The Air Force seal took over the screen. A digital clock began a countdown from 10 seconds. Below the seal were the words: "USAF Command Master Record: August 9, 2037."

The two Air Force professionals felt the cold tingle of history grab their necks. "2037," they whispered in unison.

"August 9. The day of the Satellite War," Ike said, even though they both knew it.

The countdown clocks on the home screen hit zero and the screen now filled with a large electronic map. The clock was now counting forward from 08:00:00:00 EST. It took the captains a few moments to absorb what they were seeing. It was the master map from the Strategic Air Command headquarters. These files were obviously the official recording of everything that went on in that room. Every hour of every day for a highly classified number of years.

The default setting of the map was of the Northern Hemisphere, tracking the movements of everything that wasn't touching the ground: civilian and military aircraft, satellites, even flocks of birds if they were large enough. And if it came to that the flight paths of missiles. On either side of the map were columns of data streams, plus maps of other parts of the planet that could be transferred to the main screen if an official or computer so decided. Since neither one of them had trained for this command, they had trouble grasping the meaning of all the data. Occasionally an emotionless human voice almost robotic noted the position of a satellite, a note on weather, planes in flight. Routine, almost sleepy.

"Eight in the morning. What time did the war start?" Ike asked.

"That's always classified. Best reports are around noon, Washington time."

"Could each of those files be an hour?"

"Easy to check." He closed the file and opened the next the same map, and now the clock said 09:00:00:00 EST. "What do you want to do?" he asked Ike.

The screen mesmerized Ike. "My father meant for me to have this upon his death. He couldn't have meant for me to drop it into a drawer."

"No note? Nothing?"

"Nothing."

They just watched for several minutes. The map periodically changed from the Northern Hemisphere to the atmospheric map showing the locations and orbits of multiple satellites.

Finally, Ike could not stand the blandness. "Go to the noon file, please."

Peter complied. Initially, the file was the same: the same map and the clock counting up from 12:00:00:00 EST. The same pattern: changes in the maps, data streams on either side of the screen, punctuated by a different robotic voice. After about ten minutes, an authoritative voice sounded, this voice was never a robot.

"Adjustment. Sector two-niner, 75 percent." They did not understand what that meant, but it didn't matter at that moment.

"That's my father's voice," Ike marveled. After so many years of being blocked from top secret history, Ike was now hearing his father at work. They sat mesmerized. They still didn't fully understand everything they were seeing and hearing. General McClellan was speaking the specialized language of his command. His son only wanted to hear his voice. He occasionally ordered a change in screen or a closeup of some particular blip. Then at 12:14:23, a yellow light went on and the screen immediately switched to a view of space from a low orbit. Multiple blips were moving at a steady speed satellite. The captains didn't understand the reason for the warning lights, but those airmen from long ago clearly knew what was going on. Two satellites were on parallel courses. Instead of a screen of data, there was now the minimum information about the two satellites: one US, one Chinese.

"General, one of ours has veered off course."

"Why," McClellan asked, "What's the malfunction?"

Before the officer could answer, the yellow light turned to red and the blips representing the two satellites were also red. A computer voice reported: "Collision imminent."

The general responded. "Control over-ride. We must take command of that..."

With a flash, both red blips disappeared. A scatter of blips that started as yellow and quickly turned to red replaced them. Another satellite, this one apparently a UN one, flew directly into the new debris field. It too vanished in an electronic cloud of red dots. The voices were no longer robotic, all their training had not prepared them for a cascade of exploding satellites. Like a nuclear chain reaction in which one atom splitting causes an exponentially increasing number of atoms to split leading to a nuclear explosion, each destroyed satellite became a multi-pronged weapon indiscriminately targeting other satellites. Although it wasn't obvious at that moment, the captains of 2052 knew that even some satellites not destroyed got damaged or knocked out of orbit.

After a few numb minutes, a voice rang out.

"General, the President is on the line."

"Thank you. Yes, Mr. President." The general was remarkably controlled.

The recording included the President's phone. "What just happened?"

"A Chinese satellite diverted orbit and collided with one of ours. As we were analyzing if this was a malfunction or a deliberate attack, a second Chinese satellite hit a UN satellite. Sir, this is aggression by the Chinese government. What are your orders?"

"Take all necessary action to protect US assets, including

the interception of Chinese satellites. Presidential authorization Alpha-Foxtrot-Niner-Niner-Zero-Four."

"General, voice recognition confirms. Code confirms authentic," the unseen officer reported.

"Yes, Mr. President. Implementing aggressive self-defense actions across the spectrum."

Aggressive was an understatement. The general ordered the view over China and Russia. Most of the space vehicles there were still intact. McClellan issued a rapid series of orders consisting mostly of numbers. The captains had to assume these were commands to enact certain protocols on the military satellites and space stations because some US blips shifted positions and the still undecipherable data on the sides changed color from white to red. The counterattack had begun.

Soon it was clear the US was not the only country at war. What appeared to be Chinese and Russian space stations were also launching attacks China against the US, Russia against China. The flashing red debris field soon looked like a low orbit case of the measles. Then some of SAC's own monitors failed, their satellites attacked or victims of the spreading debris. This meant the continuing stream of data had to be coming from the few satellites in a higher orbit.

And then the hour ended.

Still stunned, neither of the captains thought to start the next hour.

"Dear God," was all that Ike could say.

Peter was slowly formulating an idea. "It began when the Chinese and American satellites collided."

"Right. Like we always thought, a Chinese satellite hit one of ours."

"No, the officer said our satellite went out of orbit."

"I guess."

"But your father told the President the Chinese satellite went out of orbit. That wasn't true. The President gave his orders based on faulty information."

"Then that means..."

"Ike, your father started the Satellite War."

CHAPTER 34

They built the UNSS *Francesco Uno* on the same plan as the USS *Roosevelt*, but on a smaller scale. Its three missions were to monitor both human and natural activities on earth, conduct scientific research, and clean up space debris. As the UN did on Earth, it did in space clean up the big boys' messes. They required all space stations under the Treaty of Seoul to provide for debris clearance, but the two UN stations had been collecting the lion's share of the junk. Anything that was truly junk nuts and bolts, chunks of paneling, wires got collected and shipped back to Earth for recycling if possible.

Any human remains if they could establish identity got returned to families. But every once in a while, they recovered something spectacular; computer hardware, or items that looked suspiciously like a weapon. Because of the possibility that some junk wasn't junk, the Treaty of Seoul also required the UN to have representatives of key countries on the stations and they had first rights to review the trash. Thus, both stations had at least five highly educated crew members who were garbage pickers. Those provisions didn't extend to the national stations. If the *Roosevelt* found a chunk of a Russian computer, well, too bad.

Commander Luiza de Souza, a Brazilian, ran the *Francesco Uno*. She was primarily an astronaut, then a naval commander, then a scientist. But now she was giving an interview.

"The United Nations has two stations moving in sun-synchronistic orbit, one over each hemisphere. Our standard orbit is 75 degrees north to 15 degrees north. Our sister ship in the south, the *Al-Khwarizmi*, has a similar orbit. Most of the time we are on opposite sides of the Earth, we can alter our orbits slightly if there appears to be a need."

"Such as?" asked the EuroNet reporter, McBride.

"Indications of a massive, dangerous weather pattern, tidal activities, storms forming. In space, we may encounter a particular large cluster of debris. It takes a lot to alter the course of a space station, so it's rarely done. Mostly we leave that task to the cleaners. We have no weapons or military applications, of course. The Treaty of Seoul bans space-based weapons, either on stations or satellites. Other than that restriction, we work to take on as many duties as possible."

"You're still collecting debris from the Satellite War. How much debris do you collect?"

"About a metric ton a month. It's undoubtedly the least glamorous job in space, but we all have to do it. Every space station UN, nationals have to do it, not only because it's the right thing to do but as a simple matter of self-preservation. The 1967 UN Outer Space Treaty required all nations launching anything into space to take responsibility for what they put up here. Earth-based monitors have been evolving now for almost 100 years, so they provide us with back-up. Being approximately 2,000 kilometers up, we're above the debris field so we're not collecting as much. The stations that are lower down, collect much more. Before the war, debris pushed out of Low Earth Orbit got ejected into High Earth Orbit, but now that range is essential for the communications satellites, so the UN has a ship up there doing nothing but collecting pre-war debris. Any damage to the HEO satellites would be catastrophic.

McBride felt he had enough for the moment and signaled for the camera to be turned off. "Thank you. That's enough for now. We'd like to see more of the station now."

"Certainly." She motioned to a crew member to take over escort duties. "What are you going to do with all this material?"

"Probably use it in a series of short documentaries. As you know, EuroNet started out as a teaching tool for high school students and we just kept growing, so now we have some pretty complex shows. But we still focus on being as accessible as possible."

"Well, looking forward to seeing the result. What's next?"

"We are heading for the *Theodore Roosevelt* next. Contrasting a UN station to a national one should be an interesting program."

"Also, a risky trip. You understand you'll be passing through the most treacherous part of the debris field."

"Oh, we know," he said, trying to be as nonchalant as possible.

"Going to the Moon?"

"Not us, but another team will head there, next cycle."

"Exciting place. New discoveries every day. You've consulted with my navigation office about your course?"

"Yes, Commander. *Francesco* and the *Roosevelt* will be in closest proximity at 700 GMT, and there are no major debris fields on the flight path."

"Well, you're lucky then. Better stick tight to that schedule."

CHAPTER 35

Even social animals needed quiet time. George and Maggie were alone with the lights down and only their essential phones nearby. The long silence was like a vast blanket that they could hide under.

"George?"

"Yeah, Mags?"

"Umm..."

Umm could not be good. Umm was hesitation. Maggie never hesitated. Resigning himself to the inevitable, he asked, "Yes?"

"Victoria's under arrest again."

Cranston was glad for the darkness. "Where?"

"That stoners' warehouse on the Potomac."

"Drugs, I assume."

"Sure. You know the drill. They cut them all loose after one night. Issued an order to appear in court, they never do and the courts couldn't care less."

"So where is she now?"

"You don't know?" There was only one person in the world who could get away with asking that question.

"I haven't seen her in a week. Face-to-face is too frustrating for both of us. What am I supposed to say, 'Daddy will take care of everything when I'm in charge?' She's only two steps away from spitting in my face as it is."

"Cut off her money?"

"She has her own accounts."

"She's still a minor."

"A legal detail."

"You know what's at the heart of this, right? You let it slide because deep down you agree with her. With them."

Maggie the operative couldn't help but make the political calculations, and of course had the sense to keep them to herself. In past decades, a junkie teenage daughter would have been a career killer. "How can he run a country when he can't run his own family?" This was now a big glass house syndrome. Nearly every political family had a Victoria. Anyone raising questions about Victoria could expect the reply, "Why exactly did General Hayden's son resign his commission?" or "How come we don't see Ailes granddaughter anymore?" It was a permanent stand-off. Ironically, one of the few people with clean windows was Lilly, and she was the last person to exploit it. Besides, Maggie was right: Cranston agreed, understood. No more "what's the matter with kids today?" Cranston knew. And Victoria knew what her father believed. And she had no intention of letting him come up for air. She would hold him underwater as long as she could.

CHAPTER 36

Theo arrived back at base just before the EuroNet crew arrived. The EuroNet jet was three times the size of Theo's sand-hugger. They designed it for intercontinental travel with extra seats for visitors or dignitaries. On this trip, one of the least glamorous possible the ship carried only the documentary crew. Once the jet had descended onto the landing pad, the roof slid shut and Theo entered from the passageway. "Welcome to UN Biogeological Station A4. I hope your trip went well."

"A bit of turbulence, nothing special. Thank you for asking."

Sam was a black man, but the accent instantly pegged him as a Londoner. Brixton maybe, Theo thought. He wondered if EuroNet sent him because he was black or if it was his idea. Then he got annoyed at himself for spending two seconds on nonsense.

Theo led Sam into the station as the crew started removing their equipment.

They had warned Sam about Theo, so he started with the simplest question he could think of.

"Station A4 is pretty bland name. Other places we've covered give their facilities nicknames. Do you call your station anything else?"

Theo stared blankly at the reporter, unable to comprehend the thought behind the question. "No."

"Ok, now, as I'm sure you know, the EuroNet webcasts are designed for high school students in Europe. The casts are about climate adaptation and coping strategies. You know, encouragement for the home front. We have a wider audience around the world, but that's our target audience. When you speak, please don't talk down to the viewers they're not scientists but they're not children either. For example, when you refer to species of trees don't use only the scientific name, use the common name too."

Theo did little to hide his boredom. "In what language?"

"Whichever you prefer. We will add subtitles in various languages later."

"So, this won't be live?"

"No, we can transmit live, but that uses up valuable satellite time, so we only do that for special occasions..."

"And this is not a special occasion..."

"Well, no, it is very rare..."

"Don't apologize, I'm not offended." He really wasn't.

They entered the conference room where Raj was waiting. The table was empty except for pitchers of water and glasses. A large projection dominated the wall. It was obviously their part of Africa, but with a patchwork of images and colors. Sam approached Raj with an outstretched hand. Raj, well-practiced, had already extended his left hand, giving Sam plenty of time to correct without being embarrassed.

"This is Dr. Raj Gupta, formerly of the Galma station," Theo said, "Since the station is closed, he has been seconded here until we can decide what to do with him." Even Theo realized that sounded like an insult, so he quickly added, "I mean, we have had to close his station. It's not a reflection on Dr. Gupta, it's a reflection on the soil of Galma."

Everyone sat around the table facing the projection. Theo picked up the remote. It was easy to recognize this middle swath of West Africa from Morocco down to Nigeria/Cameroon border, with its withdrawn coast and lack of interior cities. The map showed Katsina and Galma, marked with bright red spots. There were several other such spots in a line extending from Tan-Tan in southern Morocco, southeast through Mauritania and leveling off at approximately 15-10 degrees north, eastwards. There were irregular areas of green near many of these spots including Katsina but excluding Galma. In addition, there was a yellow line beginning at Tan-Tan; it broke after a few hundred kilometers but then there are other sections of yellow along the parallel. There were none near Katsina.

"I understand you wanted a briefing about our work before you saw the nursery or went into the field. Correct?"

"That's right."

"Every time we explain to visitors why we are trying to reforest in the middle of the desert, they always ask why here. To save us both of some time, let me first explain why we are here."

Hesitating a bit, Sam answered, "Actually, that was going to be my first question..."

Ignoring Sam, Theo was already in professorial mode. "First, remember that until a few decades ago this wasn't desert. It was the Sahel, a vibrant ecosystem of plants and wildlife that kept the Sahara at bay. The desert finally won, but there is arable soil underneath all this sand.

"In many parts of the world, we are planting genetically enhanced trees derived from native species that should be more adaptable to the changed environment absorbing more carbon, using less water, resisting insects and extreme heat, even providing timber and firewood, but that's secondary here we need the trees alive more than dead. We're having some luck in former rain forests. Despite the deforestation, vast areas of soil were never fully depleted or polluted. Here it's different. While 70 years ago Katsina was savannah, the desert had been close for centuries and the land was never especially suited for a concentration of trees. The soil is poor and for a region never densely populated, an unusual amount of pollution. For decades, toxic wastes from industrial countries were secretly dumped here. We had a promising site near Galma, but it turns out nuclear waste had been dumped there decades ago. No one knew. What little soil and water we might have been able to exploit is permanently useless."

"So why even try?" Sam asked.

"A desert can grow so a desert can shrink. There's nothing special about this place in terms of agronomy, but there are other considerations." And now he finally turned to his colored map. "The red spots are bio stations and agronomy centers. The irregular green shapes are trees, as you can see, they are not large. The yellow line is the Sahel water pipeline. You've seen the purification plants on the Morocco coast?" Sam nodded, but Theo didn't care. "It's been reasonably successful in desalinating and cleansing water and pumping it into the interior in limited quantities. However, it uses too much energy and the pumps and filters get constantly overloaded.

"Then there are the political problems of running a pipeline through so many countries. Too many authorities, too many bribes. See that strip east of Bamako? It doesn't connect to anything else, no water, no pumps, just pipes. They built that section of pipe was built as a bribe for something else I don't want to know about. Someday it may connect to the end stations, but that time and money could have been better spent on the purification plants or contiguous piece of the pipeline."

"No water, no pipeline, so why are you here?"

"Katsina has advantages: If we can grow a reasonable,

healthy forest without the pipeline, then we have a chance of a mature ecosystem by the time the pipeline is ready. That will lead to an exponential growth of the ecosystem once water is at hand. Timbuktu and Niamey have the same potential.

"We are tragically only recreating what we lost some 30 years ago. At the beginning of the century, when climate change was finally accepted, there were major reforestation projects undertaken all over the world. The programs in the Sahel a name that really doesn't have any meaning anymore since the Sahara has taken it over, were among the most successful. On the one hand, they left the trees alone, farmers planted food crops among them and on the other, they planted millions of new trees. Gao, doum, baobab was planted across the region. It was a success story. But the Great Drought, followed by the changing patterns of Sahara winds, except for a few trees. A few trees were saved. Many of our trees are direct descendants of those unlucky trees."

"But why here? Don't areas of more fertile soil allow for creating better carbon sinks?"

"Yes, that's what's happening in the Amazon, the temporal forests of Canada and Russia, and where possible, Indonesia. These trees make inefficient carbon sinks, but that's not the point the point is to improve the arability of the region, recreate the ecosystem, thus encouraging people to move back into the interior. The trees make it worth it to build the pipeline through here, the water in the pipeline helps the trees, both help the people. But it has to start with the trees."

"Seems to me it should start with water, meaning the pipeline."

"Logically, of course, I agree. But the pipeline is a piece of bureaucracy, trees are trees."

"And animals are animals. You said ecosystem that means

more than trees. You need animals, birds, insects, burrowing mammals. What about those?"

"Exactly." He didn't want to admit Sam's insight impressed him. "We are carefully introducing indigenous insects and a few birds. It's difficult to replicate nature's balance, but we are having limited success. Of course, when the Galma trees died, so did the insects. The birds flew off. A few made it to here. But the rest..." And he gave his characteristic shrug.

"I'd like to see some of Katsina itself."

"Suit yourself. Not much to see anymore except the Gobarau Mosque. That is fascinating, built of mud and palm with hardly any wood, no stone, and it's the second sturdiest building in the city."

"And the first?"

"My station, of course."

CHAPTER 37

Zhidoi was as miserable a place as Mosel expected. Everything, even the people, was in place to service the industries of the city. Both because of pollution and neglect, there were few trees. Some people had a valiantly tried to maintain small kitchen gardens, but they produced more frustration than vegetables. As an American, she had to register at one of the better hotels something she would have done anyway, even if it was out of her own pocket.

Her contact was through a classic dead drop. The drop followed a pre-arranged pattern. There were four benches in a park at roughly the four cardinal points. The hours overlaid the points but in reverse thus north was six, not 12, and so on. Following on from that, the message "NN" meant to pick up the data on the north bench at 6pm; "EW" meant the east bench at 3pm. They encrypted the data was on a fine wafer that was small enough to fit on a fingertip and not fall off. A plain plastic adhesive kept it attached to the bench. Since they introduced these chips into spy craft, the standard procedure if compromised was to swallow the wafer. It would eventually pass through, but the data likely would get eaten away in the digestive tract.

They advised operatives to consume as much citrus as possible to aid the destruction. Therefore, Mosel had a bottle of hard-to-get grapefruit juice in her room. She knew they were developing a biodegradable wafer that would vanish after less than an hour in the stomach. But this was not a priority case, thus the grapefruit juice.

Once back at her hotel, the wafer fit into a traditional drive that the computer could read. Every day, there was nothing special to report. On the fourth day, there was nothing at the drop. Same on the fifth. On the sixth day, a twig with its bark scraped off stuck in the slats of the bench. The contact was finished. Mosel went back to her room, reported, deleted all her files, the wafers flushed immediately after downloading, and the delete folder "burned."

She was more curious than startled when someone knocked on her door. She put the computer in the desk drawer and went to the door. A Chinese state police captain and a civilian were standing there.

"Ms. Erica Mosel?" said the captain.

"Yes."

"This is for you," he said as he held out an envelope. Mosel couldn't remember the last time anyone had handed her a paper envelope.

"There must be some mistake. I'm an attaché at the US consulate in Shanghai, you can't arrest me."

Arrest? Oh no, this isn't a warrant. It's an invitation," he said, exposing the most mirthless smile imaginable.

"A what?"

"An invitation to an official briefing at Site 755. Please be at the main gate at 1330 hours. Please do not bring any record-ing or communication devices. I understand you know the way to the facility."

Arriving at the appointed hour, Mosel wasn't surprised to see her invitation was not exclusive. Official cars from Japan, the

EU, Russia, the United Nations and Brazil all arrived at the same time. Discreet small talk revealed that no one had any enlightening information.

First thing when they entered the compound was to deposit all phones and other communication devices with the guards. This was a superfluous condition no one was fool enough to turn their equipment over to the PLA, everyone had left their phones with their drivers. Since she didn't have a driver, Mosel asked the EU driver to hold on to her phone. It was a request for show. Mosel had left her real phone in Shanghai. She was carrying a new, cheap phone that contained only the number for the consulate. It was not even possible to tell it was Cheng who sent her. But she didn't want to be the only one to give her phone to the army. Next was the optic scanner to ensure they were in fact the people invited. Finally, a body scan to detect hidden communication devices (like a chip in an artificial kneecap?).

Under armed escort, they all walked at a pace designed to be uncomfortable until they reached a room marked "Conference Room 4." Mosel wondered if the other delegates noticed that the nameplate was newer than those of the rooms they had passed. They entered a sterile conference room with room for 100 but with just enough chairs for the officials invited. There was a low-rise stage with a simple podium off to the side. A massive panel took up most of the wall behind the stage. They painted everything in an industrial anti-color. The only color was the Chinese flag on one side and the PLA flag on the other. After everyone sat down, the guards took positions at the main door and a small side door. Then a guard opened the side door, and a general hurried to the stage. They had placed the podium on the opposite side of the stage from the door, so the general got to walk the full length of the stage as if in a parade.

"Good afternoon, ladies and gentlemen" he was able to say "ladies" because besides Mosel, the EU, typically, had sent a woman. "Thank you for arriving so promptly. My name is General Xi Xuan of the Scientific and Innovation Bureau of the People's Liberation Army. I know you are all reasonably conversant in Chinese, but I have my reasons for speaking in English. I will ask you no questions, there is nothing you can tell me I don't already know. I am here to answer questions." And on cue, the panel lightened and became a window.

On the other side of the window was a factory floor dominated by a long, sleek machine with a massive appendage jutting out from the top. It was the Chinese Device. The air was buzzing with mental notetaking for the inevitable future debriefing: the size, how many components, any way to tell what materials they used, what were the dimensions of the appendage was it stationary or mobile? It was larger than we estimated, Mosel thought, and wondered again if anyone else had as much information as did the US. The variant converter was also larger than expected, making the device at least ten times larger than estimated.

"The machine you see behind me is the latest advance in Chinese technology. It is based on revolutionary principles of physics. I understand in the United States, this is referred to as the Chinese Device. While the name demonstrates a profound lack of understanding as to the nature of our invention, that name will suffice for this briefing.

"The Chinese Device represents an exponential leap forward in essential technology. While the power source is a simple nuclear reactor and the superstructure is constructed of basic alloys, the technology within is unlike anything else produced anywhere in the world. Once construction is completed and the Device is operating at full capacity, we will demonstrate to the world the next magnificent contribution the Chinese civilization has created for the betterment of the human race.

"Computer and laboratory tests have been underway for eight months. We fully expect to conduct an actual test by the new year the Chinese New Year, of course.

You may report to your capitals now. Anyone remaining in Zhidoi after 1200 tomorrow will be deported as an undesirable alien. Thank you for your attention."

The window turned into a wall again. Walking marching across the stage, General Xi left by the same door, not deigning to glance at his audience. Once he was off the stage, the guards wordlessly opened the doors.

CHAPTER 38

Ruth was in her quarters. It was a breezy room filled with as much non-scientific stuff as possible: art from Borneo, China, Kenya, India; the traditional family photos holographically projected from her clock; a much-ignored flute; and stuffed animals, mostly of primates. A toy orangutan coincidently the same size Rabu was at that moment propped up on her pillows. It was down time, a quiet moment. She was on the computer, talking to her mother who was half a world away.

"Mom, are you sure you don't want me to come home? I feel strange being here while you're campaigning."

"I'm sure," Lilly said, "Your work is too valuable..." She didn't know about Rabu, the need for secrecy extended to opensource communications "... And we know what this is really about. Your reality needs to take precedence over my symbolism."

"Well, I still don't think it's symbolic. This is a real campaign with a serious chance of victory."

"I'll leave that to Senator Cranston and his team. I know what I need to do and will just keep plugging away until Election Day. So, what's new?"

Don't say it. "The couple I've been monitoring seem very happy, no signs of stress. What's most interesting at the moment is that their range is expanding, meaning they're feeling more secure. Very positive."

"She's child-bearing age, isn't she? Any sign of a new arrival?"

"Not yet," as she hurried on to the next subject, "The

signing is advancing. I'm going to introduce more abstract words soon and see if they take hold."

"You see. Why would you walk away from all that?"

CHAPTER 39

They were waiting in a small conference room at the Academy.

"... Maybe there's a new assignment..."

"I already told you I know nothing," Peter said, "Stop speculating."

"But..."

Peter stopped him. Holding up his phone, he waved it around the room. The room was likely bugged, so silence was best. Then, without warning or formalities, General Adams entered the room. The two captains snapped to attention.

"As you were, gentlemen. Have a seat." He motioned to the men to sit on either side of him. "Captain McClellan, you've opened the box from your father and viewed its contents?" Ike stayed silent. "Don't worry. Rank has its privileges. All listening devices are turned off. This is a private conversation. If someone has taken it upon himself to ignore a direct order, I have this." He took out a small device and laid it on the table. "If any communication device is on, this light will turn red." He turned it on, and it immediately showed red. The captains stared at each other nervously. Adams was concerned. "Your phones are still on, I assume?" Embarrassed, the two turned off their phones. The red light went out.

"Now then, Captain."

"Yes, sir."

"And you needed Captain Reilly's help to interpret the contents?"

"Yes, sir."

"So, you both know. And what did you think?"

Well, sir. It's hard to absorb. It sounds as though my father... My father had a role in the Satellite War that... isn't in the history books."

"A very subtle way of phrasing it. Fine. Why do you think he did what he did?"

"He saw the signs. He saw China as the Beast rising out of the East. The floods, hurricanes, plagues, the End Times. He struck at China before it could strike us."

"Exactly. The Earthly authorities could not see it, but your father knew where true authority lies. And the Great Darkness, how else to describe the loss of so much communication that followed, and not only prevented the inevitable attack, but gave rise to more signs? And then the India-Pakistan nuclear war followed a year later. More Darkness, more plagues."

"But the End Times did not come," Peter interjected.

"'You shall not know the time and place,' admonishes the Lord. The signs are still here, growing stronger even. How can you know the End Times are not here? Look at the Mars Mission, countries working together to reach into the heavens. How is this not a modern Tower of Babel, that God struck down as punishment for man's vanity? And now we have Cranston, a traitor who wants to bring the Chinese right into the White House. A woman, a soulless scientist."

"But General Hayden will win. It's inevitable," Ike said.

"Never say that," he snapped, "The Devil is real and ready to take advantage of anyone who lets down his guard. That is a rule for the soldier and the Christian."

"What do you want of us?"

"Before I answer that, one more thing. Ask, you know you want to ask."

"Were you with my father at the Pentagon on that day?

There's no sign of you on the computer files and your official biography is vague on that period."

"You will find the records vague on a number of people. I was your father's second-in-command. I was at Cheyenne Mountain. What your father did, he could not have done alone. He needed someone who would walk with him and the Lord. That's an important lesson. And now to your question, what do I want of you?"

"Yes."

"To fulfill the will of both your fathers." Turning to Peter he asked, "You're a 360?"

"Yes, sir."

"Interesting. A 360 and a Christian. A valuable combination. You'll be on my staff. You'll be my 360."

"Begging the General's pardon, don't you already have one?"

"I do, but he's about to get promoted and transferred." Turning to Ike, "I can't do the same for you we're always under surveillance. If any of us pull together too many Christians onto our staffs, alarm bells go off and they preempt us. Adding a 360 who is a Christian is fine, but two, especially when one of them has your last name, that's too obvious. It probably isn't even necessary. What is required of you is already in you. No training necessary. But you," looking at Peter, "You, I need you with me. God has a special task for you, and you are providentially suited for it."

"Pardon, sir. Is Washington necessary?"

"You don't want a transfer?

"It's not that, sir, but won't too many changes spark someone's interests?"

"Very good, that's how you need to think. In one sense, you are right, that's why we're making as few overt moves as possible. But for our plan to work, you have to be in Washington."

"And that plan is?" Peter asked.

"Strictly need to know, for the moment. I won't keep you in suspense long. Have either of you heard of Zhidoi? Industrial city in the Chinese interior."

"No, sir." The two spoke in unison.

"You will."

CHAPTER 40

Ron was in his tin can when he spotted something unusual. "Bridge, I see something approaching at heading 1212. It's quite large. If it's debris, we're going to need boosters."

"Roger that. Unidentified object is EuroNet vessel on scheduled rendezvous with us. No action required."

"Roger that, Bridge." Muting the radio, he marveled to himself. "Space tourists. Still can't get used to that. Still, would be nice to get Mom and Dad up here someday."

The EuroNet ship had cut its engines and drifted towards the docking arm. The arm caught the ship and gently swung it into position near the airlock. Once the ship attached to the station and the arm released before the docking protocol began. Since all spaceships designed for re-entry had tapered noses, by necessity the Universal Docking Ports had to be placed near the rear. For a ship like EuroNet's, designed for durability not speed, or distance, this was not a problem. Most of the fuselage was large enough to stand in, so once the two vessels were attached it was a matter of walking from one to the other. A space version of a gangplank. Smaller ships such as the Moon-to-Station shuttle crafts and the so-called sports cars had narrower bodies, so the UDPs took up a larger proportion of the ship, which meant people practically had to crawl to move between the vessels.

An ensign was waiting for McBride and his team outside the airlock.

"Welcome aboard, ladies and gentlemen. Ever been on a space station before?"

"We've just come from the *Francesco Uno*."

"Of course, you did. I mean, before this trip. I've checked your programs and didn't see anything from space for a while."

"That's right. It's been well over five years. Still not especially safe, as you guys well know. But with the technology making such tremendous gains and the Mars mission gearing up, we thought we focus more on space. Of course, that's a pretty expensive operation, so we have to make the most of what we get."

"That would have taken some nerve back then."

"Wasn't me. Don't think I would have been able to risk it. They didn't come in their own ship, came up with one of the cargo rockets, better chance of surviving a hit. And it worked fine."

"The *Roosevelt* itself took quite a hit in '41. Lost a docking port."

"I remember. Say, could we talk to one of the cleaners? It's not glamorous, of course, we want to talk to the commanders of the station and the candidates for the Mars mission, but how about one cleaner? Nose to the grindstone and all that. Their work is making space safe for space travel like ours."

"Sure, fine idea. Let me run it by the captain."

CHAPTER 41

The next morning, Theo and Raj escorted the EuroNet crew around Katsina. It wasn't even close to noon, but the heat was already creeping into their pores. They were wearing loose, white garments made of a blend specially designed for this climate. Even though they were well-fed and hydrated, the desert heat had grabbed them by the ankles and was pulling them into the sand. "What must it be like to live here?" Sam thought.

Katsina had not been a thriving city for centuries. But the last few decades had driven it down even more. The visitors and their hosts stood in front of the Gobarau Mosque just as the muezzin calls the Adhan call to prayer from inside the Mosque. A few people come out to pray, but not many.

It was obvious to Sam right away that this wasn't a vibrant city, but the lack of men surprised him. "Does this mean a lack of the faithful?" he asked.

"It means an abundance of heat. Most people are inside this time of day. It still counts. You should come back after sunset. The evening prayer is much more public."

Sam felt ashamed for judging them when he had just told himself he could never handle this heat. He was already glancing around for some shade. Then he stared at the prostrate men and wondered if they would ever get up.

Theo's phone rang. He listened silently.

"We have to go back to the station. An urgent message is coming in from Lagos."

He turned and headed out with no further consideration of the rest. They had no choice but to follow.

CHAPTER 42

They returned to the conference room, but instead of a projection of plants and pipelines, the screen showed an elderly, worn man wearing crumpled white clothes. He was sitting at a plain desk with the UN and World Health Organization flags behind him.

"Dr. Asanti, how are things in Lagos?" Theo asked, even before he sat down.

"Theo, a pleasure," although his face showed none. "Excuse me, but who's that with you?"

"A crew from EuroNet. Is that a problem?"

"I'd prefer our conversation to be private."

The bluntness startled Sam and the crew, but they silently left the room without waiting for Theo to tell them.

Once the door closed, Theo turned back to the screen. "This sounds ominous."

"Last week, a community hospital in Ikorodu district reported six cases of a virus. Four died within 24 hours. We've isolated the strain, and it's a mutation on the A3N4 flu..."

"It's mutated already?"

"Exactly. Which means it's impossible to develop a vaccine before it spreads too far. The mutation turned up in Mawere yesterday, that's a neighboring district so that doesn't mean it's jumping. But a lot of day laborers live in Mawere so they could be spreading the virus by riding the bus to work. Today, there are reports of illnesses from downtown Lagos, but we don't know yet if it is the mutation."

"That's fast."

"A city-wide quarantine may be necessary within days if this trend continues. You see why I didn't want that EuroNet crew around. We need you to come to Lagos with all the air and water purification equipment you have, and vaccinations."

"We only have capacity for 80 people, a few more when you divert the purifications systems for the trees to humans. That's nothing compared to your needs."

"Everything is something. There are US and French navy ships en route, and a private hospital ship. But none will be here for at least three days. You can make it in one day. We can deploy your equipment to one of the neighborhood hospitals. It's enough for the local hospital in Mushin or Onianu. If we can create a buffer there, that might be enough to slow down the virus in that area. A little may buy us a lot of time. We have to use everything."

"Then I'm going to have to tell the EuroNet reporter."

"Why?" He knew Theo well enough to know this wasn't a whim.

"They have a newer model airship, it's faster, larger and can reach altitudes our sand-huggers cannot. We need their ship."

"I suppose. The news would get out shortly."

"I have to wait until morning. We can't just pack up the equipment, it would traumatize the plants. We need to leave enough water behind for a skeleton crew and the saplings. We'll leave at first light."

"Be careful, there are sandstorms in the forecast."

"There are always sandstorms in the forecast," the fatalist said.

CHAPTER 43

"Mr. President, General Hayden is here."

"Send him in."

The Chief was the only person in the Oval Office with Ailes, so it was all very cozy. "Jack, Jack, great to see you again. Everything is going splendidly."

The President sat in his chair with Hayden next to him with the Chief at a comfortable distance on the couch. "Thank you, Mr. President. I wish I could share your enthusiasm. There are cracks in the system."

The Chief hid his annoyance that Hayden had got straight to complaining when chit-chat would have been in order. This was supposed to be his election. The Chief thought it was unseemly for Hayden to keep running to the President for help.

Ailes didn't seem bothered at all and picked up on Hayden's lead. "Nonsense. Money, media, momentum. You've got it all. The Chinese Device is even working in your favor. The only thing they've got is that Cranston acts like St. Francis in public and acts like Genghis Khan in private. He's a ruthless son of a bitch, but he can't carry this thing alone. McDowell is worse than useless."

"O'Brien is going to let slip just enough information about the Chinese Device soon; we'll be ready with just enough information every day for a week. Then day after day, its Chinese device equals McDowell equals Expendable. Who serves whom?"

"What if the Chinese Device is a big nothing?"

"So, what if it is? No one will know for sure until after the election."

"Are you telling me..."

"No, I'm not telling you anything. No one knows what it is. Don't worry, we've got the deck; they've got a deuce and the Suicide King."

"Still, it would help to get rid of those hackers. I don't like uncontrolled factors. And what the hell does SID mean, anyway?"

"And that's brings us to why I asked you here. Don, bring the boys in."

The Chief went to the door that connected his office to the Oval and motioned a small group of four three men and one woman into the room. They were all slightly nervous and awestruck. They had been working for the President for two months and this was the first time seeing him.

With a well-practiced expansive gesture, the President said, "Please, everyone, sit down." As one, they headed for the chairs and couch but halted in a panic: sit where? Was there a protocol? Who sat closest to the President? The Chief was standing where he had he been sitting? The Chief settled that by directly each to a seat, placing the team leader in the second chair closest to the President.

"Jack, here is your brain trust."

"Pardon me, sir?"

"Best 360s in the country. The White House's best. They are yours for the duration. Tight security in the White House can cut both ways. Nothing unauthorized can get out or in, but sometimes you need a little maneuvering room, you'll have that at party headquarters. A loan from the White House. Thank you, ladies and gentlemen."

The Chief was the only one practiced at this. He stood

instantly and said, "Thank you, Mr. President." The team followed his lead, but Hayden was confused whether this dismissal also referred to him.

The Chief subtly but firmly settled that question. "General, we'll continue in my office." The Chief walked the General out as the team followed. Once in his office, the Chief continued, "As the President said, we'll set up shop at party headquarters. While the General is here, give him the highlights of your research."

The team sighed a collective sigh of relief that this part of the meeting had been mapped out. The team leader immediately projected a map of the Earth, Moon, and a few key satellites and space stations before turning his attention to the group.

"Bottom line: It's impossible that it's one person, it has to be a network of hackers. We are working on the assumption that this is being led by Americans, but it is extremely unlikely that it is only a US operation. Avoiding exposure this long means they have the entire planet to hide in." He then rotated the screen 45 degrees. It was flashy and meaningless, but he hoped the two old men would be impressed.

"The physical infrastructure cannot be too large there is no one central point. Like a terrorist network, it has no capital city, no headquarters. Such a set-up would be dangerous if found, we could destroy the network in a flash plus unnecessary since six supercomputers linking a near infinite number of personal computers could do everything SID does."

He closed the screen and concluded. "We've done linguistic analysis of all written and verbal communications, looking for clues in syntax, word choice, etc. to narrow down the options. We're certain they are running all transmissions through computer screening to remove any trace of individuality. The longer communiqués read as though a computer wrote them."

Hayden had had unpleasant experiences with computers during his career, so he flipped the conversation elsewhere. "I understand the political threat SID poses, how serious is the national security threat?" He meant of course threats to his election.

The Chief jumped in, knowing what Hayden wanted to hear and knowing the techies would not understand the subtext.

"Extensive. SID has been more of a nuisance than a threat. But it has shown a capacity to hack into virtually every computer system on Earth. As you know, there are constant failed attempts to hack government and military systems. They fail and we can't be sure if SID or some facet of SID is behind any of them. But they do seem to succeed more than they fail. That SID has not, say, forced space stations out of orbit or crashed a large bank is more likely a case of lack of desire than lack of ability. But, as you said, it's the uncertainty that's the real danger."

"Is it Cranston?"

The politician continued. "Highly unlikely, he's got people who would be very good at this, but so does every important person. The scientific community loves him and McDowell, so there's a deep well of talent that they could tap. Ethically if you can use that word about Cranston, he is of course capable, but we're watching too closely. If there was any hint of a connection, we would have picked it up by now. Throwing suspicion on Cranston is good politics, but it doesn't get us anywhere close to truly solving the problem."

"Ok, but is there anything SID can do to us?"

Before he could answer, the Chief's phone emitted a quick three-note signal. Rather than answer his party's presidential candidate question, he answered his phone. Hayden was shocked but the Chief didn't notice or apologize. The Chief looked at his phone, scowled and showed the phone to Hayden.

"This a special link exactly 18 people can access it. When that goes off, there is something urgent." His faced darkened as he read. "SID is at it again. It hacked a game show and every answer on the screen was 'Zhidoi.'"

"Could be worse."

"It is. Before SID closed down, the last answer was 'Ask Ailes about Zhidoi.'"

CHAPTER 44

All the 360s and politicians involved would have been amused to know – and would probably invoke the chaos theory – that Sean and his team were plowing the same field as Ailes' people at the same time. The senator wasn't there, so the mood was far less formal and more freewheeling. Plus, they learned long ago that isolating computer geeks to themselves didn't deliver the best results. While everyone in the room knew their computers, there were also experts on religion, philosophy, history, a whole range of disciplines that allowed them to examine problems from different angles. Still, Sean and Worth were running the show, so discipline was the order of the day.

"SID. Not a person's name, wants us to think that but clearly playing," prompted Sean, "So an acronym?" Sean said, throwing something out to get the brains sparking.

"Society? Science, scientists, scholars." Tamar ran with it.

"Secret," added Juan.

"Subversion," continued Tal.

Tamar took it back. "Why does SID have to be English?"

"It doesn't," Tal argued, "Except that all communications have been in English, and SID has an obvious interest in the comings and goings of the United States. Europe, Russia, even China, everything else is incidental."

Worth joined in. "What about religion? What covers the world? Politics, business, science and religion. Catholics. S for Synod? Maybe it's Latin."

Juan said, "Protestants use Synod too, the Lutherans for example."

Tal batted out. "A person's name? Samuel Isaac Davis. I don't know."

Snapping around, Worth asked, "Why did you use those names?"

"I don't know, first names that came into my head that fit."

"Samuel, Isaac, David, all key figures in the Old Testament."

"Maybe the I is God," said Tamar.

The non-theological among them – meaning all of them – stared.

"What?" asked Sean.

"God. Yahweh in Greek starts with an I, Greek doesn't have a Y."

"Now you're fishing."

"'I shall make you a fisher of men.' Peter, Simon Peter. Simon, Simon. No apostles begin with I or D," Tamar continued.

"Stop it." Tal was getting bored.

Juan picked it up. "'I' could be just as simple as 'in' or 'it'..."

"... or 'I'."

"So I Did," suggested Tamar.

"Meaning?" asked Sean.

"Don't know."

"Alright, alright, just stop it..."

"Stop it, dude."

The marine had had enough. "Shut up," Worth said, "Brainstorming is good, but we are just pissing on our own shoes. We have analyses in front of us. Language analysis shows that the English is letter perfect, meaning it is likely the people run all text through a computer to eliminate linguistic clues..."

"... Or that the entire thing is computer-driven without human control," suggested Tal.

"Please don't say that again," suggested Tamar.

"But what if it is artificial intelligence?"

"It's more likely a loose network of individuals highly skilled..." Worth continued.

"Such as 360s," Juan said.

Everyone paused and instinctively and embarrassingly glance around the room.

Worth grabbed back the conversation. "They never meet, maybe never met. At least one, probably more, has access to supercomputers. That's the key. Supercomputers must be involved to network so effectively and hide their tracks."

"Great, there's only some 5,000 such computers on Earth, space stations and the Moon," Juan said.

"6,112," added Tamar.

"At least, we can discount space stations and the Moon. They limit the traffic off of stations compared to what happens on Earth. They couldn't hide the origins of space transmissions."

Sean took a break. "This shouldn't be investigated by techies only. We're thinking like computer experts, we need other frames of reference politics, religion, even philosophy. We have to understand why they are doing this, not how."

"We need to recruit more imagination," Worth added.

"At least as much as they have. They are not doing this to prove how clever they are. They're not sociopaths creating viruses to crash computers. They could do it, but they're not. Nearly everything they do is technically sophisticated, but almost childish in content. But you don't poke the world's most powerful governments in the eye for a schoolyard prank. Their abilities and actions don't match. We focus too much on the how and who, somebody has to deal with the why."

"So, they are planning, what?" asked Tal.

Sean's special ping sounded. He bolted to his computer

and pulled up the image the ping cited. It was an afternoon quiz show.

"What's this?" he asked, puzzled by his own computer.

"Some stupid quiz show," Juan noted.

They watched as the host speaking in a language slightly above white noise prompted the contestants. But every third word was with a computer voice saying "Zhidoi." SID was playing its old game. The team stared at the screen. Finally, the announcer said, "Alright, contestants. For 200 points, what is…"

But instead of a question, SID said, "Ask Ailes about Zhidoi."

"The Great Flood!" the contestant squealed.

"Correct!"

The technicians stared at each other. Sean and Worth caught their breaths, realizing in time that they weren't supposed to know that Zhidoi had any special meaning. The others were genuinely confused.

"What the hell was that?" asked Tamar.

Speaking up from his computer, Tal read, "Zhidoi is an industrial city in the Qinghai Province of China. Pretty high elevation, 3000 meters. Population three million. Some heavy metal manufacturing. Class 5 pollution. At least two secret military sites. Major claim to fame is that it is near the headwaters of both the Mekong and Yangtze Rivers. Nothing special here."

"So, who's supposed to ask about Zhidoi?"

"I can think of someone," Sean noted.

CHAPTER 45

The sweepers' pilots were receiving their daily briefing in the assembly hall. As usual, Ron sat next to Kate. They were all checking their tablets.

"Everyone got your coordinates for the day?" the ensign asked as she updated the master screen. The screen showed a grid with the *Roosevelt* in the center and numbers in the other squares designating each cleaner's responsibility. The data transmitted to each tablet. "Sensors show nothing unusually large in our field today. The video crew that arrived yesterday will be here until tomorrow, so we do not factor their ship in. However, at VIP ship is arriving at approximately 1040 today when we are over US space. Once its trajectory gets set, they will instruct you to stand down or move further from the station to ensure no complications. One final point, that European team wants to interview a cleaner. They will inform the lucky pilot of the captain's decision after mess tonight. Finally, double check your grid. If there are no questions, you may leave."

There were no questions, so the pilots got up in unison and walked out.

Kate asked Ron, "Who do you think is going to get on TV?" She was petite. Most crew members were on the small size lanky didn't work well in space.

"Don't know. But you can bet it won't be you or me."

"Why is that?"

"I'm too junior and you, well..." Pause before punchline. "Well, you're too ugly." He got the desired slap on the back of his head.

CHAPTER 46

Sandy was determined to make it to Colorado. Most people would want to escape the putrid swamp of Alabama. There were enclaves for the rich and while climate change didn't change everything, but the bulk of the southern states along the Gulf Coast were empty of everyone who could escape. Decades of pollution from the land and sea had created a dead zone along the northern coast of the Gulf. Oxygen-sucking algae was the only life-form of any note. Pink, red, green tides would take turns roiling up on shore and leave a new collection of rot on the beaches that even the crows avoided. Shrimp and any edible fish were long gone. Attempts to create kelp and "good" algae farms got pummeled. There was nothing left to do but move inland and pretend it was normal.

Sandy had enough. She was young enough and pretty enough to find a decent job in the cool cities of the Rockies. She had to leave Alabama and cross four state lines, most likely by foot. Each state had its own methods for keeping people out. She didn't worry about Mississippi. The government didn't care so long as you kept walking. Besides, she had an aunt in Winona so she could pretend she had a legitimate reason for being there, and her accent was close enough so not to draw attention. She needed to offer some relief to a truck driver and a couple of guards at the border, but that was a small price to pay. She straightened up, rinsed her mouth with moonshine, and kept walking.

Omar lived in Russellville, and he was staying put. He had no choice; he was only eight. Besides, he didn't know any other world. Escape? To where? Sandy passed within ten miles of Omar's village but didn't notice. They designed the villages not to be noticeable, and the bulk of the populace was fine with that. The villages had fences but no barbed wire. They only locked the gates at night. The guards had no visible weapons. The residents weren't prisoners; they were there to receive help, the easier it was to make sure they had the minimal food necessary and that no medical surprises were brewing. They were free to leave so long as they went back to the Gulf.

And they were villages, not camps. Too often in history "camp" came after "internment," "concentration," "re-education." No, these were villages, with all the accompanying imagery of neo-Roman town halls, squares with a gazebo in the center, and park benches delicately placed among the scrubs and flowering trees. There were a few trees and benches.

It was also purely a matter of demographics that everyone in the village was black. Occasionally, a white person would be among the team of doctors or aid workers who visited. Omar was five before he saw a white face. He stared wide-eyed at the doctor, tugged at his mother, and asked, "What's wrong with her face?"

By the time Sandy got to the great river the next night, Omar was engaged in his favorite past-time staring at the stars. It was a rare privilege he didn't know he had. No light pollution. Unlike so many others, he could see clearly into space. On nights with a weak moon, such as this one, he could also see several large stars moving quickly through the blackness. When he asked his mother about the stars that ran so quickly, she told him those were space stations. That people lived up there and looked down at the Earth. Why? To see what is happening here. Why don't they just ask us?

Arkansas was a problem. The Ozark watershed gave the state a bit of an advantage, but they wrapped the state on three sides by Mississippi, Louisiana, Texas, and Oklahoma. Arkansas was like an icicle in a bowl of warm water it was still an icicle, but not forever. As everywhere across the South, mosquitoes were the prime enemy, they could spray all they wanted, but the mosquito populations grew larger and more aggressive every season. Arkansas couldn't stop mosquitos, but every human at the state line got checked for cholera, Zika and the rest. She needed a lot of moonshine mouthwash to get across the border.

When she got to Oklahoma, she was getting excited despite her embedded cynicism. But then she faced the awful reality that she was in Oklahoma. Everyone knew a scorched scar ran ragged through the Great Plains from Texas to North Dakota, but no one warned her of the boring hell-scape of this place. What water and soil they had they had poisoned, there was no defense against the temperature rises, what soil hadn't blown away baked. The state was a giant brick. A regular round of earthquakes over the decades had cracked the brick, what water underneath was a witches' brew of unidentifiable chemicals identifying the chemicals would have been an unnecessary burden. At least there weren't any mosquitoes there wasn't any water. Sandy might have been able to fake her away so far, but there was no one here to con.

She was lucky when the first sandstorm hit. She saw it coming from miles away and found an old gas station in time. What had been the checkout counter became her bomb shelter. Before squeezing herself under the counter, she took one more look at a monster she never imagined possible. The sandstorm was first visible as a billowing cloud of sand, but as it got closer it grew. Instead of a cloud, it was now a tower. Instead of being brown, it was now black. Mesmerized, she watched it snatch up more dirt and sucking it up as if it were a giant, angry straw. It grew meaner and howled louder and she realized what she was facing a sand tornado. She had enough experience with traditional tornados to know that the path of destruction was very narrow, but very thorough. If it missed her, it missed her. But if it hit her, every bit of sand and dirt would strike like a tiny piece of buckshot traveling at the speed of a missile. It wouldn't matter how many counters she was hiding behind.

The force of the storm was so great that Sandy was certain the ground cried. She heard what the gas station windows smash left behind. The tornado was closer, but she didn't dare peek at how close. Her ears bled from all the howling. She didn't notice exactly when it happened, but after a few minutes she realized her ears weren't ringing. The rattling was quieting. She dared peek over the counter. Sand and debris were still swirling through the air, but now there was also some sunlight. The tornado had moved on.

She headed for the main highway, assuming that if another storm came, there would be more place to take shelter. But there would also be more people. She calculated that talking her way past people was better than risking turning into sandpaper. She should have realized from a lifetime of being invisible, no one would pay any attention to her. So long as she kept walking, didn't loiter around any cars or grocery stores, avoided eye contact, she was in good shape. A police or Border Control car would slow down occasionally to examine this unusual specimen, but ultimately decided it wasn't worth it to leave their air-conditioned cars.

The tornado also caused Sandy to decide against sleeping in the open. That was another reason for the highway. One day near Tulsa, she saw a larger building ahead. It looked like it would be a good place for the night. She could see some windows freshly covered. Small solar panels scattered around the roof. In the dying light, she could already see some lights in the windows. Whatever this building's intended use, it was now a squat. The sign was well-battered. Chunks of the lettering were missing. She might have been able to figure out what it had said if she cared. " he J am s . Inh fe Cent o Religi nd Sc enc ."

She snuck in unnoticed. Her hope that everyone would be too stoned to pay attention was dashed. No one was. She had stumbled on some kind of purity cult. Advertising herself as an orphan seeking solitude and enlightenment in the isolated Rockies, the residents pointed her to a mattress, offered her some tea "Don't worry, we have a filtration system" and asked discreetly if she had something to share. Seeing that all she had were a few protein bars and the booze, she made excuses. They were disappointed but not aggressive. She collapsed on the mattress and slept through the night. No one touched her.

Omar found the knife half buried in the mud on the steam bed. It was ugly and corroded but to an eight-year-old; it was treasure. Pirate treasure. Charging and slashing at a suspicious overhang of kudzu, Captain Omar vanquished the enemy, collecting all the gold for himself. He twirled the knife in the air to demonstrate to all his confidence. But he caught it by the blade and cut a couple of fingers. It hurt, but he was a brave pirate who would never complain to his mother, so he hid the knife under a rock and went home for dinner. He washed his hands of course so he knew the cuts were clean. He thought nothing of it until he woke up the next morning, his fingers swollen and green.

Sandy's luck held up so well that she truly believed that she would make it to Colorado. By necessity, she had to turn northwest as she got closer to the border. But that meant entering even more desolate land. There were a few old signs laying claim to property here, indicting she was now on Indian territory. The land looked exactly the same. Equality at last. The illusion was a speck at first, no more than a black smudge on the horizon. She knew it wasn't a storm rising, no wind, no sound, which was a relief since there was no place to take shelter. It clearly wasn't a car, not wide enough. Maybe a motorcycle? The smudge took on more form as it got closer. It was a man on a horse.

He was going the opposite direction of what Sandy wanted, but still it was a potential ride. She wasn't afraid that was a useless emotion, but she didn't know exactly what she would do when the moment came. And then the moment came, and the rider revealed. The rider was an Indian. Of course he was. What else did she expect? That would not help her. Asking an Indian for help was a ridiculous waste of energy for a white person. Her special skills would not be useful with someone who would undoubtedly hate her on sight. He rode up to her, deliberately, steadily, never breaking pace, never veering off course. He stopped in front of her.

As bad as the situation was, it was now worse. He was a tribal policeman. Huge chunks of the Plains returned to the First Peoples, now that the Second Peoples had worn them out. Sandy thought the Native Americans were fanatics for accepting such a deal. But she like most non-Indians had heard stories about Indian magic that was restoring the land. Nonsense, she thought. The rider sat motionless his black eyes stared at her. She wanted to say something, but she didn't know what. Asking for help would undoubtedly result in an ironic chuckle. Before she could open her mouth, he looked down on her whiteness, took out his rifle and pointed it west.

"Keep walking."

And he rode off.

CHAPTER 47

Once a month during the new moon when the heavens were the darkest the Prairie Grass Evangelical Church sponsored a sky watch. They rented a high-resolution telescope from the university, and a professor volunteered her time to point out the stars and the galloping planets. But what everyone was most interested in was brighter and faster than any planet. They wanted to see the USS *Theodore Roosevelt*. All the space stations were large enough and viewable with the simplest telescope, but this was more than an astronomy class: it was a celebration of one of their own.

The Andersons were uncomfortable with the attention vanity was not among their sins but Rev. Hang convinced them that this was not only about Ron but the hope and energy that Ron represented. In this sense, he wasn't just their son but the son/big brother to everyone. Ron although not thrilled, had the option of switching off the radio.

Civilian radios could not be too powerful, so conversations were a series of brief intervals. There wasn't even enough time for an uninterrupted prayer. Plus, they could only see the ship for some 12 minutes. Still, they could see the *Roosevelt* long before they heard anything. When Ron came on, the little ones always squealed: "A voice from outer space!" And there was always a know-it-all ten-year-old who said, "It's not outer space, he's in low earth orbit, outer space begins…" "I can see him!" "Is he waving?" He would tell them what he and his friends were doing, what interesting piece of space debris he had found fortunately the little ones still hadn't thought to ask why there was so much stuff up there, what Minnesota looked like from space, how bright the moon was, explaining why the moon didn't have phases in space.

Finally, after an hour meaning two orbits, the congregation formed a circle and held hands to pray. If it was warm enough, they knelt. Some knelt anyway. "Heavenly Father," Rev. Hang spoke, "Some say 'The poor and the earth are crying out. O Lord, seize us with your power and light, help us protect all life, to prepare for a better future, for the coming of your Kingdom of justice, peace, love and beauty.' Jesus Christ our savior told us 'Blessed are those who hunger and thirst after righteousness, for they will be filled.' We hunger, we thirst, but through your mercy our needs are of the soul, not the body. We pray for our brothers and sisters whose hunger and thirst are the immediate needs of their bodies, victims of a world turned against them. Our dear son Ronald tolls high above your Earth, doing your work to help protect and renew your beautiful creation. We pray you protect Ronald and his brothers and sisters. All glory to You. Amen."

CHAPTER 48

Ruth sat before her video screen, trying to speak without using the words she wanted. Her conversation was with the Interior Minister. He was a colonel in full uniform but insisted on the fiction that he was a humble government servant, therefore should be addressed as "minister," not "colonel." Captain Jamal was sitting quietly to the side, outside of the range of the camera.

"Mr. Minister, our security team says they have heard rumors that some men with reputations as poachers and smugglers are moving inland in our direction. Someone in the ministry must have leaked the news about the baby."

"Why my people? Why not yours?"

Jamal clenched visibly.

"There are very few people here compared to the ministry. I trust them. And even if the leak was from here, wouldn't it be easier for someone already here just to steal Rabu?"

"Who?"

"The baby orangutan. The last report of the selling of a kidnapped orangutan was half a million dollars. Anyone here could snatch the baby and disappear. Why go through the trouble of recruiting poachers?"

"I see they hired you for your scientific skills, not diplomacy."

"I suppose this is the wrong time to mention that the nature zone needs to expand. The more successful we are at replenishing the population, the greater the temptation to invade."

"We'll investigate your rumors." And with that, the screen went blank.

Jamal moved his chair to face Ruth. "Liar. He knows full well that the news is out and where it came from."

"Could they get half a million for Rabu?"

"Sure. That was three years ago. Rare animals are getting rarer. You only need a handful of billionaires to keep the market alive. And orangutans are a hell of a lot safer to capture than tigers." He paused before turning to his least favorite subject. "You know, my offer to give you rifle training still stands. Karen ..."

"I know how to shoot."

"You know your way around a firing range. You don't know how to shoot."

CHAPTER 49

I t wasn't true, but the air seemed so much fresher at the Colorado border. The Dust Bowl winds were still blowing, but they were blowing against her back. She wanted to believe there was snow on the mountains she saw in the distance. She wanted to believe she was mere steps away from being able to sit under a tree. As was her strategy, Sandy aimed for a minor crossing point, but the minor crossing points meant dangerous mountains or deserts. She could have tried slipping in through Kansas, there was essentially no border between Kansas and Oklahoma, but she had had enough dust. She could have tried slipping in through New Mexico, but she had had enough of Indians.

The only safe crossing between Oklahoma and Colorado was the main crossing at Campo. So Campo it was. Sometimes blending into a crowd was the best option, but these days Sandy often found herself to be one of the few white faces, so that wasn't the best idea. Desolate posts worked better: bored guards willing to accept her favors because what else was did he have the energy for?

The Campo crossing was the busiest she had seen in her travels. She looked around the trucks, hoping for a hitch or to hide in the back. But everything was locked tight. And there weren't many of them to begin with who had anything to ship into Colorado? Most of the traffic went the other way.

She had no choice but to walk through as if it was something, she did every day. She was ready to find the opportunity to offer her services, but that ended as the door slid open. The agent was sitting behind a Plexiglas wall, massive arms folded across a massive chest, waiting for the next slob to enter. Grim, squat. And female. Going forward was Sandy's only option.

Looking Sandy over as if she were a fish that might not be quite fresh, the agent asked through a speaker, "Where are you from?"

Sandy had been practicing her accent. "Tulsa, I'm here to visit friends."

"Friends," the agent repeated with absolutely no conviction. "And you walked? Nice friends." She just kept looking at Sandy. She had tried to clean up a few hours before. She knew she smelled of the road, but she couldn't have been that disgusting. The agent slid open a small door and commanded, "Hold out your hand, palm up."

She had no choice, but she did it as slowly as possible. For someone who barely moved, the agent was fast, grasping Sandy's wrist as soon as it was through the door. She took out a small, pointed tab, and again with a practiced swiftness, pricked Sandy's finger. Sandy instinctively tried to pull away, but the vice was firm. Once the tab was red with a few drops of Sandy's blood, the agent let go. She put the tab in a small device that looked like a scanner. After one minute or one hour, the device flashed. The agent looked at it and for the first time showed an emotion other than boredom. "Whoa." She looked at Sandy again, this time it was a sharper appraisal. Then she hit the intercom. "Security. One for quarantine."

Sandy was fast.

The guards were faster.

CHAPTER 50

"""B""ridge, this is RV 3. Ready for launch."

"Stand down, RV 3. VIP ship approaching through sector N-0046. They're ahead of schedule. Once secure in the docking port, you will receive permission to release."

"Roger."

He sat back and waited. Since all he could see out the window was the docking bay, he studied the blips on his computer instead. The small, slow-moving blips were the other cleaners. He could see some larger chunks of debris, but then there was something moving oddly. It was the same size as the cleaners, but it was moving much faster and heading straight at the *Roosevelt*. This had to be the VIP, but what the hell was he doing?

"Bridge, this is RV 3. Don't want to be telling you your business, but isn't that ship approaching fast?"

"Right on both counts it's approaching too fast, and it's none of your business."

"Roger that." Someone was nervous. He probably had Hightower leaning over him, breathing fire while watching some idiot zeroing in on his ship. Ron resolved himself to staying put for a while. No one was going to be thinking about him.

The technical procedure was the same for *Apollo XX*, but the protocol was distinctly different. This time Captain Hightower himself and two junior officers were waiting at the airlock. Their VIP had arrived. He hated the political part of the job, but it was part of the job. First the EuroNet crew and now a civilian. This was not a hotel. He didn't want both parties, but the EuroNet visit got scheduled months before and this new one was an addition he couldn't reject.

The door opened and out strode a tall young man. He took in his surroundings with darting eyes that never fixed on any one thing. He looked at the people, but never in the eye until he focused on Hightower. Then he looked the captain up and down, a bit quizzically.

"Welcome to the USS *Theodore Roosevelt*, Mr. Prescott." Hightower extended his hand. Prescott was a civilian, so this was all the formality Hightower felt he needed. The young man took his hand, glanced into the captain's eyes, but immediately drifted to their joined hands.

"Thanks, Captain. An amazing trip."

"I see you piloted yourself. Very impressive." Even though Hightower took an instant dislike to the young man, he grudgingly admired his skill. We do not design ships like his to fly this high into space, he thought. Joyriding just below the debris belt, say 600 kilometers above the Earth, was the typical extent. Even though his ship was top of line, to surpass 1,500 klicks without spinning out of control, it needed a sure hand to ensure a safe trip.

Prescott didn't so much as release his handshake as let his hand slip, as if he had forgotten it was there. His eyes were now roaming the corridor. When he spoke, he had stopped looking at the captain and instead seemed to look at all the computer panels along the wall.

"Been flying since I was a kid. This is my third trip into space."

"Amazing, I know a hundred people who would love to make even one trip."

"Yeah, well, everyone's not me, are they? What's your first name?" He still wasn't looking at Hightower when he said this.

The captain was taken back. The escorting officers stole glances at each other. He didn't read up on the *Roosevelt* before he left.

"Charles."

"Mind if I call you Chuck?"

The escorting officers tried to make themselves small.

"Mr. Prescott, you are on the USS *Theodore Roosevelt* and I am its captain. I prefer, Captain."

"Absolutely, absolutely." It was as if he heard the words, but not the slap back in the voice.

The two walked down the corridor with the junior officers following as far back as safety permitted.

"I don't get it," one whispered

"His dad is a friend of Ailes," said the other.

CHAPTER 51

Ike didn't think it was possible, but Peter's new office in the Pentagon was more loaded with computers than his old one at the Academy. Peter couldn't have been happier than if he had gone to heaven, which in a temporal sense he had. But at the moment, Peter's bliss centered on their leader, not his machines. "This is truly extraordinary. The General tells us to watch out for Zhidoi and in only a week, the news is out all over the world..."

"But the news came from SID, not the White House or Pentagon."

"It doesn't matter. It's the hand of God at work. The General knew what was going to happen. He saw everything we all saw, but he saw more. Your father's passing brought that data file to you and General Adams to you. And he knew about Zhidoi. Even the fact that you needed me to read the data file fit the plan: The General needed someone like me. This is not a series of coincidences. Remember when he said your father could never have done this alone? He needed General Adams at Cheyenne Mountain, but we've progressed so that the help doesn't physically have to be in different places. Under his instructions, I've been able to reprogram several computers to act at our command without ever leaving the Pentagon. We are missing only one more element..."

Peter didn't finish his thought when the general entered. Both captains came to attention.

"As you were. Peter, you've explained everything?"

"All the technical arrangements, as you instructed."

"And?"

"About the hand. I was about to tell him about the hand. But I thought you would, rather."

The general motioned for the men to sit. Then he sat, pulled his chair closer and leaned over. And with that movement alone, he ceased to be a general but was now family. A favorite uncle. Adams was very good at persuasion. "Ike, think about all the humble men God has called to his service. Even Moses considered himself unworthy. But think for a moment. Why should the all-powerful God need men to perform his deeds? Could not God had freed the Israelites and parted the Red Sea without Moses? Of course, he could. He didn't need Joshua to destroy Jericho. He created the Flood without man, why could He have not saved Noah and his family and the animals without the ark? Why?"

"Because God created man in His own image and called on man to test him, to test his faith in God. God could have freed the Israelites without Moses, but without the will to act by Moses and the Israelites, they would not have proved their faith in God. God calls on man to show his faith."

"Exactly!" Adams quickly reached over and in a surprisingly swift and strong motion, he grabbed Ike's right hand and thrust it skywards. His gaze followed his movement and the captains instinctively followed the general. At that moment, all three were staring at Ike's raised hand.

CHAPTER 52

The EuroNet plane made several wide, low circles over the Galapagos Islands. The team had been here three times before over the previous seven years, so they knew what they were looking at. They saw the expanding patches of green on some islands especially Isabelle and were sure a few of the smaller islands were definitely lost beneath the ocean. All the shorelines were under stress, but it would not have been possible to judge how successful the re-planting of the mangroves and creation of artificial nesting platforms for birds had been.

Much of the new green was due to Scalesia trees more whimsically known as daisy trees were the most common genus on the islands. Clear-cutting for farmland and introducing goats and pigs that ate saplings decimated the trees. Aggressive efforts to protect the trees reversed the trends, but as El Niños started lasting longer, the growth cycle of the trees was disrupted and the balance between mature plants and seedlings were knocked out of balance. So, it wasn't a matter of planting more Scalesia. Other indigenous species were carefully planted to aid the daisy trees and take their place if the islands' climate changed too much more.

The mangroves were the most valuable and abused trees on the islands. Taken for granted for centuries, mangroves were powerful tools in maintaining habitable land. Their ability to extend their roots through salt water and anchor themselves in the shifting, silty soil below meant they were feeding ground for fish, nesting for birds and a bulwark against the wind and waves. But from Louisiana to Bangladesh, they were decimated as humans tried to master the environment. It was as if a medieval knight went into battle by removing his breast plate. At least in the Galapagos, they weren't uprooted in the name of progress, but still climate change pummeled the stands, exposing the retreating land and robbing reptiles, birds and fish of food and nesting areas.

After they had shot enough footage, the plane began its slow and almost silent descent to Santa Cruz.

Electricity or biofuels now powered nearly all transportation. Oil-based internal combustion engines were mostly used for air travel and propulsion into space and a few nostalgic car races, mostly in the United States. The gas engine was still the most effective way to counter Earth's gravity. Russia's attempt at a nuclear-powered rocket to reach space ended with 5,000 dead and a landscape that made Chernobyl look like the Garden of Eden. The amount of gas used decreased even as the launches into space increased due to more efficient engines and lighter but stronger alloys used in the launch vehicles construction. Finally, launch vehicles were no longer the skyscraper sized rockets but were instead sleek air ships that piggy-backed spaceships up to the outer atmosphere where the spaceships separated and launched themselves into space.

Airplanes had gradually shifted to solar generated electricity. It wasn't easy, and it was scary not to hear the roaring engines at take-off. But the designs were so elegant and evocative that the public fell in love with the idea of sitting in a plane that didn't look like it should exist.

EuroNet had to make the most energy efficient aircraft possible. The dual goals of global travel and reducing carbon required a fleet of specially designed aircraft. Unlike commercial air travel where speed was a major selling point, EuroNet sacrificed efficiency for speed. That they couldn't cross the Atlantic in three hours wasn't the issue, doing it with zero emissions was. They were also free of the need for bulk. Commercial crafts needed to transport hundreds of people, no EuroNet design accommodated more than six people. EuroNet adapted its technology from commercial and military designs. But they added tilt rotors that added weight and slowed things down but eliminated the needed for landing strips. The rotors rotated 45 degrees and allowed the ship to land vertically like a helicopter. This was an important consideration when teams were visiting remote locales or areas where paving over land for an airstrip was not a popular notion.

Which was why the EuroNet plane arriving at the Galapagos had tilt rotors. While there was still one traditional landing field at Puerto Ayora on Isla Santa Cruz, all other airstrips had been torn up and replanted leaving only a room-sized patch of concrete for vertical landings. Even though they would have landed at Puerto Ayora, the crew opted for the soft landing in deference to their host's distaste for swooping landings.

The first off the plane was Elsa. A 30-something Dane, whose athletic stride made her look taller than she was, looked around and spotted Sanjeet. She was followed off the plane by Marta, a Czech who was the camera operator/producer, and Pol, a Belgian, who was the pilot and doubled as the sound and light engineer when needed.

Sanjeet embraced Elsa. It was not a casual embrace. "Welcome back."

"Thanks." She was in no hurry to let go. "From the air, it doesn't look like much has changed."

"These days, that's a compliment." They finally realized they had not let go.

"Are things any better?"

"Minor recoveries, mostly terrestrial. I have some hopes for some marine life, but we need more than one cycle to be sure. There has been little recovery from the last El Niño. At least three tortoises drowned during the last rainy season, but the mangroves on the eastern side of the islands are doing pretty well." They started walking away, with the other catching up. "There's a lot to show you. It's about time you came back, I thought we were your most popular documentary last year."

"Second most."

"And the first?"

"'The Last Polar Bear.'"

CHAPTER 53

The helmsman had gone through his routine when a ship was leaving the port and heading away from the *Roosevelt* in this case, heading back to Earth. He monitored the ship, waiting for the moment it was officially outside of his station's responsibility. But the routine ended too soon.

"*Apollo XX*, this is *Roosevelt*. Do you read me? You are off course, your speed is 20% too fast, please change course or you will leave the safe zone eight minutes early."

The voice coming out of the comm was calm. "Man, you guys in a space station just cannot appreciate speed. Do you have any idea what I'm feeling?" His tone of voice let everyone know that "space" wasn't just something outside the ship.

Captain Hightower decided his intervention was necessary. "You're going to be feeling decompression if you hit anything out there. We've got two sweepers out there, and there's potential for debris. Stay within the corridor we plotted for you."

"Ok, ok, but this is the greatest rush ever..."

"Then do it when you're out of my jurisdiction... *sir.*"

The ship did not change course but increased its speed.

"Helm, what's he heading into?"

"He's heading straight for a cleaner, sir. Also, debris."

"Warn him."

"RV 3, RV 3. Do you read?"

Ron's seriously annoyed voice came across. "I read you. What's that ship doing?"

"He's stoned, flying outside his coordinates, and too fast.

He's heading for you." "I can see that. I can't outrun him, what's my best maneuver?"

"Heading 43.3 is the best way to avoid him, but there are bogies over there."

"Doesn't look like there's anything big. Do you read it the same way?"

"Roger that."

"Guess I'll take my chances with the junk rather than the junk-head."

"Stay in constant radio contact."

"Get the second ship nearby just in case he gets damaged," Hightower commanded.

"Aye, sir. RV 6, RV 6. Do you read?"

"I read you." It was Kate.

"RV 6, do you see RV 3 and the civilian ship?"

"Affirmative on both."

"Change your heading to 0042 and rendezvous with RV 3. He is taking evasive action to avoid the civilian. This is sending him into a bogie field but prepared to assist."

"Copy that."

"Captain, we lose visual contact in 90 seconds."

Meanwhile, Lt. Tanaka was escorting McBride towards the climate control chamber when he noticed crew members hurrying by. Stopping one of them, he asked, "What's going on?"

"That rich kid was on the station is flying off course and forcing a cleaner to move towards debris to avoid him."

"What rich kid?" McBride asked.

"Name's Prescott. Was on the station for... something."

"Prescott? Prescott Aeronautics?"

"Yes, the old man's son."

"We were on the station at the same time and no one thought to mention that?"

"Not my responsibility." Which wasn't exactly true: his captain had ordered him directly that the EuroNet crew and Prescott should never meet. Hightower had no interest in the journalists knowing he was baby-sitting.

"Good lord, where can we get a look at that?"

"The forequarter. But I need authorization for that." He turned on his radio. "Bridge, this is Lt. Tanaka, escorting the EuroNet crew. We understand there's a problem outside. They want to observe from the forequarter. Do you authorize?"

"I doubt it. Stand by." After a brief silence, the bridge was back. "Captain says ok, captain says we may need witnesses in case something screws up."

"They can hear you you know."

"Oh. Signing off."

"Witnesses to what?" McBride asked.

"Umm, well, a ship hitting a ship, or a ship being hit by debris... or both."

"When was the last time that happened?"

"Two ship colliding? Not since the Satellite War, I suspect."

⸻

The *Apollo* XX passed so close to the RV 3 that Ron swore he could see Prescott and that his eyes were closed. As long as he didn't veer any closer, he would be clear in a few seconds. Then Ron felt a thud on his side and yellow lights in the cockpit started flashing. Ron checked his controls and saw that a chunk of debris about the size of a loaf of bread had bounced off his ship.

"Bridge, something just hit me starboard."

"Affirmative. About a quarter meter across. You okay?"

"So far so good." He checked his instruments and looked out the window. "Looks like our friend is about to leave our sector."

"Good, we've got enough rubbish to deal with already."

What neither one of them noticed was that the chunk bouncing off RV 3 had directed it towards the *Apollo XX*. Unlike a cleaner, these sports cars didn't have a thick skin. They were trophies, show horses, meant more to show off wealth without being burdened with too much boring practical accessories. They also were mostly for stratospheric travel zoom out of the atmosphere and then zoom back down to some place on Earth. Space stations were as far as they could travel, they didn't have the range for the Moon, but they seldom got that close to the debris ring. So once the ricocheting chuck hit the *Apollo XX*, it was more than a bump. It hit near an engine and either a bit of the junk or a piece of the ship itself bent the exhaust. That was enough to knock the ship off-balance.

"What was that?" a suddenly alert Prescott asked.

"A piece of space debris hit you. It appears to have damaged your starboard engine. What are your readings?"

"Readings, right? Um, yes, the starboard engine is out of commission. And, huh? Fuel level is dropping?"

"Your fuel lines have been compromised," Hightower told him.

"Oh man, I've got to get out of here."

"Don't power your engines!"

He powered his engines. The leak became a tear and the warning lights on the control panel went berserk.

Since the *Apollo* wasn't one of his ships, Hightower had no link to Prescott's controls, but he recognized the sound of the alarms. That they were now out of visual range increased the frustration.

"Cut your engines, you idiot! You're starting a fire!"

"You can't have a fire in space!"

"You can have one inside a spaceship. Now shut up, power down, and do exactly what I say. Are you wearing your space suit?" He knew the answer was yes because it was regulation, and his crew would never have allowed him to board without it.

"Yes."

"And the helmet and gloves are in the rack behind you?"

"Yes."

"Put them on. Now."

Although unaccustomed to taking orders from the help, the rattled Prescott unbuckled his seat harness and stumbled into the equipment and scurried back to his seat.

"Ok, now what? I see smoke at the back. I can smell something too."

"Stay calm. A rescue ship is on the way." He cut the radio and turned to the helm. "Who's closest?"

"Still RV 3."

"What's the pilot's name?"

He had to check the log. "Anderson, Ron."

"Open a frequency. Ron, this is Captain Hightower. Do you read me?"

"Aye, sir," answered the calm, youthful voice.

"Listen carefully. They crippled the *Apollo* XX. There's a fire and it could explode at any moment. There is one person on board. Move yourself into position and prepare for a spacewalk. You may be able to retrieve him with your hooks, but you have to be ready for anything. It's not one of our ships, so we don't have any readings from onboard. Ron, this could be dangerous, I can't pretend otherwise. It could blow at any moment. Do you understand what I'm saying, son?"

A space walk from a cleaner? Had they ever done that

before? Basic training included space walks outside the station, but stepping out of a moving spaceship? Ron's mind raced. He had to start calm. He was a professional. He was a spaceman. Since the dawn of aviation, every pilot, regardless of language or vessel involved, had one imperative when speaking. From the guys who broke the sound barrier to the pilot on a commercial jumbo jet to every astronaut ever, there was that golden rule. Stay calm. "Aye, captain."

"We'll do everything we can from here. Keep this channel clear and don't forget to turn on the radio in your suit. We'll be back in range in… eleven minutes."

"Aye, sir." Eleven minutes? An eternity of time in the eternity of space.

Ron moved into position. This part wasn't hard at all approaching a floating hulk was something he did every day. But none of them had ever been on fire before. He couldn't get close enough, so he prepared for a spacewalk. Normally these rare events were fun, but now again there was a fire in space.

Ron got within range of the sports car, cut his engines and put on his helmet and gloves. He attached the tether and performed the irreversible act as he popped the cockpit. The void of space rushed into his miniscule ship, instantly sucked out the puny scoop of air that spread like so much dust into the blackness and tried to yank Ron into the nothingness. The tether held and Ron worked to regain control of his ship and suit. Using the control panel on his suit, he slowly let the tether out. His jet packs directed him toward Prescott's cockpit. He could see Prescott. Panicky but still, Ron saw he was wearing his gloves, but his helmet not secured. The cabin was filling with smoke. It must have smelled awful in there. Ron pounded on the window and motioned for him to secure his helmet.

"Captain tell him to secure his helmet and then pop the

emergency escape. I don't think he understands me."

"Got it." The helmsman relayed the instructions. Ron could see him following the instruction, so he prepared to help pull him out of the crippled ship. The cockpit screen popped off, but Ron didn't need to reach in to retrieve the man. Prescott had forgotten to reattach his seat harness when he grabbed his helmet and gloves. Releasing himself into space was like an ant getting swooped up by a tornado. He flew out into space, banged into Ron, who got thrown back towards his own ship. Ron grabbed an arm of his ship to right himself and propelled himself towards the fool.

"Ron, are you alright?"

"Aye, sir. The integrity of the suit and tether are intact. I got hold of a claw and have pushed myself in his direction. I think the collision slowed the speed of his ejection. I'm moving closer. I'm going to let out the tether the entire length and fire the jet pads. I should be able to close in on him." As he executed the moves, he added, "I'm worried he's panicking too much. He could hyperventilate."

"Under the circumstances, him unconscious is probably the best option. RV 6 is approaching your position. The UN station will be within visual range in five minutes. We have notified them. Don't take any unnecessary risks."

"Aye, sir. I think I've hit the limit on risks."

Ron suddenly realized that he had forgotten about the burning ship behind him. He looked back and saw the sleek hulk floating in space. Of course, he realized, no more oxygen, no more fire. At least he didn't have to worry about having his suit ripped apart by an exploding ship. He fired his jets again and moved closer. With unspeakable comfort, he saw Kate's ship approaching. For a fleeting moment, he envisioned the embarrassment he would face being hauled back to the station in Kate's claw, like a mother dog grabbing the errant pup by his neck. That vision passed quickly when he realized the alternative was dying. Prescott was still out of range so Ron did what he promised himself he wouldn't do: he released the tether and emptied the jets so that he shot straight at Prescott. Ron caught him. But now they were both floating in space.

"What the hell are you doing?"

"It's the only way I could get to him. RV 6 is closing in it'll be easier to grab both of us."

Ron could hear the helmsman talking to Hightower. "There are a lot of bogies there. Those suits will not withstand an impact."

Four minutes before the *Roosevelt* could see the ships. All the remaining RVs were ready to launch.

Prescott had passed out. Ron felt a ping of something hitting his helmet. And then another. No warning light went on, so he knew he was safe. For the moment. On the bridge of the *Roosevelt*, the captain and helmsman could hear low sounds coming from the pilot.

"What? What is he saying?" Hightower asked.

"He's praying."

The next thing Ron knew was that he was no longer drifting. A claw of RV 6 had grabbed him by the boot.

CHAPTER 54

Mr. Anderson drove across the Minnesota plains towards the South Dakota border. Windmills and bison herds ruled the landscape. There were cows out there too, but the most valuable animals were penned in far out of view of the road. This was Lakota land. Most of the land returned to Native Americans had been used up, akin to donating a bone after it had been used for stock. But this patch of Northern Plains where North and South Dakota and Minnesota met still had life.

Decades before, the Lakota had made a deal for this land with both sides knowing the aquifer was poisoned. What the Lakota did was create a water and power system that sustained the minimum of live and then made the minimum enough. When it was clear, the prairie was still alive, Ailes tried to grab it back through eminent domain. This strategy had worked before in claiming private land in the name of combatting climate change, most notably in Vermont. But in a rare defeat for Ailes, the Supreme Court ruled that eminent domain could not be evoked since the Lakota were doing as Ailes claimed he wanted to do.

There were few cars on the road. Those that were, were like Mr. Anderson electric cars using the solar panels embedded in the roadway. The number of windmills increased as he got closer to his destination, a power plant. When he arrived at the gate, robotic security scanned the car while a human security guard checked Mr. Anderson's retinal scan and other

ID. Once cleared, he drove to the main office where the plant manager was waiting for him.

"Sorry to bring you all the way out here," Mr. Nasky said.

"Not at all, I enjoy getting out of the office occasionally. I grew up out this way, I love the air. I love looking at these things, he said, gesturing towards the wind farm. "Well, I'm glad you're in a good mood now, you may not be when you see what I have to show you."

"Obviously, this has something to do with a visa I issued."

"Actually, two visas."

"Runaways?"

"Yes. They appeared to have taken separate vacations but were actually coordinating..." Mr. Nasky continued to speak as they walked past a workstation where the crew was not doing their jobs but were instead watching the news. A single phrase coming from the TV punctured Nasky's explanation: "... the USS *Theodore Roosevelt*."

The ever-present fear of a parent grabbed him. "What, what was that? What happened? My son is on the *Roosevelt*."

One worker turned around, not sure how to reply to the stranger. "Don't know for sure. The reports are pretty sketchy. Someone said there's been an accident on the *Roosevelt*."

CHAPTER 55

Andresh Rajabov was old enough to remember the glaciers. The snowpack shone in the winter light. His glaciers faced north, so they rarely reflected the golden glow tourists always "ohhhh-ed" over. But because they faced north, meaning they got less sunlight, they retreated slower. The country's largest - Fedchenko Glacier still held that title, but only because the smaller ones were melting faster. Fedchenko was half the size it was when the 70-year-old Rajabov was a child. His glacier in the Pamirs Mountains drained away a decade ago. He saw it nearly every day of his life, but somehow couldn't remember the exact day when he looked up and saw nothing but rock. The last specks of white were finally, irretrievably, gone.

They foresaw the death of the glacier decades before, but it was as inevitable and unstoppable as a flood or landslide. The glaciers fed the rivers; the rivers fed the lakes and Aral Sea, and they all fed the people. The glaciers were in Tajikistan, but its waters eventually flowed to Uzbekistan and Turkmenistan, who all needed the dwindling supplies. Wars, border grabs, dams, sabotage centered on securing as much water as possible until there was nothing left to fight over.

There was a false spring, a phony peace during Rajabov's youth. For a few brief years the valley had water. But it was the last gasp supply. The last of the glaciers had melted, the rivers filled, but there was nothing behind that. They had eaten their seed grain. He would look up at the mountains and saw the bare rock. It's probable that no one in human history had seen these mountains without ice. But here he was, at the precise moment in human history and speaking the words that should never have been spoken: the glaciers were gone.

Tajikistan had been cooking for most of the century. The land cracked. The crops withered. Soil gone, water gone, food gone. And now it was the humans' turn.

In most countries, the United Nations had a headquarters known as the UN House. In industrial countries, the House was more about information and public relations. In what they had referred to as developing countries, the UN House was the collective headquarters for all the aid and relief agencies working in that country. As more countries deteriorated, the number and sizes of the UN Houses increased. Partly it was need, partly it was security: all UN agencies in one building were a tempting target but it was also easier to defend.

Countries hosting UN Houses rarely bothered to specify what UN agency was involved. Partly it was shorthand, partly it was a resignation that to spell out the names sounded absurd. Development Program? Nothing left to develop. World Health Organization when no one was healthy? Food and Agriculture Organization? A sick joke. Refugee agency? No one in Tajikistan dared used the word. These people were not refugees. They were crossing borders but left of their own free will to go to Kyrgyzstan, which had lost a population of its own and was open to repopulating with ethnically similar Tajiks.

This was part of a phenomenon that no one wanted to talk about. Countries nations were disappearing. No one could pretend that the island nations still existed. Fiji, Vanuatu, Tuvalu were all underwater, no pretense was possible. Small, low-lying countries like Bangladesh were little more than a city, slums and a nameplate in the UN General Assembly. Still, national and international officials could not bring themselves to name the reality. Policy experts used phrases like "decelerating economies" and "impaired sustainability." But there was the name everyone knew but no official would ever speak: "empty countries."

Rajabov's country was about to empty.

He, his family and the remnants of their village were packing up the last of their belongings. As least their journey was short. Only a few mountain-passes to Kyrgyzstan. Most people wanted to go there. China wouldn't let them. No one wanted to go to Afghanistan. Since a land crossing was the only option, that left Turkmenistan and Kyrgyzstan. His family had ethnic ties to Kyrgyzstan, so it was an obvious choice.

They were not the best trucks, but they were all that were available. They were among the few diesel trucks left. For all the advances in technology, the worst terrain was still too much for anything but the lumbering polluting monsters. It was the final kick that the Rajabov family's last breath of Tajik air would be loaded with diesel fumes.

CHAPTER 56

The campaign planned Lilly's rallies in as academic-like settings as possible. Her singular value was to motivate the people whose votes would be most difficult to steal. She stood at a podium made of a translucent and bullet-proof polymer. Several dignitaries are sitting behind her. Behind them a full wall projection of US and New Mexico flags. It was not a stadium, but a lecture hall. Lilly spoke without passion but with conviction, addressing the audience, connecting with them personally, more like an inspiring professor than a rousing politician. Rousing crowds were not the goal, even if the visuals would ever really get out.

... "'There is nothing new under the sun.' I never fully understood why people embrace that line. In the original context, it's clear that the author of Ecclesiastes was not a pessimist, throwing up his hands over the puny existence of humans and of our inevitable irrelevance, but a meditation on reason, contrasting the existing with the potential. But people still use it in a literal sense, free of context, a cosmic shrug. Is there 'nothing new under the sun'? Is there anything that is *not* new? Under the sun, under the sea, even under the Moon. Core samples just this past year show three possible new elements on the Moon. One so far labeled only M-12, the 12th new substance identified on the Moon shows properties of being a metal of enormous strength and flexibility. If it exists in abundance, it could revolutionize manufacturing even space travel. More than one hundred years ago, Bertrand Russell wrote, 'Science may set limits to knowledge, but should not set limits to imagination.' Marie Curie wrote, 'Nothing in life is to be feared. It is only to be understood. Now is the time to understand more, so that we may fear less.' This is an accurate interpretation of Ecclesiastes, the realization of potential.

"Aldous Huxley revitalized a phrase, but again the original context meant something else. 'Brave New World.' Huxley's brave new world was a horror, the phrase clearly ironic. Because as Shakespeare wrote it, it was a cry of discovery, full of wonder, even innocence: 'How beauteous mankind is! O brave new world/ That hath such people in't!' That wonder should still be with us, because, after all the horror and pain of the past decades, this is still a world with people such as ourselves. It is past time to reclaim the phrase from irony and despair and proclaim it as a badge of honor this is a brave, new world, and it is a wonder still that it has such as ourselves!

"Thank you. May God bless and keep you and bless the United States of America."

The applause would have made a university professor proud. Any other political candidate would have slouched out of the room defeated.

CHAPTER 57

L ike all indigenous peoples, the Dyak did their best to survive and adapt in a world they did not create. Like most indigenous villages in the 2050s, this Dyak settlement maintained obvious traditions of dress, tools, diet, houses and mixed with modern facilities. Here, most of the houses were at least partially made from concrete and there is a solar tower/radio transmitter near the center that provided power to the homes and wells and let them communicate with the outside world. That "outside world" part didn't interest them much except for the doctor, who made a regular "visit" to the village. Three men approached the outskirts of the village. Ethnically, they belonged to these islands, but the clothes and especially the weapons truly identified them: poachers.

The leader, burlier than the other two, silently signaled them and they split up, looking for windows of opportunity. With a whistle from the leader, the three charged out of the bush and grabbed the closest child they could find. A shot fired into the air punctured the screams of children. Immediately the other children ran away, some adults ran towards the captives while other men and women poured out of their houses carrying rifles.

"Everyone out into the center! Bring all your phones and weapons! Pile them at the tower! Do it now or we shoot!"

Everyone froze with their weapons pointed in dangerous directions. The poachers could have shot the children then, but then they would have been shot without their bargaining chips. The poachers weren't here for children. There were a few precious moments to find out what they wanted.

An elderly man, clearly the village elder, walked straight towards the leader. Following one step behind him was a muscular young man, likely the elder's son. Both were unarmed and strode straight towards the lead poacher.

Facing each other without blinking, the two sized up the other. Neither was bluffing. With a hand gesture to his son, the young man signaled the others. They dropped weapons, and villagers disappeared into their houses and brought out guns, computers and phones and piled them at the base of the tower.

Still unblinking, the poacher said, "If we searched your houses, would we find more guns? Would we have to kill a few children?"

"They know what I told them to do. What do you want?"

"Where is the place the government calls Station G4?"

"That means nothing to us."

"It's an orangutan station near the Tarakan River."

"It's a hundred kilometers northwest of here. If you leave that way, after 40 kilometers you reach the river. Follow it upstream to the Song bridge. The orangutan camp is another 20 after that."

"Very good. Very smart."

The poachers pushed the children to the ground. While one threw a grenade at the tower, the others fired into the air. The tower and equipment erupted into a fireball as the villagers scrambled. The poachers disappeared in the panic.

It was too late in the day to cover 40 kilometers before night, so the poachers' immediate goal was to put as much distance between them and the village as possible. Trotting quickly in single file over the barely visible path they were, children of the jungle they covered the first ten clicks in less than an hour. A drink of water, a bite of dried fish, a consultation with the compass, and they were ready to move on. Suddenly one poacher cried in pain and fell to the ground, clawing at his neck. The other two dropped into a defensive position as several Nyak led by the elder's son emerged from the trees armed with the one weapon the poachers forgot to consider blow pipes. The poison in the dart had already immobilized the first poacher. After realizing what they were facing, the other two fired wildly at the invisible men in the trees and started running. The second poacher dropped to the ground in pain. Without looking back, the now troop-less leader ran deep into the woods, far off the path. He had an hour before nightfall.

CHAPTER 58

The Isla Floreana had a landing pad but Sanjeet insisted on going by boat. He never flew among the islands. This was the best island for underwater life fish, sea lions, even coral. There was little by way of scientific equipment on Sanjeet's boat, this dive wasn't for science. Wearing only swimsuits, the pair clearly knew their bodies well. They put on masks, snorkels and fins. One set of scuba gear laid unused on the deck. The canopy of solar panels both powered the boat and shielded the humans and gear from the elements.

"So, when can we take a vacation together?" she asked.

"What are you talking about? This is one of the greatest places in the world!"

"Va-ca-tion. As in away from work. Like New Zealand, or Mexico, or hold your breath in Europe. We have water in Europe too, you know."

"We were together in Malaysia last year."

"That was a conference. God, you're doing this on purpose."

"Doing what?" he teased.

"Let's dive. That way you can't talk. And I do want to use the tanks at some point today. You know I can't hold my breath as long as you."

"Suit yourself, but that makes you more machine than human."

"It keeps me alive, thank you very much."

What they saw underwater gave them some comfort. Pushing out of their minds the knowledge of what they had lost, they focused on what remained. The fish stock was reasonably healthy, even a few sea lions zoomed around them. They dove towards the coral. Elsa wanted to believe that she saw a few hopefuls' new white outcroppings among the brown amputations but wasn't sure if she should ask Sanjeet. They held hands as they swam, with a hand occasionally stroking a back or inner thigh, sending an electric tingle through the salt water. Then Sanjeet dove even deeper, teasing Elsa to follow. She didn't. Instead, she headed for the surface. She knew he would have to follow her, eventually. Once they were back in the boat, exhausted and thrilled, they kissed wet and deep.

Sanjeet wrapped his fingers in her soaked hair. "And you want to go somewhere else."

CHAPTER 59

The Lopez household was more nervous than usual. She wasn't there yet. It wasn't her fault; she told them they should come to the rally, meet Dr. McDowell, get out of the house. No, we'll wait. Mrs. Lopez re-fluffed pillows and re-rearranged knickknacks while Mr. Lopez, pretended she wasn't doing it.

Finally, the door opened, and Elena walked in.

"Oh, thank God. What took you so long?"

"Mami," Elena said through the chocking embrace, "I just can't walk away. I had to stay until Dr. McDowell didn't need me anymore."

"Let the girl sit down."

"Are you ready to eat? Dinner is ready. Are you eating well?"

"I live in Washington, yes, I eat well."

"But not fresh tortillas. Sit down, you look tired."

Trying to steer the conversation, Mr. Lopez said, "The campaign seems to be going well."

Exhaling, she said, "Yes, the rally in town was very successful. We're still behind, of course, but we are chipping away at several districts, especially in Texas and the Plains the cities, mostly."

Mrs. Lopez couldn't even pretend that politics interested her at the moment. "Go wash up for dinner."

"I'd like to see Papi first."

Embarrassed that they hadn't thought of that, Mr. Lopez said, "Of course." Then in the hope of softening the blow.

"He's not doing especially well."

"I saw the videos, I know."

Never convincing, Mrs. Lopez said, "But we're sure you'll get through to him."

"Sure."

Elena walked in quietly, as if she were preparing for confession. A penitent, she hadn't been in this room for over a year. She sat down in the chair near her grandfather, put on latex gloves and held his hand. She looked to the monitor to see if there was any reaction. Of course, there wasn't.

"Papi, it's me, Elenita. I finally made it home. I've seen all the videos Mami sent, and I know she's been showing you the videos from the campaign. Senator Cranston sends his prayers. How about that, Papi? The next president of the United States is asking after you. He says one of the first things he will do as president is give all you guys another medal. How about that? Maybe you can even meet him." There weren't too many words left blocking the tears. "Would you like that?"

Finally, to herself as much as to him: "*Te quiero mucho, Papi.*"

CHAPTER 60

Ruth was worried. Jamal had never called her in from the field before. Not only was it important that she and the apes direct the research with minimal interference, but also that she loved this, so Jamal was loathed to break in. But he had, so Ruth had to assume something had gone wrong.

He was sitting at the computer bank. For once, the main screen focused on a satellite map of their region and not on Rabu. Ruth immediately noticed that deep in the jungle a red blip was flashing. She hadn't even sat down when Jamal, pointing at the blip, said, "We have a report of a radio tower being destroyed in a Nyak village about 100 clicks southeast from us. There's been no severe weather or earthquake that could account for it. It's most likely the poachers trying to prevent the Nyak from reporting their movements."

"Why should they give away their position by destroying the transmitter?"

"Maybe they thought they were hiding their position, preventing the Nyak from warning us. They didn't know the towers have an automated distress signal."

Ruth enlarged the map so that the red blip was in the lower right corner of the screen and their base in the upper left. "It's not very rough terrain between here and there. They could easily do this on foot in two, three days. They would most likely have to cross the Song bridge, could they be intercepted there?"

"We don't have the troops for that. HQ won't agree, and I

can't send my own men and leave the station at risk. Besides, there are several spots where the river isn't that deep. They are just as likely to cross there than at the most obvious place."

The two contemplated their dwindling choices. "We must bring the family in," said Jamal.

"No, the whole point of our work is to reintegrate them into their natural environment. That'll never work if we keep snatching them away. Besides, the poachers would just look for someone else."

"Your alternative?"

The choices had truly dwindled. "I guess I will need a refresher course with that rifle."

CHAPTER 61

anjeet and Elsa weren't alone this time. They had gotten to Isla San Isabela by boat, but Elsa's team insisted on flying since they had all their equipment and the spot Sanjeet had selected was on a cliff. Marta and Pol had no interest in hauling everything off a boat and up a mountain. Elsa and Sanjeet walked along the cliff, from where they could see other islands in the archipelago as the crew unpacked.

Looking over a panorama that caught most of the islands to the east, Elsa asked, "Do you want to do the interview here?"

"Yes, this is it."

Elsa set up two folding chairs for them so that the late afternoon sun would not be in their eyes, but the background would be as expansive as possible. Marta and Pol set up, pinned mikes on the pair, and Elsa began.

"Just so our viewers know," Elsa began, "I'm not blindsiding you with these questions – you've already agreed to speak about your personal life. In fact, this was your idea."

"That's right. We all have our stories, but I thought your audience would be interested in how I arrived here."

"I was born on Fiji in 2018, part of the last generation born on the island. By the time I was born, most of the climate change deniers had quieted down, the sea levels were rising and changes in oceanic and atmospheric temperatures were making matters worse. Stronger storms at unpredictable times, loss of fishing stocks, sea water intruding onto freshwater reserves. And of course, once we understood the full impact of the Tipping Point, the efforts that should have been several decades earlier began in for earnest. And too late, of course, especially for the island people. Fijians started migrating gradually, some to other small islands, most to the mainland or the larger islands like Australia and New Zealand. The tsunami of 2031 sealed the fate of Fiji and many of the people. My family emigrated to New Zealand the next year. Fiji is now on average eight centimeters below sea level.

"Ever since the warnings started going out some 80 years ago, we were told that the first national victims of climate change would be the small island states. The combination of sea level rises, extreme weather, loss of fish would doom the most vulnerable islands. And that's what happened. Fiji, Tuvalu, the Marianas and some other Pacific islands were among the first. That Ring of the Fallen at the UN you know that circle of flags permanently at half-mast for the nations that have disappeared, Fiji was the third flag raised.

"I emigrated to New Zealand and studied oceanography and marine biology, a pretty obvious choice. I worked on the Mediterranean Basin Project for a few years, but really, I belong to the Pacific Ocean. This ocean is my lifeblood, my parents and grandparents, and we have wounded the largest body of water in the world most grievously. My life is science, but it is also penance to apologize to the Ocean and to repair what I can."

"And why the Galapagos?"

"There's the obvious reason: it is unique and one of the most endangered ecosystems on the planet. Preserving it even regenerating it is one of the highest aspirations of humanity."

"You talk about the Ocean, these islands, nature as if they were human. Not very scientific."

"What could be more scientific than understanding that

the world is alive? Treat her as the living organism she is. If all you see is water, rocks and carbon-based life forms, you don't truly understand what is happening. Meaning you can never cure her. The most destructive thing a person can do to the planet and to themselves is to act as if there is a disconnect between the human and natural world. That arrogance helped get us to this state; understanding what it truly means to be a part of the world is a step out of this. That is a fact, and what is science if not facts?"

CHAPTER 62

Presidential candidates didn't campaign in person very much anymore. There were practical issues that transcended partisanship the danger of air travel, people avoiding being parts of large crowds for fear of infection or violence, candidates' fear of infection or violence. Holographic appearances became the default. And since they didn't involve the messy problems of actual human beings, the appearances became spectacles. Holographic fireworks and roaring crowds, cost nothing. A typical Ailes rally involved a patriotic background, usually the White House since he could use it for free, a small crowd enhanced by holographic multiplication and fireworks at the end. Ailes loved fireworks. So, Ailes had made virtual campaigning the norm. He hated having to spend time near the people he led. He led, they followed. Public appearances were a waste of time. His previous Federalist opponent knew he was a sacrificial sheep. He acted like it. And they treated him like one on Election Day. Hayden followed the same pattern. He couldn't appear more dynamic or braver than his boss.

But Cranston played it a bit differently. First, and he would never admit it, his father would taunt him for being a coward. But secondly, it was not in his nature to step back. He had to look into the eyes of the people he was talking to or confronting. Finally, he had to distinguish himself from Ailes and Hayden. He was the underdog. He had to dig just to prevent getting buried.

Since the public appearances had to be limited, each time he went out into the country, the appearance had to count.

The idea was to be provocative. Go to Ailes country. Draw a crowd that had a heartbeat. Plant himself in the middle of the damned country, open his arms, clear his voice, and shout, "Here I am."

Lilly would have been perfectly comfortable with holographic seminars. That's how she taught most of her classes. Cranston practically pushed her out the door as he rushed out. The Chicago rally right after Labor Day was exactly what he wanted. Real people. The "real-est" Americans. The "stormy, husky, brawling, City of the Big Shoulders" of Sandberg, Mailer, Turkel, and Mamet. The people you denigrated at your peril. Cranston stood on a stage with the Arts Institute of Chicago at his back and the putrid wind of Lake Michigan at his face. Chicago and its lake were dying, the lake fighting the heat, pollution, and parasitic species and the American prairie at the front door was gasping as the dust ate at its vitals. Everyone backstage pretended not to see the nurse with an oxygen tank and basket of wet towels sitting with nothing to do.

He shouted out to Emilio, to Hanna, to Mario, to Maureen, to Hans, to Kim. He embraced the overwhelming America of the broke-back city; the stench of stockyards and bosses; the black, white, and brown pug face of the American that never bowed. "Come and show me another city with lifted head singing so proud to be alive and coarse and strong and cunning." He didn't have to call them to fight, but he called on Hayden to fight. Hayden wasn't a fighter Chicago would recognize. Cranston told him he was. The crowd believed him. They needed no holograms. Individual recordings zapped around the internet. Even America's Network was compelled to report on him.

Cranston was a political animal that could not let Chicago be the end. He had to up it. He had to go to some place spectacular. He had to do something that no one else not Hayden would ever do. He had to slap everyone in the face. When he announced his decision, his father smiled, Lilly blanched, Sean maintained his professional composure, Mei almost hugged him, Maggie did. No ceremony, no explanation. None needed. He walked into the room and said the name. Still, nearly a century later, the name sent chills throughout the political body: Dallas.

No national candidate had campaigned in Dallas since Ailes did when he was running for vice president. The party wanted him to go, and he wasn't yet in a position to say no. Texas was so fractured, so unruly, so unpredictable that no one wanted to chance it. Trying to engage Texas was like playing chess with a mountain lion. All the large states fractured, but most like New York and California kept some center of gravity. Texas was a free-for-all. Now 18 years later, the state settled into something that looked like government, but not enough to make a non-Texan politician want to walk into the middle of it. There was no advantage to Hayden to go to Texas since whatever he could get out of the state, he would get. But Texas fit Cranston's campaign strategy of forcing eyes to turn towards him. Dallas was the perfect "what the hell is he thinking" venue.

He flew into the city around noon for the early evening rally. An outside event was out of the question even in October, an outdoor rally was a health risk for the audience. So they booked a sports stadium. The campaign booked the site through a shell company. By the time the owners found out who was really going to use it, it was too late to back out. People began arriving a few hours in advance. That was newsworthy. Once they passed through body and retinal scans, everyone got a filter mask even if they had brought their own gloves, a bottle of water, and a couple of protein bars. In the old days, if you knew you won't fill a place, you would pack the audience in tightly upfront and hope the cameras didn't pan out over all the empty seats. Getting people to attend was a triumph, so if it wasn't a massive crowd, it wasn't a death knell. Tightly packed humans were a death knell. People had an absolute terror of being around too many diseases carrying potential unhinged murderers otherwise known as fellow human beings. It was a great excuse for politicians not to hold rallies "the people do not want them," the solemn servants of the people sadly explained.

And now Cranston had arrived and kicked them in the shins. Holographic images sprung to life from the classic American tableaus with some Texas specifics thrown in. And then the music. Rather than the hyper electronic sounds designed to tingle nerve endings, Cranston always used the same old, old song with a lush synthetic orchestral arrangement. First the solitary drums, then the solitary horns, and then the crescendo of "Fanfare for the Common Man." When he started using it, nobody knew what the hell was going on. Where was the soaring electronic swing? Where was the white noise blast? But when people found out the name, everyone wanted to claim it. Which was Copland's point. Which was Cranston's point.

Cranston appeared before the holographic scene. At first, he looked like a hologram; it looked like the audience had been double-crossed; it looked like an ordinary campaign event. Then the screen went dark and Cranston stepped into the light. "It is the real man," the audience thought as the "Fanfare" cymbals crashed.

"Good evening, DALLAS!" It was as much a dare as a greeting. "God bless you and God bless the great state of Texas!" Sociologists would undoubtedly ponder for years why the audience started taking off their masks. Ailes, watching from the White House, didn't need a sociologist. He knew what Cranston had done. He had done what the audience didn't even know it wanted. It was a classic political move. He did what the people could not stand but deeply, truly wanted. George Cranston touched them. They wanted to be touch. So, they dropped their physical and metaphorical masks.

"We are not living the American Dream. It is a founding principle of this country, a belief, a conviction, that we will always be better than we are today. It was a trust handed down since the very start of this country. John Adams said, 'I am a soldier so my son can be a politician so his son can be a farmer so his son can be a poet.' We always looked to the next generation, and the generations beyond, committing ourselves to something greater than ourselves, committing ourselves to an ever-strengthening commonwealth."

"Think about that word: commonwealth. Common. Wealth. 'Common' is not ordinary, 'common' is community. 'Wealth' is not money. 'Wealth' is the bounty of our efforts to improve heart, mind, body, and soul. The commonwealth is the united strength of our nation. I found this little piece of wisdom floating out in cyberspace. They probably wrote it sometime early this century.

"'We owe each other a debt. We owe each other an obligation. That is the thing to which we truly commit ourselves if we follow our Constitution. It is a charter that enumerates individual liberties, but it is not a license for unbridled greed or reckless political solipsism. We owe each other a debt and we owe each other an obligation, and because of these fundamental American imperatives, there are things that we own in common with each other, and that we are obliged to protect for our posterity.'

"Keep that in mind while I read you something else. This is an old quote from a politician. The name isn't important, but just to give you a flavor of the time, they considered this guy to be a serious contender for the presidency. 'As far as a law that we can pass in Washington to change the weather, there's no such thing. If we pass if you took the gift list of these groups that are asking us to pass these laws and did every single one of them, there would be no change in our environment. Sea level would still rise.' Let that sink in. The cynicism, the aggressive I don't know which ignorance or denial of reality. The cosmic shrug of 'oh well, it's going to happen anyway.' Is that any way for an American to talk? Is that any way for a human being to talk? Since when is fatalism a virtue in a president?

"And this isn't just old schoolbook stuff. How different is it from our current president? President Ailes has made the deep sigh national policy. He often says, 'Some things are beyond human control.' That's policy? True, some things are beyond human control like the tides, sunspots and phases of the moon, but are we supposed to be passive victims of our own fatalism? Are we supposed to just sit back and count how many methane bubbles popped yesterday? Take bets when the next chunk of Greenland calves? Just sigh when another species goes extinct and we comfort ourselves knowing DNA is preserved in some lab?

By now the audience was cheering and shouting "no" at each question. It took a certain skill to make DNA an applause line. Cranston and the audience were marching together. Each question was really a challenge, each "no" really a promise.

"So, what has happened to the American Dream? The same thing that has happened to every dream. It fell under the Tipping Point. The generation that could have done something didn't. Now gone, but we're still here. Each succeeding generation violated that trust and left the world worse off for their children. Our children, my child. No more. No longer."

"No longer. No more fake solutions, no more fraudulent data, no more deep sighs of inevitable regret. 'Some things are beyond human control.' No, no. Not these things. We are not stones helplessly rolling down the side of a mountain. We can still be agents of our destiny. We *will* be agents of our own destiny!"

Cranston had turned "no" and "not" into affirmations of life. He had convinced people that there was still hope. And he had done it in Dallas.

Ailes was watching on a private feed. Long after the commercial stations and most bloggers had cut off, the President watched the stadium until the last person left and the lights went out.

CHAPTER 63

There were advantages to squatting in these buildings. The walls were thick, the foundations as solid as possible under the circumstances, and the roofs since they were two or three stories up were more or less intact. The last legal owners had taken everything of value when they evacuated: art, precious metals, furniture, even gold leaf. The next wave striped out the cooper, kitchen and bathroom fixtures, eventually even the wiring. They were empty hulks. But they were large and strong, empty hulks.

Juanita and Jose laid claim to an upstairs room facing away from the ocean. Most windows got blown out by various storms, but the few that remained faced inland. Besides, facing west gave them a bit of protection from the evening heat. Luckily, they had found a roll of window screen, so they managed to screen in a few windows thus letting in some air but not too many mosquitos and flies no small feat. Other squatters had installed solar panels. The police ignored their conspicuous arrival, so they bartered for access. Once settled, Jose would apply for free solar panels. They qualified, but without a stable place to install them, they would be useless. And the government offered those panels as a one-time grant. Once they felt secure, Jose would go to the county welfare office.

The barter was food. The owner of the panels was a drug dealer. Such people are almost by definition not, cooks. Tony wanted more from Juanita than *arepas*, but Jose had a lot of practice squatting, so Tony never pushed too hard. Even if he had, Juanita the cook was handy with many types of knives.

Up and down the Florida coast, billions of dollars of real estate were water-logged. The rich had moved inland. But "inland" was a relative term since the Gulf was attacking from its side, making "inland" more of a fantasy than a refuge. All the cooks, gardeners, pool boys, and nannies got cut loose like so much flotsam from a sinking luxury liner. A couple generations of these folks wandered the state, picking up loose work. Somehow there was never enough money for simple housing. A little here and there, to ease pressure or in response to a recent outbreak. There was an army of climate refugees, blocked from entering Georgia, shot if they entered Alabama, they picked camps where they could and found shelter in the mansions that had yet slipped into the Atlantic.

Palm Beach was no different from the rest of the communities. Juanita and Jose's "home" was on the North Ocean Boulevard, on the north end of what was left of Palm Beach's island. It was only a matter of time before the sea completely covered the island. The increasing frequency and violence of hurricanes combined with the absence of any natural or man-made barriers meant the end of garish mansions. Soon Atlantis would not be a fable. There really would be a lost city under the sea.

For months, they built up the room. Cleaning, installing the solar panels and running "found" wires into the room. There was a city water line nearby where they could draw clean water the fear of cholera was an excellent motivator for civil projects which they supplemented with cisterns. What little real money they can make went into buying basic foodstuffs for their own use and their barter products. Sanitation was always a problem: urine went into the ground and fecal matter got deposited in an outhouse that hopefully flushed out into the ocean. It was almost a home.

Finally, Tony had enough. He had moved in first. He was the boss. He was on a nasty high when he kicked in the door. Juanita was always cooking, always ready. By the time Jose got home, Juanita had cleaned the knife and packed the bags.

Jose climbed up to the roof and took the solar panels.

CHAPTER 64

Wendy Villar had the second most miserable job at Marbury Point. The title of the first most miserable job went to the guy who washed away the vomit the morning after. A cynic would say that at least he could see results. Wendy also never saw results. Her mission was to rescue the kids from killing themselves here and try to convince them they had a reason to live. Most people would have bet on the vomit.

"Haven" was the name of Wendy's storefront. The bulk of the building was an open space filled with chairs and cushions. Sometimes just taking a nap without having to worry about what was going to crawl on you was haven enough. Water, juices, synthetic fruit of course, the real stuff was out of reach, coffee, high-calorie protein bars were available for the asking. The bars tasted like fruit or candy. They had come a long way from the bars handed out to refugees to ward off starvation. The origins of the bars could be tracked back to old military k-rations, and the food early astronauts took into space.

By the turn of the century, relief agencies had developed high-energy biscuits that they used in the early stages of disaster to provide victims with a basic level of nutrition. The original biscuits didn't have much of a taste, focusing instead on a quick shot of calories and vitamins. When food scarcities became a global phenomenon, someone realized that they could have a use in less catastrophic settings. Bars got produced for a variety of needs and tastes. There was a range between bland and sweet. Although they rarely contained the real thing, they could taste like meat or fish.

Regional preferences were taken into account, for instance, curry in India and chilies in Mexico. They added the non-essential but very enticing caffeine. In the US, they were first manufactured for internal refugees; handing them out to the poor and self-destructive came later. They altered the bars to make them tastier with more fructose and more visually appealing with some coloring. They favored vitamins over calories. Refugees' stomachs were literally eating themselves from lack of food calories were the first line of defense. As bad as things could get in the States, starvation was rarely the first consideration, so the goal was to prevent the body from getting so weak that disease could take root. Minimal health as opposed to not dying was the modest goal.

The Haven had back rooms for private consultations about mental and physical health. Wendy's staff were qualified for this work, but a nurse or doctor from a nearby hospital would stop by some evenings. Not all of their advice and services were legal, but the government didn't look too closely. Places like the Haven did what the government wanted while pretending they weren't involved. Their purity heartened them.

There were still remnants from past lives scattered about. Wendy thought these incongruous bits would engage addled imaginations and get her clients to think about innocent nonsense. Nothing too sharp. A sign saying "Video Rentals" whatever that meant, bits of bicycles and machines the major chunks sold off for scrap years ago mounted on the walls or arranged in abstract designs, a few torn paper posters for movies. One drew attention. It was the eyes that did it. They were women's eyes floating free of a face, lovely but weary, wary. What looked like hair was actually a circling ring of cigarette smoke, Wendy assumed from the age that it must have been tobacco. Following the wisp of smoke downward showed the cigarette in the hand of a shadowy man wearing a very old hat. One girl became so obsessed with it that Wendy considered taking it away. "There's nothing to see here, there's nothing to see here," the girl would chant. When Wendy asked the girl what she meant, she turned to her with a sick grin and said, "Forget, Jake, it's Chinatown." Wendy did not understand what that meant, but it truly unnerved her.

There was no money, no drugs, no weapons. Not even a stun gun. Wendy had one a few years ago but a guy had found it and shot his girlfriend point blank between the eyes. Her frontal lobe fried. Wendy took her chances.

She was used to hustlers wanting to use the Haven as a drug drop, but the police helped her on this front. If they approached her, the police turned up the next day. Wendy was a bulwark against collecting more bodies and filing more reports. Muscling dealers was far easier than writing another autopsy report. So, when a shaky guy with Iks-stained teeth walked in one day with a proposition, Wendy wasn't surprised at first.

"I've got a deal for money."

"I don't pay for information."

"No, I get the money from someone else. A reward."

Wendy knew where this was going. It didn't happen much anymore, but occasionally well-connected parents would offer a reward for the safe return of a runaway child. As the years wore on, most people gave up on the quest.

"So, go collect it yourself. Why do you need me? I will not help you find her."

His limited grasp of the situation was shaken. "Did I say it was a girl?"

"It usually is."

"Well, it is. Rich. Big reward. Some old chick posted an alert, promising serious money. I've seen the girl. I can find her. But she'd never come with me. She'd come with you."

"Not interested. I'm not a bounty hunter. Besides, how do I know this isn't kidnapping?"

"Because she's the daughter of the stiff running for president. He could afford a real kidnapper. Now are you interested?"

"Cranston?"

"Yep."

She knew Cranston had a daughter but didn't know the girl's name. That was easy to find out. What would not be easy was finding out her club name.

"No," she said, "I don't do that. People come to me. I don't go searching for them."

He turned, muttered the usual obscenities, grabbed a bar and left.

CHAPTER 65

Most of the food was canned, vacuum-packed, or some other form of preservation. The only fresh foods were those of clearly local origin cheese, eggs, seasonal fruits and vegetables, lake fish, bison steaks, chicken and turkey. Mrs. Anderson quickly collected some basics mechanically, the products she bought all the time. Afterwards, she entered, somewhat semi-hesitantly. A section was isolated from the rest of the store and had a guard stationed at the entrance.

These guards were well-attuned to potential thefts. It was harder to distinguish between gawkers and nervous shoppers working up the nerve to walk inside and spend money. Inside there were few people. Display cases are all closed. Nothing was sitting out in the open. She seems a bit abashed, like a pauper in a jewelry store. These were the now exotic and expensive food stuffs: prime cuts of beef and veal, salt-water fish, shellfish, roe, not caviar, fine wines, avocados, mangos, kiwi, bananas. Most large stores had some version of this section. Some stores rubbed their customers' noses into it: "Platinum Club members," "Restricted Area," "Elite Shopping" let everyone know their place. Mrs. Anderson liked the Minnesota-nice version in her store: "Specialty Items." Yet she suddenly felt embarrassed by the ordinary food in her cart. Finally, after window shopping, she stopped in front of the fish counter.

"The salmon, it's farmed, right?"

The clerk answered, "Yes, we don't have any wild salmon. And if we did, it would be double the price."

"That's clearly out of the question."

"Sure, I only sell about two kilos a month."

"The haddock?"

"Wild."

"My son loves seafood, but he's, well, usually pretty far away from the sea." Her little joke amused her. "But he's coming home for a visit and I have to make fish." As she studied the fish pretending, she knew what she was doing the clerk was studying her.

"Haven't I seen you on television?"

She was taken aback. That was not a sentence she ever thought she would hear about herself.

"I suppose so. It wasn't very long, though."

"Don't tell me. It was about... your son! That's it, your son is the space hero!"

"Well, yes, but I'm not really, you know, looking at him that way..."

"Ron Anderson! That's it. Saved the Prescott kid and now he's assigned to the Mars mission."

She responded with a mix of pride and terror. "Yes, he's going to Mars."

"Well, well. Amazing. So a celebratory dinner? I think I can give you a break on the salmon, I can recommend a great white wine for that. But I'm afraid I can't do anything about the prices of the wine."

"I know. It's overwhelming, but few occasions can be more special than this."

"Absolutely."

That night, Mrs. Anderson was handling the salmon as if it was the Dead Sea Scrolls. "What? Salmon again?" came the mocking voice behind her. It was so strange to hear that beloved voice without static. She turned to see her boy with his silly grin and tightly trimmed hair leaning against the doorway. He was dressed in civilian clothes and had a small bag at his feet.

"Oh, praise the Lord!" She embraced her. "You looked famished. Why didn't you tell us what time you were arriving, your father could have met you at the airport?"

"And waste fuel? Mom, the government's paying for this trip. I'm allowed a leave, under the circumstances."

They both heard the running feet on the second floor and then the stairs. His father dashed into the kitchen and joined the hug. Tugging his wife and son into the living room, he said, "Come on, come on, we can cook later." Ron didn't resist, but he did cast a wistful eye towards the fish. He restrained himself from saying, "Don't let it dry out."

Settling on the sofa, the father said, "God, we can't tell you how proud we are of you."

"Dad, I saved a rich man's idiot son."

"It also took bravery and skill. Do you think you're less deserving than most of the rest of the crew? Do you think they are all there because they are the absolute best in their fields? Politics had nothing to do with anything. Money. You're a hero and this is an election year. Ailes needs a hero, even one from the wrong church, but that doesn't change who and what you are."

Mrs. Anderson finally took her eyes off her son and looked to the floor. "That's a pretty small bag. Can't you stay a while?"

"A few days, but I'll see you again. The Mars launch is three years away; until then, I'm only going to be on the Moon."

CHAPTER 66

Following the grand tradition of believing whatever happens in Africa doesn't matter elsewhere, the resurgent old diseases and the exploding new viruses were largely ignored when they wiped out tens of thousands of people in a blink. Anyone who might have thought AIDS might have changed that mindset wasn't paying attention. As Africa got hotter and her people poorer, it became an even greater incubator of horror. It wasn't until SARS III jumped from Congo to Mississippi that it finally dawned on most people that the Earth was one planet. But even then, there was the cosmic shrug that magically absolved the leaders. "Some things are beyond human control," President Ailes would say.

As promised, the ships left at first light. They had spent the night carefully dismantling the equipment, taking care that the station had the minimum needed to maintain plants and humans until resupplies could arrive from Nairobi. Fortunately, since they had closed the Galma station, there was an uncharacteristic surplus of supplies. Theo divided up the supplies to keep the three ships balanced. The EuroNet jet was twice the size of the sand-huggers, so they loaded the larger purification system that was the most essential need for Lagos in there, plus a mix of medicines, food, and other supplies. Theo's ship got the smaller Galma purification system and some medicines. The sand-hugger Robert would pilot had the bulk of medical supplies and food.

They lifted off in a simple formation: the EuroNet jet above and slightly ahead of the sand-huggers so they could see any dangers human or natural approaching. Theo and Robert maintained a safe distance from each other but stayed within sight of each other. Raj was with Theo, and Robert's companion was the staffer with the most medical experience. Altogether, eight people. They all knew but decided not to state an uncomfortable detail: none of them had any military experience.

Theo spoke to all three ships over the radio. "Forecast, as always, includes sandstorms. This time of year, they usually come out of the north, so pay attention in that direction."

"How high up do these storms usually go? Our ship should be able to rise above them," Sam popped in over the radio.

"Varies wildly, could be as high as a kilometer. But our ships can't fly that high, they're made for near ground observation, not long-distance flight."

"Where exactly are we heading?"

"The World Health Organization compound. We offload our equipment and the WHO takes it to wherever they feel it will be of the greatest use. The idea is to get the purification equipment to a small hospital or clinic where the spread of the virus can be contained. In effect, a firewall. Once it's safe to leave, we leave."

"Safe?"

"The government doesn't have full control of Lagos. Warlords hold quite a bit of territory, especially to the north and west. Among other things, they extract taxes..."

"Bribes," Raj translated.

"... from anyone passing through their territory."

"But we're flying," asked the Brit, who probably had spent little time in Africa.

"They have surface-to-air missiles," Raj explained.

"Of course they do," said Sam, feeling rather naïve.

"So, leaving is a question of security and health," Theo explained, "If the virus is as viral as Dr. Asanti suspects, the UN or the Nigerian government will be forced to declare a general quarantine."

"When was the last time an entire city was quarantined?"

"Calcutta was the first, Sao Paulo, Kula Lumpur after the '34 tsunami, even Lagos has been quarantined once before. I guess Sao Paulo was the most recent, '43."

"I remember São Paulo. Seem to remember that it worked reasonably well."

"The cholera didn't spread, but 30,000 people inside the zone died before a vaccine was developed. Success is gauged on whether you were inside or outside of the quarantine zone."

"I assume this is your tactful way of saying that by tomorrow, we could be in a quarantine zone."

"Perhaps. Since it's not safe to fly at night, the sooner we get there the better. We'll take the long route, circling to the east out over the Atlantic and come into the city from the coast. It's longer but safer."

Sand, sand, sand. Mixed with grit and organic bits. The expanse was unbroken. Bland but still ominous, the hot sameness lulled the pilots into a light stupor despite themselves. The computers were sent to warn them if they were hypnotized into flying off course or too close to the ground. This was new desert, solid ground was only a few generations below, but there was still enough sand to course across the ground like a burning hot blanket, billowing and waving. Beckoning the flyers to come closer. Occasionally, a bizarre reminder that humans are stubborn. The smallest of villages dug in, clinging to a few resilient trees. A goat or two, something that had to be a well. And then it was gone. There were more abandoned villages than living compounds, trees blasted, roofs pulverized, useless walls holding up nothing. Someone's grandfather tended cattle on this land.

The only thing that could break such monotony was terror. And it arrived.

Raj saw it first. "Theo, look at the radar, 38 degrees north."

"Yes, that could be one."

"One what? Sandstorm?" Sam's voice asked.

"Yes. If that mass continues on this trajectory, we need to change course about ten degrees southeast, that will take us a bit off course, but it might keep us out of the path."

It did not. The computers reported that the tidal wave of sand was six kilometers wide and at least one klick high. It was impossible to know how deep it was.

After some mental calculations, Theo told Sam, "I suggest you fly above the storm and keep heading for Lagos, you have the settings, so you don't really need us to guide you."

"No, we can't abandon you out here. What's your plan?"

"We land on relatively firm ground. Cover the ships to protect the windshields and the intake and exhaust chambers and wait out the storm."

"We can do that. We can seal all the vulnerable components."

Raj had some good news. "There seems to be an abandoned building or compound just ahead. It might provide some protection."

It was the best shelter under the circumstances.

CHAPTER 67

While Theo was waiting out the storm, Emeka Idu was dying. She had noticed the rash the week before; it meant nothing unusual to her. The water was soiled, the food rotten, cleanliness absent. She got rashes all the time. The local clinic would give her some cream. It would help, but not much. The fever was different. Rash, yes. Fever, yes. But together was unusual. Plus, the fever got worse. Her joints ached. Bright lights caused terrible headaches. She finally went to the clinic on her day off. The nurse took one look at her, pretended not to worry, and took her to a back room.

Her first hint that this wasn't normal was when the nurse put on long, thick gloves instead of the thin latex ones that they always used. Then the mask. Then the glasses. Then she got nervous. Then the doctor came in. He was already armored up. They took blood and saliva samples. They asked her to urinate. She couldn't, it hurt too much. She was placed on a bed and told to wait. Ten, maybe twenty minutes later, two people wearing what looked like space suits entered carrying something rolled up. They pushed her and the bed in the corner and unrolled the package. It was a kind of inflatable tent that they constructed around her. Then they stood guard around her, their backs to her. No one had said a word.

Emeka was so nervous that she didn't even realize that they hadn't given her any cream, or medicine, or even water. One spaceman must have had a phone in his suit because she could sometimes make out words "too high," "too late" but they never spoke to her.

Then the nurse brought in an IV drip and attached it. Giving her a glass of water, she said, "Please drink, it will help you sleep." Emeka didn't know she was supposed to sleep.

When she woke up, she thought she was in a different room but couldn't be sure. It looked like the clinic the walls were white; the lighting subdued, but something was wrong. Then she realized that there was more equipment than she had ever seen in the clinic. She couldn't find any word to describe what she saw. She lifted her head to get a better look. It was then that she realized her headache was gone. Cured? Was it possible? How long was she unconscious? Where was she? Did her family know?

A doctor she didn't know came in. He was suited up, but not as anonymous as the spaceman. He looked at her chart and started tapping on his computer. When did she first notice the rash? The joint pains? Where did she work? Do you handle food? When was the last time you bathed? Where does the water come from? What does her stool look like? Where do you dispose of your waste? The anonymous doctor prepared to leave.

"Wait!" she called with more strength than she imagined she had. "What's wrong with me?"

"You have a virus."

She knew enough to know that meant nothing.

"Why doesn't it hurt anymore?"

"We gave you a sedative."

"What about medicine?"

"We're working on it." He was practiced with words that said little.

She tried to remember what little she knew about hospital

medicine. Aren't sedatives for sleeping? Narcotics kill pain. Why narcotics and not medicine?

The answer came before she fully understood. With only the faintest hint of pain, she vomited and vacated her bowels at the same moment. Pain and shame strangled her mind. The doctor had stepped back. She thought he said something, but she was crying too hard. "What... what..."

The spacemen entered the room with sample cases and a large hazardous waste container. They lifted the tent, collected samples of her waste, vomit, blood, and saliva. They lifted her dress and took photos of her breasts, abdomen, genitals, feet. She didn't object. Emeka had died 30 seconds before.

CHAPTER 68

The storm struck like a trillion ravenous fleas. The dry flood morphed from grey to black, but by then the humans didn't want to look. Even if they wanted to, they couldn't. Looking directly into the storm meant their eyeballs would have been shredded. Hunkered down in their ships, they could have watched from the ships' monitors. But there was no motivation to look at the monster trying to devour them.

The walls did a decent job of protecting the ships. It didn't take long to dig out and there was minimal damage.

Theo was shaking sand out of his boots when he heard Asanti's voice over the radio. "Theo, how are you? I saw the storm on the satellite. Were you in it?"

"After a fashion. But we found some shelter. Everything survived intact, but we had to clean the intake and exhaust valves on two of the ships. We'll be airborne shortly."

"I see that. So if all goes well, you'll be crossing into Lagos airspace near sunset."

"Afraid so. Does Savimbi still control the northern district?"

"Yes." Elaboration was unnecessary.

"And that's the most direct route to you."

"Yes."

"If we go around, we're flying over Lagos at night."

"Yes." The weariness of a positive word.

"Savimbi it is."

"Want to explain that?" Theo turned around to see Sam at the door.

"Explain what?"

"Savimbi, of course. Who is that?"

"He controls the northern slums. Flying over his territory has its risks."

"He has surface-to-air missiles?"

"Of course." He did a few mental calculations. Then he called out to Robert. "We're not leaving yet."

"Why not?" Robert asked from behind a dune.

"We have to rearrange the cargo."

CHAPTER 69

Wendy walked carefully, avoiding the used condoms and discarded wrappers at least she had the satisfaction of knowing the trash included the condoms she distributed, Iks vials, smashed booze bottles, various human excretions, even a few bent needles, indicating a heroin user. This surprised her a bit. The Point was not known for its heroin users. Heroin was the champagne of drugs. With such a storied history, its heroism in beating back even climate change, it was the connoisseur's drug of choice. The heroin user looked down on the amateurs and posers who favored this season's designer batch of chemical. Marijuana was lame, your grandfather's crutch. Besides it was legal. Cocaine was no longer pure enough to maintain the supplies as the Andes dried out required chemical boosts. It was a mongrel drug, unworthy of serious consideration. But heroin, ah that was the only drug if you knew what you were doing. The shadow people of the Point couldn't have cared less.

Wendy was well known around here. This strip of corroded storage tanks was the poor part of town compared to the club scene. This was where kids too broke for the clubs fought, screwed and died. Wendy was one of the few people to come down here who wasn't looking for a fix. Even if no one knew who she was, she would still stand out. No one who spent time at the Point could ever be as, well, round as Wendy. Her full face and stout hands marked her as an outsider.

She counted off the tanks, looking for the one with a vulture painted on the side. From the shadows, she heard an uninspired groan, a junkie's orgasm. Someone was opening up for a fix. It was an *Iks* trick.

Wendy found the vulture. No guarantee she would be here, but that's what the dealer told her. She wouldn't give him money and he didn't even bother to ask for drugs, so he must have assumed helping might benefit him further down the road. Maybe he thought he could start a side career as a rich kid bounty hunter.

"Slasher?" Wendy called into the darkness. "Vik?" She instinctively knew not to call out for "Victoria," impossible that a girl in her state would allow herself to be called by such a regal name. Wendy didn't know how right she was. Vik never called herself "Victoria" and not "Vicky." Even though she was named after her grandmother, she always felt her parents naming her Victoria was a cheap shot, a lifelong mocking of what she could never be. "Vik" sounded like the noise you heard when the high slammed your brain.

An addled young man rose from the heap. "I'll be Vik if you've got some Iks."

"Here's some food," handing over a bar. It wasn't drugs or sex, but he was hungry, so he took it. "Where's Slasher?"

"She a wasted little kid?" he asked, as if that narrowed the search.

"Yes." Why not, keep him talking.

"Hey, Vik, we've got a new batch!" He grinned a stupid grin of satisfaction at his cleverness as he held out his hand. Somehow, he was surprised that all he got was more food.

A reedy cough preceded a crumpled shape.

"Gimme."

"Come on, Slasher, I want to show you something." Wendy led her out of the tank and towards some open space. Vik slumped and Wendy handed her a bar and a bottle of water.

The girl stared at these exotic objects as Wendy took out her phone and called the number.

"You have her?" the sharp female voice said.

Wendy paused, wondering how the mystery woman knew before realizing, of course this is a person with resources, it's probably a number she used only for this enterprise. "Yes, ma'am."

It was the woman's turn to pause. "'Ma'am'? Who are you?"

"My name is Wendy Villar. I run the Haven at Marbury Point. I was told you were looking for Victoria Cranston."

"Do you know who she is?"

"Yes, ma'am, Senator George Cranston's daughter."

"And you want the reward. Or maybe score a few points with the next president? Don't try it. Trying to blackmail me would be useless."

Wendy had a great deal of tolerance for junkies, not so much for bullies.

"Look, ma'am..." It was getter harder not to spit out that word. "I run a kind of shelter here. I feel bad enough that I'm making this effort for a rich kid when at least three poor kids are going to die tonight. You can take your money and stuff it... you can keep it."

There was an oddly long pause. "The Haven, you said... Yes... I see." Wendy realized the woman must be reading about the shelter on her computer. "Wendy Villar. *Sister* Wendy Villar. Interesting that you didn't introduce yourself that way."

"And I find it interesting that you haven't introduced your-self at all."

"Do you have a car? How soon can you get to the southeast corner of Lincoln Park?"

"Half an hour."

"Fine." And she hung up. Wendy was sure if she called

again, she would get a recording to tell her it was not a working number.

Wendy and Vik arrived at the corner, a business neighborhood where everything was closed this late at night. Vik was stirring from her stupor, uncertain if she was still high. "Come on," Wendy said, dragging her out of the car, "You need to walk."

"Shuddup."

"Come on." She was practical at the art of forceful persuasion.

"Whodahelluryou?"

As she propped Vik against the wall, a heavy dark car pulled. Shielded, no doubt. A woman got out of the back seat. Pretty much what Wendy had envisioned. Lean, a stride like a panther, well-dressed but not flashy. Wendy did not, however, expect a blonde; she pictured a flaming redhead.

The woman walked over to the pair. "Sister Wendy?"

"Yes."

The woman looked at Vik. For a flash, Wendy thought she saw a genuine emotion cross the woman's face. "Victoria," she said, trying to sound gentle.

Vik, maybe roused by the sound of her full name, stared into the darkness. Muddled by everything around her, it took a long time before something from her past surfaced. "You," she hissed, the verbal equivalent of a claw to the cheek. "He sent you. Too weak to do it himself. Sends the bitch-in-waiting."

"Get in the car, Victoria." Ah yes, she was used to giving orders. Vik turned on Wendy, "Bitch, you koched me!" Filled with a rage she knew she couldn't use, she turned back to the blonde. "I'm not going to that house."

"You're right, you're not. Now get in the car." When she repeated the command, the driver got out of the car, his bulk rising high above the three women. Someone else used to giving orders.

Wendy couldn't decide if it was resignation or fear that propelled the girl forward. The black car swallowed her. Once certain that her charge was secured, the woman turned to Wendy.

"Thank you," she finally said, "Father MacIntyre will stop by tomorrow. Do with it as you wish."

She worked fast, Wendy thought. She had to admire the efficiency.

CHAPTER 70

It was late afternoon when Theo announced over the radio: "We're entering Lagos airspace, which means we're entering Savimbi airspace. You have the coordinates for the UN compound. Separate, fly as fast and high as you can. The next five minutes will not be pleasant."

"See you in half an hour," Sam said encouragingly.

"Sure." Sam could hear the shrug over the radio.

The three ships were still flying in close formation, with the EuroNet jet restraining its ability to fly faster and higher. With Theo's last shrug, the EuroNet pilot let loose, climbing high and fast, veering away from the city. Within minutes, the jet would change course again and make a wide loop towards the UN House. But by then, they would be out of sight of the sand-huggers.

Theo and Robert put as much distance between their ships as possible. The unspoken strategy was to ensure if one ship was hit, the shrapnel was less likely to hit the other. It was a well-timed maneuver because an aerial blast went off exactly where Robert's ship had been. The weapon wasn't an old-fashioned anti-aircraft "gun power" explosion, but a mix of traditional explosives and electromagnetic pulse, meaning the actual explosion was small but the shock waves were potent. The next blast was more accurate, spinning Robert's ship out of control. He was just regaining control when they heard a voice over the radio.

"You are flying unauthorized through our airspace. Land immediately to be inspected for contraband."

The sand-huggers were painted with the universal UN coloring all white with a large blue "UN" on the sides and wings. The voice knew who he was talking to.

Theo answered immediately. "We are United Nations ships on a humanitarian mission. It is essential that we reach the UN House quickly." Flipping off the radio momentarily, he turned to Raj. "Call Asanti on your phone, it's not likely they can monitor it, tell him where we are. He might get police out here."

"You think the police would come out here?"

"No."

The voice from the ground replied. "What you say means nothing to us. Land."

As if to punctuate the demand, a second explosive pulse clipped the wing on Robert's jet. He was still unstable from the first shot, the second sent the ship spiraling to the ground.

"Stop firing. We are landing," Theo said, with undisguised horror in his voice.

The business-like voice continued. "Look starboard. There's a beacon signal in a landing pad near you. Land immediately."

The pad was actually the courtyard of a large walled complex. It wasn't very large, but big enough for Theo to execute a vertical landing without problem. As soon as he cut the engines, raggedy soldiers in cast-off uniforms but brand new rifles surrounded the craft. Theo and Raj came out with their hands up. Two soldiers motioned them away from the ship as the rest swarmed inside.

"That way," the first soldier said, pointing with his rifle towards the main building in the compound.

The four walked across the field and into the building. There were soldiers on the roof and guarding a large metal double door, with a deliberately visible laser array crisscrossing the doorway. One of the guards pressed a button on a handheld. The lasers turned off, an electronic lock snapped, and the doors swung open. The four walked in and the door was shut, and the laser reactivated instantly.

Despite high ceilings, wide corridors, and the abundance of windows, the building was stifling. There were few lights. The spaciousness of the building, the interior courtyard large enough for multiple vehicles and a landing pad suggested to Theo that this was once a hospital. The windows were glass-less, but there were thick metal plates above that could eas-ily drop to seal the windows from any human or mechanical enemy. A series of ceiling fans provided the only relief from the stagnant air that covered everything. Other than that, a scat-tering tables and chairs, there was no furniture.

There was no shortage of soldiers, however. Every few meters, at least one heavily armed militia man watched them. Their eyes followed them slowly, cautiously. Even though Theo and Raj had no weapons, but their escorts were armed. The wall-leaning soldiers still gripped their rifles when they passed. Out of boredom or caution, it didn't matter to Theo. The men-ace was there.

As they walk down the hall, all the rooms that had doors were shut. They walked up a flight of stairs to a room with a large double door. Again, the lasers, and there were even more sol-diers. These men had the better rifles. Standing in front of the door was a man wearing a better uniform and insignias meant to suggest some high rank. He had a side arm but no rifle.

One soldier saluted. "Our guests, colonel."

The colonel glanced at them, like a bored cat noticing a dead mouse, and then motioned to the guards, who turned off the laser and opened the door. The colonel walked in first, followed by the prisoners, then the guards. Theo and Raj looked around.

They were in a large room. Originally it was probably an office of a high-ranking official or many a conference room. Unlike other rooms they had seen, this one had tall windows covered by translucent glass, undoubtedly bulletproof. Some light got in, but no air. It wasn't stuffy, but they both noticed the air was much cooler. The tingle on their sweaty skin told them an air conditioner had been on recently. It had been turned off in anticipation of their arrival. Comfort was not a priority.

Besides the windows, some light was coming in through a skylight. The sole electric light was on the huge desk at the far end of the room. The lack of light made it hard to make out everything, there were many shadows. Boxes were stacked in the dim corners with weapons. Loot. The only furniture besides the desk was a beat-up conference table with eight beat-up chairs and one very nice chair at the head of the table. Also, unlike the rest of the compound, the room was spotless.

The desk was monumental, the accessory of a president or general. It was a classic "back of the cave" set-up for the arrangement of a boss. They set the desk back opposite the door. Anyone had to cross the open room to approach, making them both metaphorically and physically vulnerable. "You must come to me." The desk was both a barrier: you can't touch me and an altar, you shall not touch me.

As large as the desk was, it was dwarfed by the man sitting behind it. A huge, roiling tank of a man. Even sitting, his bulk was unmistakable. He was leaning back in a tall, cushioned chair, his face hidden. But his hands resting on the arms of the chair were clearly visible. They were strong and thick, instruments of murder.

Nothing was on the desk except the lamp, a water bottle, a few papers, and a gold-plated pistol, positioned under the lamp so that visitors had to notice the glint of the weapon. As he leaned forward, his face came into the light. Heavy angry eyes, surrounded by a deeply scarred face. Theo couldn't decide if the scars were war wounds or ritual. His mouth was shut tight. He was clean shaven and wearing a crisp military style uniform, with the stars of a general on his shoulders. His right hand moved noticeably closer to the golden weapon.

The party walked towards the desk; the colonel stopped the men a meter short of the desk close enough for the general to see them but far enough away that if either of them were insane enough to lug at him, they wouldn't even get close. The soldiers stood a few paces behind the prisoners.

The colonel shouted at them, "This is General Marcus Savimbi. You will stand at attention!"

The civilians did their best imitation of standing at attention. It wasn't impressive. Savimbi didn't care. "Who are you and why are you in my airspace without permission?"

"I am Dr. Theodore van Bissem and this is my colleague Dr. Raj Gupta. We are attached to the UN Biogeological Station A4 in Katsina. We are on a humanitarian mission, bringing medical supplies to the WHO. We are unaware that anyone other than the government of Nigeria has sovereignty over Lagos airspace."

"'The government of Nigeria' how quaint. If you work in Nigeria, you know that there is no such thing. So now you've insulted me twice. Give the colonel your IDs and let's see if you've insulted me three times."

They obliged. The colonel scanned the embed on their UN-issued ID cards. He was unimpressed and handed them back. "Legitimate, sir."

"What about their ship?"

Again, the colonel checked his hand-held.

"Nothing inconsistent with their story. Medical equipment, medicines, rations. No weapons, no contraband. Their supplies are being brought up now."

"Sounds like you're going to get off with a fine." Casting about to find something else to interest him, Savimbi settled on Raj. "What happened to your arm?"

"My mother had the bad timing of being pregnant during a nuclear attack."

"Nuclear attack? You Indian or Pakistani?"

"Indian."

"Hindu or Muslim?"

"Indian."

"You're bad luck," he said, motioning to his soldiers, "I don't want him in my presence."

Suddenly, the soldiers cared deeply about Raj's appearance and hurriedly poked their guns at him to move him out of the room.

"What are you going to do with him?"

"He's cursed from the womb. I don't want his curse here," was Savimbi's non-answer.

"What are you going to do with him?"

"Don't worry, I not going to have him killed. I don't want that blood touching my ground."

The colonel had no interest in this stage of the drama. He had been studying his hand-held. "General, we found the other ship. Most of the crew was alive. We sent them on their way. Not much in the ship."

"Who's alive?" Theo asked.

The colonel stared at him blankly, and Savimbi answered for him. "What makes you think he's obliged to speak to you?" He made a great show of studying the colonel's computer, satisfied that Theo understood the general now knew more than he did. "So, the valuable cargo was in the third ship. What are you carrying?"

"I told you, air and water purification equipment, some medicines. We put the bulk of the medical supplies on the larger ship, figuring they had the best chance of getting through."

The door opened and a line of soldiers brought in the supplies from Theo's ship, and placed them neatly before the general's desk. Savimbi took his time examining them.

"And this? It's labeled penicillin. What is it really?"

"Penicillin."

"Does this mean the rumors of a new flu are true?"

"Most likely."

"Then this penicillin will be worth something to someone."

"Most likely."

"You're traveling very light."

"It's only enough for a few people. A US Navy ship and a hospital ship are on their way with adequate medicines." He winched slightly. "US Navy ship" was not a term to endear someone whose power base is only a few kilometers inland.

"You risked your lives to vaccinate maybe 20 people?"

"I'm not a medical doctor, I don't know what they planned to do with it."

"So, what kind of doctor are you?"

"Agronomist. I plant trees."

"Planting trees. What a lovely hobby. Do you plant tulips as well?"

"No, tulips aren't indigenous to the Sahel."

Savimbi wasn't sure if he was being mocked. "An adventurer, agronomist. Flying over lawless Lagos on a great humanitarian mission to save as many people as died since you landed here. You really think you're some kind of hero?"

"No. A friend asked me for a favor. No hidden meaning."

"'No hidden meaning.' So, you're a cynic and a hero. And a fool Africa is nothing but hidden meanings." He finished studying the supplies and motioned for the soldiers to remove everything. "Fortunately for you, your cargo is boring. I have no further interest in holding you. Let's go."

They walked out side-by-side with the two guards a few steps behind. Soldiers snapped to attention as Savimbi took his time, slow-walking his prisoner past the armed audience.

By now they had exited the building and crossed to court-yard towards Theo's ship.

"Don't make the mistake of assuming I'm an ignorant war lord. Penicillin for the flu? Nonsense on both counts. I know we're looking at something much worse than the flu. What is really in those vials?"

"Penicillin. We don't have any vaccines that could be of use for any flu, so I brought along whatever I had. What is truly valuable is the purification equipment, and that should be at the UN by now."

"No. You're lying. You've insulted me again. There's something bigger going on here. There are extra layers. No one is fool enough to put themselves in this much danger for so little. You're the first sign of something bigger, aren't you? So great a risk for so little medicine. Something worse is coming. Something that will terrify people. Somebody is going to get very desperate soon. Desperate is good for business. You're not worth the bother now. Here's your ship."

The ship looked fine from a distance, but as he got closer, he could see how it had been diminished. He knew what had happened, but he checked even though he knew it would entertain Savimbi. The door was missing, so he leaned in to survey the wreckage. It was stripped of anything that might have value metals, circuits, supplies, computers. It was little more than a shell. A shell he was sure would soon have a new life as a cell, or worse.

"Guess I'm not flying anywhere in this."

"Probably not." He was enjoying this. So much more fun that simply slitting his throat.

"Mind telling me which way it is to the UN House?"

Still smiling, he pointed west. "That way. I guess you have about an hour before it gets dark. Not that it will matter much for you."

By now, Theo's shrugs were as much to annoy Savimbi as they were his natural reaction. So, with one final shrug, he looked at the gutted ship, didn't look at Savimbi, and walked out towards the setting sun.

CHAPTER 71

Ike arrived at General Adams' office at the appointed time. He had gotten to the Pentagon quite early, expecting the same elaborate security checks that he always had to go through on the few occasions when he entered that building. He had hoped that saying his appointment with his former classmate rather than with a general would ease things a bit. So he was surprised when security was eased quite a bit. His appointment had already been approved and the security check was routine. When he entered the outer office, instead of an NCO or civilian sitting at the front desk, it was Peter. After greeting his old friend, Peter did the next surprising thing after locking the door with the standard desktop button, he took out a handheld and pressed another button. Ike could hear the snap of another lock although he saw nothing and the lights in the room dimmed.

"I've reduced all the power in the room, including communications," Peter answered the obvious and unasked question. "Follow me."

They entered the general's inner office. Again, Peter pressed a button and again Ike heard an unseen lock snap.

General Adams was sitting behind a grand general's desk. It was a magnificent cherry masterpiece, not a hint of metal or polymers anywhere. That and an easy chair were the only traditional pieces of furniture in the room. Ike noted the lack of other chairs or meeting table the general probably didn't have too many visitors. What was left was high tech. A large monitor with a bank of smaller monitors, all blank and multiple panels and speakers, and a few switches that made no sense to him. The pair of locked metal cabinets seemed out-of-place in a general's office. Too utilitarian, bland, something for an unseen storage basement. The lighting in the room also caught his attention. It was bright but somehow muted. Then he realized the windows were almost opaque. Light could get in, but no distinct shapes could be seen. Ike knew that most windows in the Pentagon has special blast-proof windows, but this was something more.

"Turn off all your phones and give them to me."

They instinctively complied. Adams opened one of the steel cabinets and placed all of their phones and then removed four weapons: a military issued taser rifle, and four old-fashioned guns, three standard pistols and a larger machine weapon that Ike recognized from history lessons as an Uzi. Adams handed each of them a pistol, gave the taser to Peter, and he kept the machine pistol. "Sir, why such old weapons?"

"A modern gun issued in the Pentagon has a computer chip that will send out a signal when activated, we can't risk any unwarranted transmission. In addition, since the C Ring massacre, Pentagon security can override any active weapon and shut it off. These weapons lack those features." He paused, deciding whether to share. "It took a lot to get these into the Pentagon."

He looked at the clock on the terminal. "We will have less than 15 minutes, possibly no more than 10 minutes, once the program boots up. Correct, Peter?"

"That's probably right, sir. I've embedded a few decoys, nothing too elaborate, but it should be enough for anyone tracking us to think we are in several locations. It won't hold long, but it will give us a few minutes." He placed his thumb on a panel near the keyboard and the monitors sprung to life. At first, the screens showed only test patterns, but then images popped onto the smaller screen: a shot of Adams' outer office and two shots aimed at both directions of the corridor. The fourth screen showed what looked like a trimmed down version of the SAC radar it showed the daylight side of the northern hemisphere meaning North America and the tracking lines for only a few orbiting vehicles space stations, Ike assumed. Peter pressed another button and a countdown clock showed 15:00:00. The large center screen maintained the test pattern.

"Excellent. Ike, we've run a few computer simulations. Best case is that we need eight minutes, but that requires that once activated the program will continue on its own. 'Dead hand,' if you will. Realistically, we will need 12 minutes. Gentlemen, it is virtually impossible to complete our mission and remain undetected. Once I turn this computer on, we are in God's hands. We will leave this room heroes or in shackles. If either of you has the slightest doubts, now is the time to leave. If you leave, leave with God's blessing." Neither moved. "Ike, I suppose I should tell you the full nature of this mission."

"I would appreciate that, sir."

"You are going to fulfill your father's mission. God placed him on Earth to fulfill His divine plan. He was stopped but God is patient, and He has sent you in the name of your earthly father and your heavenly father. The Beast is upon us and God's will must be done. You will place your hands on this computer and smite God's enemies. The armies of the Devil and of Jesus will rise up this hour, but we will give the Lord the humble advantage of which we are capable. We will strike the Devil's minions with a bolt from the heavens. Your father was wrong only in the hour. Let us pray."

They dropped to their knees and bowed their heads.

"Heavenly Father guide the hand of your servant whom you have sent to us to fulfill your will. The righteous shall be uplifted and the corrupt damned. Your Son will return to us and the angels in heaven shall rejoice. We humbly ask that you guide your son to complete your divine plan. Amen."

"Amen," the comrades said in unison.

Peter shifted to business. "Ike, everything is programmed. Sit down. At 0:55:00, General Adams will place his hand on this scanner, you will place yours on the other. Once the authorization reading is accepted, this panel will be activated. At precisely 0:00, you press this button. Understood?"

"Yes."

"Now we wait."

CHAPTER 72

Goa was always a place apart. A small alcove sitting quietly while the world whipped around it. The only piece of the Portuguese empire on the Indian sub-continent, it was the last piece of the jigsaw puzzle that was modern Indian to be absorbed by the giant state. As a result, it held onto its non-Indian-ness in many obvious ways: the use of Portuguese, the proliferation of Christian churches, eating pork, and drinking beer.

After the war, the prevailing winds carried the fallout and hot debris east across the continent from Delhi and Mumbai. The attack on Bangalore, being inland, didn't send any fall-out Goa's way. So relatively speaking, Goa had a future. The worst sea level rises were a couple of decades away, but climate change had messed with the Indian Ocean and rain and wind patterns had become unsettling. This meant those lovely beaches were no longer habitable, but the fancy hotels on the cliffs could still function. The workers who could no longer live in villages on the shore moved inland but to land that could no longer be farmed. Goa gained farmland by cutting down tropical hardwoods and selling the lumber cheap. Anywhere they could grow rice, they did. Other land went to soybeans. It still wasn't known how far the populations of India and Pakistan had fallen, but it was known how much arable land was lost so anywhere that could grow food was used. The consequences of the loss of the trees and their roots systems and canopy would have to be dealt with later.

Many of the hotels had been commandeered for

government and corporate use. The hotel owners didn't mind since there were hardly any tourists anymore and those who did come were foreigners pushing deep into the jungles to experience the lushness before it was gone. It was another example of a perverse eco-tourism. People were rushing to experience and mourn the death throes of nature's wonders: rain forests, glaciers, coral reefs before they vanished forever. The largest hotels also had the advantage of having self-contained power and water systems the need for preventing water-borne diseases was paramount. The hotels kept recycling the same water. It looked awful, but at least they knew what was in it.

And then there were the pigs. Nowhere else in India did pigs abound. Unclean to Hindus and Muslims, appalling to vegetarians of any or no religion, only Christian Goa had swine in any number. After the war, the government thought to feed the starving people pork, food was food, but the revulsion was swift. So, the pig population dwindled. It dwindled further when pressure for land increased. While pigs are low-maintenance animals, they will literally eat anything, including human feces they still needed some land. It was essential and faster to use the land to grow grain to feed people. They ate but didn't replenish the stock. They tried to export suckling pig to China, but "food from India" was literally poison. So, except for a few hardy adventurers cultivating free-range pigs to sell to the non-Indians working in the hotels, raising pigs dropped from the culture.

Which is why no one could think it odd when the pigs started coughing.

It was a witches' brew of swine flu, germ transmission through diarrhea, and a hotel water filter past its prime. It started with the people who tended the pigs. Their coughs carried it to other humans, the resulting diarrhea carried it further, and the not so purified water ran the virus through the hotel. Within two weeks, everyone who spent any time in that hotel was wrenchingly sick or dead.

Every pig in Goa was slaughtered and burned.

CHAPTER 73

Ron and Kate were sitting in the mess aboard the *Roosevelt*, eating something that looked like creamed chicken when the siren went off.

"Red alert, red alert." It was the First Officer's voice. "We have detected an unauthorized power surge. Possible generator breech. All emergency personnel report to stations; all pilots report to their vessels; all other personnel report to secure positions. Repeat: red alert, possible generator breech, this is not a drill."

Confused but calm, everyone left the mess hall.

On the bridge, the First Officer snapped to attention as Captain Hightower entered the room.

"What the hell is going on?"

"There's been an unauthorized power surge, sir. We thought the generator was breeching but we've isolated it to Quadrant 2."

"The surge is coming from Sector 101!" the helmsman said.

Hightower was knocked off his stride. "Sector.... That's impossible. I gave no such order."

"Is there anything in there that can generate that kind of power?"

The helmsman stared at the data in disbelief. "The sector is decompressing, exterior doors opening. Doors? There are doors?"

CHAPTER 74

The Situation Room was barely controlled chaos: lights and alarms going off, people running in and out, talking on phones, writing into computers. The officer in charge was an army general, Alan Monroe. The master screen was split into thirds:

Air Force General Miller with the Pentagon seal behind him took up the center screen; Captain Hightower to the left; and the right screen showed the interior of Sector 101. It was a grainy image that showed a chamber loaded with electronics. In the lower right-hand corner of the screen, a finger of darkness was visible. The sector looked quiet but in fact doors were slowly sliding open to reveal a hint of space and that finger also appeared to be lengthening.

Ailes charged into the room, followed closely by the Chief of Staff.

The Officer of the Day needed all of his strength to shout over the riot. "Attention!"

The President waved them off before they had a chance to stand. "Everyone as you were. General, report."

"There has been an unauthorized activation of Sector 101 on the *Roosevelt*. It has powered up and the exterior doors are opening."

A second lieutenant new to the job made a mistake and asked a question. "What's Sector 101?"

Monroe spun around furiously. "Who gave you permission to speak! What's your duty?"

"Sir, monitoring communications from the UN and

European space stations, sir."

"Then do it and speak when addressed!" He resumed his briefing. "The three command centers the Pentagon, Cheyenne Mountain, and this room are secured and in our hands. All are manned, none have given the order."

Gesturing toward the main screen, the President said, "Explain."

"Mr. President, General Miller, the Air Force Chief of Staff you know. This is Captain Charles Hightower, the Captain of the *Roosevelt*. The other screen is Sector 101."

"Can you hear me, Captain?"

"Yes, Mr. President."

"Explain yourself."

For the second time in less than ten minutes, Hightower was blind-sided. "Sir, begging your pardon, there is nothing to explain from the *Roosevelt*. Protocol clearly states and it cannot be overridden from the station. Sector 101 can only be activated from Earth. The security codes pass to the captain of the *Roosevelt* only if two of the three command centers in the United States are destroyed. This obviously is not the case. The security breach is clearly coming from Earth."

"Can you stop it?"

"No, sir. I have no control over Sector 101 in any, way, shape or form. They designed it that way."

"The president of Russia and the UN Secretary-General are calling inquiring about the power surge," the lieutenant dared to add.

"What could they know?" Ailes was obviously not speaking to the lieutenant.

Monroe answered, "Only that there is an unusual power surge on the station there are any number of explanations. But if this continues, every decent sized monitor on Earth or in orbit is going to see it." He stole a glance at the image of Sector 101. The doors were fully retracted, and the dark finger was growing in the chamber. "They're going to know within three minutes unless we override it."

Turning to the colonel sitting next to Monroe, Ailes said, "Report."

"The White House and Cheyenne Mountain are secure. The transmission is coming from the Pentagon."

General Miller exploded. "Impossible! I'm sitting right here in the command center. I'd stake my life that the signal is not coming from here."

"He's right, sir. It's not coming from the command center it's coming from some other location. We have narrowed it down to ten locations..."

"Ten!" Miller was turning redder by the second.

"... some are decoys, some may be echoes. There must be only one genuine transmission point. We just have to pinpoint it."

"And why wasn't I informed of this before now?" Miller demanded.

That was a question he was far too junior to answer. He turned pleadingly to his superior. "General?"

Taking a deep breath, Monroe said, "We weren't sure your security had not been breached, we could not risk transmitting the information to the Pentagon and have it intercepted."

That popped the last blood vessel. "Breached! You pompous ass! How dare you..."

He seemed to have forgotten the President of the United States was present. Ailes reminded him. "Stand down, General!"

"Yes, sir," he growled.

"Transmit all the coordinates to the Pentagon."

"Yes, Mr. President."

Miller took to regaining his professional composure. He addressed someone in the center invisible to the Situation Room. "Deploy all SWAT. Red Alert. Dispatch with prejudice. Orders directly from the President."

Monroe split his attention between the image of 101 and his monitor. "The cannon is being extended and is powering up."

"Cannon?" The lieutenant apparently had a death wish.

"Shut up!"

Ailes stayed on point. "How much time before it is fully extended and powered?"

"Four minutes, five tops."

The President addressed the colonel.

"Will the *Roosevelt* still be over the United States in four minutes?"

"No, sir, it's over the Rocky Mountains now. In four minutes, it will be over... oh dear God... China."

For the first time in uncountable years, Ailes was stymied. "No, no, no, no. Alan, we have to stop it. Now."

Monroe turned to Hightower. "Can you shift the *Roosevelt*'s orbit?"

"Yes, sir, but that takes time. Even if the cannon is realigned, it will still be aiming somewhere on Earth in four minutes."

"Mr. President, the Chinese premier is on the hot line. He is demanding you explain the appendage extending from the *Roosevelt*," the thoroughly beaten junior officer said.

Ailes' expression clearly meant "ignore him" while Monroe continued. "We can shut down all but minimum power to the entire station. Sector 101 is integrated into the main matrix. The station can stay on minimum life support, but it would be enough to prevent the cannon from firing."

"Hightower, can we do that?"

"Yes, sir, but that's not a simple switch, it takes time to power down."

"How long?"

"It's never been done. Maybe ten minutes."

"You do have a simple switch..." Monroe said, not so much as to contradict the captain but to state the inevitable.

"That protocol is designed for a catastrophic breach. It shuts down the entire station, even life support. If I can't bring power back in time, I could kill the crew."

"Mr. President?"

Ailes silently stared at the world.

"The *Roosevelt* is over the Pacific," the lieutenant dared to say.

The peace of the righteous reigned in General Adams' office. They were all looking at the monitors. Peter was the only one sitting.

"They've narrowed the search to the Pentagon. I've set up nine decoys and echoes, and there's a false code on the outer door and this door. On the basis of last week's test, it will take them approximately two minutes to eliminate each decoy. The door locks give us four minutes, therefore we have anywhere between seven and 12 minutes."

"Twelve minutes is more than enough. But seven?" Adams asked.

"The doors on the *Roosevelt* are open and the cannon is extending. We could be ready to fire in five minutes. And we've timed it right. It will be over the target."

Ike asked, "What are their counter maneuvers?"

"Realistically, only three: cut all power on the *Roosevelt* which takes time, a space station is not designed to shut itself down instantaneously; pull the station out of orbit, which still risks firing the ray at something; or stop us."

"God is with us," their leader said.

Sector 101's camera was mounted at the back of the chamber, so it clearly showed the bay doors were fully retracted and the Earth was visible in the distance. The cannon slowly glided into the picture, like a dragon emerging from its cave, studying its next victim.

"The doors are open, the cannon is activated. The cannon's power is coming online. In two minutes, every monitor on Earth or in space will know what is happening."

Ike knew Adams was whispering scripture, but he couldn't figure out which one. Then his attention was drawn to one of the monitors. "They're in our hallway." The camera showed a heavily armed commando team hurrying down the hallway. One commando was clearly reading a computer and at his signal the team sped up and headed straight to Adams' office door. "They're at the outer door."

For the first time, there was a trace of doubt in the General's voice. "If we really have four minutes, that's enough?"

"Absolutely." Peter's confidence helped steady Adams.

The hallway camera went blank. "They've killed the corridor cameras," Ike reported. They all instinctively turned to the final monitory showing the outer office. The camera was placed above the door in their last line of defense before they would have to use their weapons.

"I'll guard the door," Adams said, "Ike, this is your moment, your father's moment. The Judgment of God is at hand."

As Adams turned to the door, a deafening explosion blew

the door off its hinges and threw the general across the room. Recovering quickly from the shock, Ike reached for the button, only to be coldcocked by Peter and his pistol. Ike hadn't even hit the floor before Peter reached under the console. Suddenly all the power was sapped out of the console. The commandos snatched up the weapons, Peter dropped his on the keyboard. Satisfied that the two officers were incapacitated, the commando leader swung around on Peter.

"What the hell were you playing at? We were supposed to be in three minutes ago. Why wasn't the outer door unlocked?" He paused his tirade long enough to listen to a voice in his earpiece. "The cannon is disarmed. Do you realize what you could have done!"

"Activating the chamber wasn't enough. The world had to see the cannon. There had to be no ambiguity."

"And that was your decision to make? You could have started a war, you idiot."

"No, God would not permit that. 'His hand is....'"

First Adams, then Ike stirred. The leader took obvious delight in barking at them through their haze. "General Adams, Captain McClellan, you are under arrest for treason."

The word "treason" snapped Ike to attention. Seeing Peter was the only one not on the floor, he realized what had happened. "Peter, how could you? We prayed together. We were instruments in the hands of the Lord. How could you? Our prayers..."

"I could because I prayed, Ike. God loves His children. This world is His world, it is our duty to preserve His blessings, not destroy them."

The leader interrupted the sermon. "On your feet, Captain."

Ike took hold of the console to steady himself and in a flash, he pushed Peter aside and grabbed his gun. With some hesitation, he pointed the pistol at Peter. The commandos did not hesitate in pointing their weapons at Ike.

Peter, fearing more for his friend's life than his own, implored, "Don't, please surrender."

Ike stared madly at his lost cause, his failure to avenge his father, his unfaithful comrade, his fallen general. The commando team turned into a massive horde of demons with red eyes, their pitchforks stabbing at him.

"Father, into your hands I commit my spirit." And he turned the gun on himself.

The frenzy in the Situation Room suddenly stopped, as if it rather than the *Roosevelt* had had its power cut. The lights stopped flashing, and everyone stood, mesmerized by the monitors and the stillness.

Ailes looked at Hightower. "What just happened?"

"The power to the cannon was cut by itself. We didn't do anything."

"Is it disarmed?"

"Yes, sir. It's completely neutralized. But I don't know how."

"Mr. President, Senator Cranston is on the phone. He wishes to speak with you about the *Roosevelt*."

CHAPTER 75

Sanjeet had called the EuroNet crew to the Galapagos Recovery Station. No explanation. When they arrived in the control room, the monitors were not showing their usual sweeps of the islands. Instead, the main screen was taken up with a space image of the South Pacific. And the dominant image there was a huge storm north of New Caledonia.

"This is not good," Sanjeet said to no one in particular.

One of his colleagues was more talkative. "On the one hand, it's still pretty far out. All computer models at this point have a margin of error of up to 23 percent. The *Al-Khwarizmi* spotted it yesterday. If their readings are correct, it's gained strength by a factor of 20 since then. Meaning it's gone from a Category 3 to Category 4 storm in less than one day."

"I take it that's fast," Elsa said.

"Not a record but certainly greater than average," Sanjeet replied, "It's currently 500 kilometers northeast of New Caledonia. In and of itself, this is not too unusual. This is the bad season for typhoons. They build quickly, but this is unusually fast. It could easily reach 325 kilometers an hour, meaning Category 5 within 12 hours. At this rate, Category 6 is certainly within the realm of probability." Once upon a time, there was no Category 6, scientists had to recalibrate the scale decades ago, just as there wasn't an indigo temperature coding until Australia started baking in the 2010s.

"The advantage is that it's not near any populated islands?"

"For the moment."

Their embrace was tight and intimate, but in no way sensual. It was late, the sky was already overcast. The winds were normal but didn't sound like it.

"What happens tomorrow if we're in direct line of the typhoon?" Elsa asked.

Typhoons crossing the Equator just didn't happen. Since weather monitoring by satellites began, no tropical storm had ever crossed the line. What was called the Coriolis Force at the Equator was strong enough to drain storms of their swirling motions, dissipating the force so much that it couldn't cross the line. Therefore, Northern Hemisphere and Southern Hemisphere storms had a limited range. This meant that the Galapagos straddling the Equator was never subjected to powerful typhoons. That changed as the oceans warmed and gave added clout to the storms. The Coriolis Force was still there, but more and more storms built up enough power to continue pressing on, even if the Force challenged them at the Equator. The islands had been hit three times in two decades with Category 3 storms, once by a Category 4. Never a Category 5 but now a monster that might soon reached Category 6 was heading their way.

Sanjeet didn't tell her any of this.

"It won't be the first time. The protocol is to evacuate people to the mainland; only the locals if it doesn't look severe, total evacuation if it's serious we've only done that once before. We also have a protocol for the wildlife. There are nurseries on the mainland for both plants and animals, as well as here. Every week we tag saplings, eggs, hatchlings in our nurseries for priority evacuation those that are unique or are in particular danger. If I decide it's necessary, we'll remove some or even all of our specimens and bring them to Ecuador for the duration."

"Doesn't it endanger them to move around so much?"

"Yes, but I'll have to balance the risks of moving with the risks of the typhoon. The animals living in the wild have adapted over the centuries to the storms, so we're only talking about a small percent of wildlife."

"Have they adapted to Category 6 hurricanes."

"Obviously not. But we still don't know if they will have to." Knowing that any real sleep was out of reach, he changed the subject, "I hope you're packed."

I've been packed all day."

Sleep finally took them. Else woke groggy from anxiety and dislocation. The dislocation was enhanced when she realized she was alone in bed. She finally focused on Sanjeet hunched over his computer.

"And?"

Without looking up, he said, "It's 50 percent stronger and has settled into a North-Northeast path of roughly 45 degrees."

"I know enough geography to know what that means. Is it inevitable that we are in its path?"

"Ask me in three hours."

Three hours later, Sanjeet's team, representatives of the islands' local leadership and the EuroNet crew were sitting in the station's conference center. They were looking at three large screens two of them were blank. The third one was a view of the coming storm. One of the blank screens came alive and showed the captain of the *Al-Khwarizmi*. Then the final screen was filled with the distressed face of an Ecuadorian minister.

Al-Khwarizmi's captain began. "As you see, the typhoon is now 100 kilometers across. There is no sign of it losing strength, in fact as it gets closer to the Equator, it is gaining force. If it stays on this trajectory, the northern edge of the storm will hit the Galapagos tomorrow morning. It'll be bad, but not the worst possible outcome. If it veers even three degrees north, it will hit the Galapagos full force, meaning Category 6."

Elsa broke the silence. "Wasn't the last typhoon to hit the Galapagos Category 4?"

"Yes," Sanjeet answered.

"Never a Category 6?"

"No, never. We're no longer talking about a storm. This is *the* storm, the one we always knew would come."

The captain agreed. "Exactly. Under the circumstances, we recommend a general evacuation of the Galapagos chain."

The government official broke in. "Forget about recommendations. As the representative of the sovereign state of Ecuador, I hereby order a full and immediate evacuation of the Galapagos and the relocation of all Ecuadorian nationals and international personnel to mainland Ecuador. This order is effective immediately."

CHAPTER 76

That morning, a motion sensor ten clicks east of the family's nest detected the movement of something large. It could have been a large cat or another orangutan, but the location and the timing of the arrival fit too well. Ruth – now armed and Jamal with his soldiers headed out towards the nest.

Examining her monitor, she stopped the patrol. "All three of them are over there. I'll go alone. They can't see you they'll never understand."

The soldier had come to the same conclusion for different reasons. Pointing east, he said, "They're likely to be coming from that direction." He looked at his men. "Deploy" and they did. In a moment, they were a part of the jungle.

Ruth adjusted the rifle over her back so that it would not be the first thing the apes saw and walked into the clearing. And absurdly, she also whistled. As she approached the nest, Kai was the first one she saw. He started to greet her and then saw the rifle. He walked slowly towards his friend and delicately touched the barrel as if it were a venomous and stiff snake. He didn't need sign language for Ruth to understand he was suspicious.

She dropped the rifle before hugging Rabu.

"Bad men are coming. We must protect ourselves."

"Bad men protect."

Ruth started cutting more branches. This was something the apes did not need to be taught. As the parents ripped up plants and turned their nest into a wall, Ruth took a branch and tried to disguise the apes' presence by removing scat and bits of food and trying to puff up the flattened grass. She held onto the thin hope that the poachers would think in traditional ways and look for the family in the treetops, not knowing that these apes nested on the ground. Useless, she thought. If the poachers have heat-seeking goggles, there was no way three large bodies could escape attention. Everything really depended on Jamal and his men. Unless she could...

Camouflaged as best they could, Ruth tried to hide the heat signature by trying to line the three of them up single file. That strategy was lost on Kai. Besides, this would work only if the poacher approached from precisely the right direction. So, with Nurul cradling the squirmy Rabu, Kai and Ruth crouched guarding the mother and child. Ruth checked her rifle. Father still viewed it suspiciously. Ruth spoke quietly into her radio.

"Jamal, we're as secure as we can be. Have you seen anything?"

"No. It's possible there's only one of them. A group couldn't be this invisible. Go to radio silence."

"Right." She turned off the radio and suddenly felt very alone. She could hear Nurul's breathing on her sweaty back. Father seemed to have somehow grown, his shoulders broader, his arms longer. Another special characteristic of the orangutan was that the male was three, four times larger than the female few species had such an imbalance. And now Kai was the largest orangutan Ruth had ever seen, still growing. His breathing was shallow as his fists clenched and unclenched. Waiting was not in his nature.

Somewhere near birds took flight, the only signal a poacher could not counter. Kai and Ruth knew that sign.

The poacher had been following the trail of scat and broken branches from the stream. He had gone up and down the bank and was finally satisfied that this was the most likely route. He entered the clearing, certain now that this was the best place for an orangutan nest. Ruth could see him. She wiped her hands and slightly raised the gun. She was hoping she could warn him off, because a shoot-out could end only one way. Kai hadn't shifted except that his hands were now firmly clenched. She could see the poacher had two rifles, one was clearly an assault weapon, the other most likely a taser. He paused, looked at the ground for signs, turned his gaze up to the canopy, and then put something over his eyes. Heat-seeking goggles.

Walking cautiously into the open, remembering the last time he was exposed, he looked left and right and up, hoping for that one signature that would mean the end of his travels. He saw the pile of branches in front of him. He could tell it was not a natural arrangement and focused there. It did not occur to him that this was not normal orangutan behavior. The heat signature was massive. "How many of them are in there," he thought.

Ruth saw him aim, but he was aiming high. He shot at a branch a few meters to the left and up from the nest. It did the job. The orangutans screamed. Nurul retreated with Rabu, and Kai burst through the brush. An orange mass of muscle, spittle, and rage charged at the poacher with Ruth doing her best to catch up. The poacher was a good shot. One steady shot and Kai fell screaming and writhing on the ground. Ruth fought her instinct to run to her fallen friend and instead raised her rifle. Her only advantage was that the poacher wasn't expecting a human with a gun. He hesitated, calculating if he should threaten, wound or kill her. The mother and baby were getting away.

"Drop it!" Ruth yelled. Her voice wasn't as convincing as her gun. He didn't drop it and instead took a clear aim he had decided on "kill." The shot that Ruth heard didn't come from the poacher's gun. The man was already on the ground, spurting blood, before Ruth realized that the shot had come from someone else. Jamal emerged from the trees with his rifle still raised as his men entered the clearing from different directions.

It still took a few heartbeats for Ruth to realize she had been saved. She then dropped the rifle and ran to Kai. He was alive, the wound was large, but it was in his shoulder.

"Base, we have a medical emergency. Adult male orang-utan with a bullet wound in the right shoulder..." She tried to talk on the radio while ripping open the first aid kit and applying gauze to the wound.

Meanwhile, the soldiers approached the prostrate man. Stripping him of both guns, Jamal examined him.

"He's alive!" Jamal shouted to Ruth, "We have a human to evacuate as well."

Ruth hesitated an obvious moment. "Right, one orangutan and one poacher."

CHAPTER 77

The western sky was already darkening as the sun rose over the bustling port of Puerto Ayora. Every ship capable of making the trip to the mainland was either getting ready to leave or had just passed over the horizon. The EuroNet plane was the last one on the runway. A large tourist ship that happened to be visiting was enlisted as transport. Civilians were shifted from the Recovery Station's ships to this one. This allowed more room on the scientists' ships for more wildlife.

Sanjeet was studying his computer as he paced the deck of the passenger ship. Elsa was with him, but Sanjeet was talking more to himself than her.

"All civilians are either on the naval ship or out to sea in their own boats. The nurseries are empty. Station personnel have loaded their possessions. All data from the computers have been backed up in the ship's computer and mainland computers. This ship has to leave right away to be sure of getting to the mainland ahead of the storm. Your airship can wait awhile, in case there's any last-minute cargo."

Elsa wasn't interested in the ship's inventory. "Why were your photos still on your desk?"

"What?"

"Your photos, in your bedroom. They weren't packed when we left the house. Neither were the books. And you're wearing rain boots."

"I have priorities."

"Why aren't your bags on the deck? You just said the ships had to leave."

He evaded. "Thought I would fly out with you. Last to leave and all that."

"The expression is 'the captain goes down with his ship.' You're not leaving, are you?"

"No."

"Why not?"

"You just said it. A captain goes down with his ship."

"Bull. This is not a ship. These are islands and they will still be here and you are not the captain."

"I am the protector of the islands. They are my responsibility. Besides, how can you say that they will still be here? Where is Fiji? Where is Vanuatu? The Maldives? I lost one home to the ocean. I am going to stay on this home. I am of the Ocean. The Pacific is my home. I simply will not retreat any further."

"Fine, then I'm not leaving you."

"If this is some kind of game to make me change my mind, it won't work."

"How thick are you? If you can care so much about water, why can't you wrap your mind around the idea that I care that much about you?"

Marta and Pol were at the EuroNet plane. Jorge was loading their gear and as much of the station's equipment as they could carry. Marta was recording the scenes at the dock. She aimed at the deck of the ship. "Look up there. I wonder what they're arguing about?"

CHAPTER 78

Ron loved this part of space travel. He was sitting, strapped in, in a seat far more comfortable than his tin can. The view from the window was peaceful, not a piece of debris, anyway. And the best part was that he was a passenger. The actual business of flying this thing was someone else's responsibility.

They were flying at such a luxurious pace, with so few indicators visible from the window that it almost seemed like they weren't moving at all. Ron's fellow passengers looked as relaxed as he did, although he knew most of them had not clocked as much time in space as he had. But they were at peace, even if they were nervous, they were exactly where they wanted to be. A few were even sipping vacuum-packed drinks. And then, so subtly, they felt a change in trajectory. They could feel a downward tug. Not a harsh grasp, just the gentle pull of a pet wanting to go for a walk.

After so many hours of zero gravity, they felt the weight of their bodies again. Not Earth weight, this was less assertive. The pull became stronger with every passing second until they knew the ship had stopped. It has landed. Ron looked out the window at the barren, dirty-white landscape. It was bright, without a hint of shadows. He could see a small section of a metal and glass dome. He craned his neck to look up, but he saw nothing larger than the stars. With a slight jerk, Ron knew the ship was being pulled forward on a kind of conveyer belt. Just before the air lock door shut blocking out the view, the captain spoke over the intercom: "Ladies and Gentlemen, welcome to the Moon."

CHAPTER 79

"Red sky in the morning, sailors take warning." Black sky in the morning? It was well past dawn and while a slice of the rising sun was visible on the eastern horizon, most of the sky was engulfed by the grey and black of the rolling storm. The natural and human world of the Galapagos had shut down. The waves were rougher and the winds higher, all the animals taken shelter.

The Santa Cruz dock was deserted, the passenger ship sailed before dark with the EuroNet plane shortly after that. Elsa had set up all the transmission equipment in the control center. She was walking around the area, shooting wide shots of the deserted docks, the landscape, the darkening sky, and Sanjeet, who was staring at his islands as he had never seen them before. Totally quiet. Not dead, he would never use that word but still, unblinking. Hibernating? Comatose?

He walked towards her as she turned off the camera. He didn't ask, but she told him anyway. "Geneva is not going to let us broadcast live. This will be transmitted to the crew in Guayaquil and Geneva headquarters. I'm going to do this as if it were live in case they change their minds."

"What did Geneva say?"

"That they are looking forward to firing me when I get home." She attached the camera to a tripod and pointed at the deserted harbor. "Do you mind?" she asked, pointing at the camera. He shrugged. The motion said, "as if I had a choice." She walked away from the camera as Sanjeet aimed and starting recording. Technically, it was broadcasting, but the feed was only going to her team and HQ in Geneva. As she prepared her thoughts to start speaking, a few drops of rain splashed her face. She reacted as if she had been sprayed with acid.

"I want to start now."

"Okay."

"It's 0900 hours in the Galapagos. We are standing on the island of Santa Cruz, the home of most of the chain's human inhabitants and headquarters of the Galapagos Recovery Program. As you can see behind me, the typhoon is approaching. Right now, the storm looks like any ocean storm. The waves are quite high, the winds have picked up and there is a bit of rain. Nothing out of the ordinary.

Theeteorological station on the *Al-Khwarizmi* says the storm is 100 kilometers due west at this time, with winds topping 200 kilometers an hour. It has not touched inhabited land for two days. There was a possibility of it losing strength once it got to the Equator, but that has not happened. There is no likelihood of the typhoon missing the Galapagos now. We will continue recording through the storm. Once it has passed, we will record how the islands and the wildlife have managed..."

Marta and Jorge had planted themselves at the naval station at Guayaquil, Ecuador's main port. A navy commander was paying little attention to the human drama but was more focused on the weather maps and reports from the space station.

"Is she serious?" Marta asked, "Does she believe that?"

"She has to say something. Otherwise, it looks like exactly what it is suicide." Jorge instantly regretted using that word.

"When are they going inside? It's the only way they stand a chance."

They watched as Elsa was worn down by the pummeling

rain. They could hear Sanjeet off screen. "We should relocate inside the station now."

Without argument, Elsa swung the camera around to face the station and followed Sanjeet towards the door. Since she wasn't speaking now, the whistling winds and growling waves were more audible. Sanjeet opened the door and ushered her in. Elsa aimed the camera inside to give a sweep of the room. By making this choice, she didn't notice Sanjeet standing at the door, looking out over the island for a long moment before shutting and sealing the door.

She let the camera roll over the scene inside. "Tell us more about this station. How it is constructed."

Sanjeet tried to mimic her just-the-fact tone. "The station is an alloy of aluminum, plastic and various polymers. The idea is that the structure can handle most weather conditions" he didn't dwell on the obvious implications of "most" "and needing minimum maintenance, thus reducing the pollution and waste that once was associated in remote stations like this. It's a closed environment, the solar windows provide all the power, human waste is recycled. Besides air, the only thing we bring in from the outside is water from the island's desalination plant.

"We have a separate greenhouse. Since foods humans tend to eat aren't indigenous to the island, we grow fruits and vegetables isolated from the environment. Most of our protein is from soy and seitan with fish and meat loaves brought in from the mainland."

The storm was gathering. They convinced themselves they had heard wind like this before.

"How long is the storm likely to be over us?"

"It depends on how large it is now. An hour or so is possible. It's moving fast, but it is large. I'll check the monitors."

"You don't have to." It was a plea more than a request.

Shaking his head, he said, "I don't want to talk on camera anymore."

Speaking again to the camera, Elsa said, "In this station, which is the central location for all scientific research and analysis on the islands, we have monitors placed around the islands to track the movements of the wildlife unobtrusively. Obviously, the wildlife has all gone to ground because of the storm, but we can still see We can still see the conditions outside." As she said that, a monitor went black, then another. Tellingly they were both from Fernandina Island the furthest west of the islands."Sanjeet, do you want to tell us what we are looking at?"

"No."

It didn't matter. All the monitors that were still operating showed the same black mass dwarfing the islands. The rain was so heavy it wasn't visible on the screens. But it was loud enough to drown out most of Elsa's attempts to speak.

The detached pose was getting harder to maintain. "There is probably no island or chain of islands more thoroughly monitored than the Galapagos..."

The building groaned, pleading against the rain. Somewhere, something snapped.

"The trick is to maintain the greatest observation without disturbing the natural balance... Sanjeet, please come over here." He complied as the last monitor went black. Then the lights on the panel itself began to go out. The lights in the center flickered. There was an explosive snap rapidly followed by a crash.

"That was probably a solar panel. We'll lose electricity any time now," Sanjeet noted.

Climate control was gone. The pair were soaked from the

rain and clammy air. The storm was vacuuming the air out of the room.

"The last Class 5 cyclone was in…"

If she was speaking it was impossible to tell. The storm sucked the words out of her mouth and flung them out to sea. She gave up, dropped the mike and held Sanjeet's hand. Like a ghost pacing down the hall banging a drum, the groans and slams grew progressively louder. It was also as if it was programmed: snap, crash, crush, repeat. Then a crash and the Furies rushed the defenseless humans.

The static from the dead screen was louder than any storm. Elsa's friends in Guayaquil simply stared.

"We're going back," Jorge said, "This doesn't mean they're dead, it just means their equipment is destroyed."

"You're not going back," the commander flatly stated.

"Who are you to tell us what to do?"

"You think that storm just vanished? Look." He pointed to a screen that was still alive. The storm had swallowed the Galapagos but didn't linger. "It's heading this way. It will hit us tonight, tomorrow morning at the latest. You have an air ship. We can transport maybe 20 hospitalized children out of the city to the interior. I have martial law authority to confiscate your ship if you don't cooperate. Once the storm has passed and we've moved everyone we can out of harm's way, you're free to head back to the islands."

"How many days will that be?"

"Does it matter?" Marta sighed as she silenced the noisy screen.

CHAPTER 80

Mr. Lopez often went to these sturdy, barren hills. Sometimes the hills called him, but usually something was happening around him that drew him here. Sometimes he couldn't even articulate what it was. But today he knew. It was Election Day.

As always, he had his broad-brim hat and large water bottle as he walked through the Petroglyph National Monument. This vast expanse of volcanic rock and little else was along the west bank of the Rio Grande at the edge of Albuquerque. The suburbs that had spread out to the edge of the preserve had now retreated. From the hillside, Mr. Lopez could look out and down on what was left of the houses. Much like his own neighborhood but more extreme since this was further from the city center, the houses were shells stripped of anything useful decades before. Anything metal, kitchen and bathroom fixtures, windows, wood paneling, roof tiles. Gone and gone. Desert animals and cacti had moved in. Drained swimming pools had layers of unimaginable gunk piling up. Dresden in 1945 was more intact. In another century or two, archeologists are going to go nuts here, Mr. Lopez thought.

The rocks were formed by volcanic eruptions 200,000 years ago. Enough of the cooled lava had smooth surfaces that invited creation. The petroglyphs were not painted, but rather chiseled art. The artist scraped away the dark skin of the rock to reveal a lighter tan under a layer that served as the canvas.

The images were a mystery. Who carved them was well known, the Pueblos carved most of them between 1300 and 1680 AD. A few were clearly done by the first Spaniards Christian crosses and depictions of animals such as sheep that they would have brought to the New World. The mystery was what they meant.

In other pictorial histories such as the paintings in the Lascaux Caves or the frescos of Cacaxtla, there were unambiguous images of fertility of humans and the earth, the hunt, worship. But here, while some were simple snakes, lizards, stars, others were more elaborate images that didn't reveal their meanings easily.

One of Mr. Lopez's favorites was a square with a variety of images that looked like sections of Mexican pyramids, the cardinal points, or a star and what? a mushroom, a nuclear explosion? Very few of the human figures were simply human. They were adorned with strange appendages, too many arms and not enough toes, squished heads. Gods or men in ceremonial costumes? The general belief was that they did not represent some formal ritual, but a highly personalized view of the world. Each artist was his own priest. If that were true, then Mr. Lopez's interpretations were as valid as anyone else's.

What he said out loud was barely more than a thought. He walked slowly among the petroglyphs, not so much because of the heat but because he wanted to. This was meditation in motion. No one could know if he was right in what he saw, but it didn't matter to anyone but himself. The Pre-Columbian version of the stations of the cross. He stopped at certain petroglyphs, his old friends, and spoke to them. It was almost a prayer.

"Man, the worshiper."

"Bird, freedom."

"Man, the warrior."
"Sun."
"Earth."
"Man, the hunter."
"Lizard, deep of the earth."
"Corn, the gift of the gods."
"God."
"The cardinal points, the directions for all life."
"Sunrise."

CHAPTER 81

Bizarrely the only person meditating in the Cranston home was George Sr. The house was brimming with aides and nervous energy. Everyone had at least two computers. They were in constant contact with the party in every state and even some congressional district. Data and more data. Did voting machines lose power? Did a station close early? Did the toll machines at certain vital locations stop working? Were any of the journalists reliable? Everything ultimately went to Maggie and Sean, who distilled the numbers, called the lawyers, flagged the inconsistencies before giving the candidate the essentials. Some campaign aides were even in the kitchen, constantly cooking whatever meal anyone's body clock dictated, which explained why there was a huge pan of scrambled eggs ready while a pot of bison stew simmered nearby.

Cranston and his core team, Maggie, Mei, and Sean were nervous, angry, hopeful. They were a mass of energy, repulsing any tiny emotions that might get in their way. The entire townhouse was throbbing. Except this room. George Sr. sat quietly in his book-lined study. This room was a full, comfortable room, obviously aged to perfection by the sole occupant. Only one computer screen was on. A platter with a pot of coffee and a bagel sat next to his chair. He was reading nothing.

It was three in the afternoon. The first polls wouldn't close for another three hours. But all the early electronic ballots had been cast and were stored. Legally, they would not be tabulated until the first polls closed. Legally. Mei was collecting reports from around the country on lines at polling stations, strategic power outages and shortage of ballots, concerned citizens at obviously random routes leading to polling stations. Any official recourse would be futile, but the data would be useful in planning a defense for next time.

George Sr. responded to the knock on the door. "Come in." It was Mei. "Anything yet?" he asked her.

"No, everything is still tentative. Sean is compiling some preliminary data he should be transmitting it to you shortly."

Normally, the instinctive reaction would be to look at the screen to see if anything new was there. But the old man didn't take his eyes off of whatever it was he was looking at somewhere beyond. "After all these years, I still can't get used to it." So, the somewhere beyond was in the past.

"Used to what?"

"Doing nothing on Election Day. When I was a boy, during the campaign we would go door-to-door encouraging people to vote for us of course and come Election Day, we would fan out across the country to monitor the vote, making sure that 'concerned citizens' didn't keep our voters from the polls. My dad even got his hand broken by some guys who had a special definition of freedom of assembly. And now it's nearly all computerized. No more, broken hands, just erased files. Who do we thank for that?"

"From what I read, counting votes by hand was not exactly the peak of democratic perfection."

"Nothing is wrong with the system, just the people running it. It's like religion there's nothing wrong with God, just the people who think they speak for Him."

"Have you ever not campaigned?"

"Never, there was always something worth fighting for. Do you know what apartheid was?" Mei left the non sequitur hanging. "There was a great novel from that bitter time. One character tells the story: 'When we go before Him, God will ask, "Where are your wounds?" And we will say, "I have no wounds." And God will ask, "Was there nothing worth fighting for?"'

"Even when there was no one worth the effort, there was always a reason, a cause, greater than the runts of the moment. And now, well, now, political perfection. Yet here I sit."

"Hardly idle. Even George Cranston needs someone like you, or in this case, you. You raised him right he's a good man who knows the world isn't good. He doesn't believe that honesty will be met with honesty. He's gotten this far because of you. Without you, he would either be a gentleman who gets stabbed in the back every day or another cynic. You will make him president. He needs a strong, honest, son-of-a-bitch behind him and that's you."

"Thank you. Please remember to engrave that on my urn." Something of a smile crossed his face. He had an impish sense of humor. Mei had none.

"Sir?"

"Yes?"

"May I be frank?"

"When are you not?

"Nostalgia is fine, but please don't go sentimental on us."

"You run, don't you?" Another non sequitur. Mei was beginning to worry. This is how crazy starts. But someone who thinks only in straight lines can't recognize a curve.

"Yes."

"Ever get that feeling as you approach the top of the hill that your entire body is just shutting down, that there's no way to make that last push? So, you start to slow down, but then you see the summit and your mind and body snap to attention, and you fly to the top? Well, I'm catching my breath, because I can see the summit."

CHAPTER 82

Someone else was looking towards the summit. President Ailes, General Hayden, their wives and the Chief were all sitting in the White House's private quarters. A few aides were standing discreetly in the background. Everyone was watching several monitors, but only one screen had sound at a time. Ailes held the control. The Chief was tapping away at his pad, making calculation, or was talking to some very nervous person on the phone. Hayden imagined what art he would hang on these walls.

The nervous person on the phone became exponentially more nervous when the Chief did the worse thing possible, he handed the phone to the President.

"I told you, I don't need details, you have a building of technicians and lawyers for that. I just want you to guarantee that the system is running."

Changing tone, he spoke to his guests. "Excellent news all around."

"Can't the vote come in any faster?" asked the future president.

"Relax, speed can lead to sloppy mistakes. Our people are very good at this, but there's no reason to force the pace and make a mistake. You've waited four years. You can wait another couple of hours."

"Mr. President, another 14 districts have been sanitized. No problems anywhere."

"See? I told you we were good at this. The polls are open for another three hours and we already have half the country settled."

———·•·———

Three hours later, the study in the Cranston house was on overdrive. It was as if *Iks* had been mainlined into the walls. Junior aides were terrified of the place. They wanted to be at the center of things but were afraid of getting burned by the sun. They didn't know if they wanted to be invited in. A few decided to invite themselves in. A very bad decision. Sean had pulled in a few junior 360s. He needed more eyes. But Cranston and Maggie in particular had no need for extra bodies. Extra bodies were either energy suckers or lunch. George Sr. had now repositioned himself in the nerve center. Sean was at the main computer. Mei and Worth were deep into calculations that no one dared asked about. Nancy was acting as the go-between for the Senator and the world beyond that door. And Maggie. Maggie's presence was so overwhelming that people forgot she had left the house an hour ago.

Nancy caught an image on one of the screens.

"Everyone, wait! It's Maggie." Sean checked the side screen and put Maggie center. She was badly lit. Dark shadows showed under her eyes, giving the impression of someone nervous and sleepless. She was neither. No matter how her mouth moved, it looked like a Halloween mask. Cranston marveled at the skill needed to make such a beautiful woman look so bad.

"We're extremely optimistic," she told the interviewer. "The events of the past few weeks demonstrate clearly that the Doctrinists have lost control of virtually everything and are flailing around, hitting at anything that moves. They've thrown every trick at us. Muddying the waters with the SID nonsense..."

"I thought we were ignoring SID," Worth said.

"I've been arguing all along that we can't ignore SID," said Mei, "Hayden keeps implying we have something to do with SID. Our innuendo has as much validity as their innuendo."

"We should have done that weeks ago," George Sr. grunted.

Maggie continued. "... This absolute scandal with the *Roosevelt*. People get it. We are clearly picking up support in numerous congressional districts that we lost in 2048..."

The interviewer interjected. "On the other hand, there are reports that the vast majority of off-Earth voters are going for the Doctrinists."

"I don't doubt that many transmissions can get garbled getting back to Earth."

"Is that an implication that the President is interfering with the vote?"

"Of course not." One beat while everyone in the study stared at each other. "He's not interfering with the voting. He's interfering with the counting. He..."

That was as far as she got. The scene switched to the anchor desk where the reporter breathlessly reported. "We interrupt our interview with George Cranston's aide for a news bulletin. By our calculations, the entire state of Kentucky has gone into the Doctrinist column."

"Definitely breaking news, that's only been the case for the last four elections." It was Mei's turn to grumble.

"Is Goldstein getting any airtime?" Cranston asked, having little faith that even a positive answer would be of any use.

Sean told him, "He breaks through occasionally, but there are strong signals on either side of him. One or the other crowds him out. Besides, I doubt he has any useful independent sources anymore."

"And SID?"

"You want to hear from SID?" Mei asked.

"Do you want to know you have a tumor or do you prefer ignorance?" Without waiting for an answer, he turned to Nancy, "Where's Lilly?"

"She's with Maggie. I imagine they're finished with interviews now." She checked her tablet. "Yes, they're on their way over."

CHAPTER 83

And in the White House, everyone was calm and jovial, as if they had just finished a magnificent banquet.

"Like clockwork. How soon before we can call it?" Hayden asked.

The President leaned back. "Polls close on the West Coast in an hour. Just in an hour and ten minutes." A huge smile that said "job well done" crossed his face. "Congratulations, Mr. President."

On the big screen, Sean was trying to make the numbers work. Maggie, Lilly and Elena had joined the party.

"Same pattern as '48 and '44. We get reports of healthy turns outs from the camps around the Gulf, but the final numbers are depressed. Florida, Mississippi, Texas. All of them, we carry a few by a fraction, but they carry just three or four more to stay ahead. The percentage of votes reporting from New York, Chicago, Seattle, all the big cities on our side pretty much matches the final announced tallies. Too many people watching. They can't sanitize the numbers in Washington without someone being able to back check from the original reports. Rural, poor districts, not so much. We've got people at some district centers, but somehow, they get locked out of the room. We've got reports that one of our guys in Oregon was even arrested for disturbing the peace..."

George Sr.'s eyes brightened at this and he cast a side glance at Mei, who refused to give him the satisfaction.

"… Conveniently timed power drops in Hawaii, Vermont, and southern California. Unofficial tallies have us down by ten."

"Remarkable restraint," mumbled Maggie, "They aren't stealing as big this year."

"No incumbent, there have to be more undecided," Cranston noted.

They studied the map where most of the congressional districts east of the Plains were colored either green or purple. Most of the rest were white unreported. As Sean and Maggie had predicted, there were a few hopeful green spots in the heartland. The eastern Gulf Coast districts despite the polls having closed already were still white. Suddenly the presidential seal took over the screen. The first thought was that Ailes was going to declare victory, but that would be too crude, he'd let the Election Commission go through the motions. Instead of Ailes, a stream of data flew across the screen, too fast for any human eye to comprehend.

Sean answered before anyone asked. "I didn't do that."

"What are we seeing?" asked George Sr., who had been watching people, not the screen.

"It's impossible to read. It's being transmitted too quickly, probably to prevent any interruption or tracking."

"Did you capture it?"

"Yes, sir. I'm decompressing it now. It is not really that much data."

"That was the presidential seal, though, wasn't it?"

"Yes, sir. Right after the seal, a set of numbers did linger. Could have been an authorization code. Got it." He tapped his keypad, and the seal reappeared, followed by a series of numbers and letter. "It does look like an authorization code."

"Can we find out if that is a legitimate security code?" his boss asked.

"No. It looks real, but we can't verify it."

The data stream continued and showed a series of names in alphabetical order followed by a series of numbers after each name: Allen, Axworthy, Chou, Cranston...

No one in that room needed an interpretation. "It's the United States Senate," George Sr. said.

The senator added, "With Social Security numbers, tax ID codes, private Senate inscription codes, personal security protocols. Those are my bank accounts, private access codes and phone numbers. Everything."

With a mixture of awe and anger, Mei said, "Ailes is spying on the US Senate."

"Ok, I know I'm getting old, but Ailes isn't doing this. This is SID, right?" George Sr. asked.

"Has to be," Sean said, "No way Ailes' people would release this by accident."

Elena asked, "Is this going out to the entire country or has someone directing this to us? Is everyone seeing this or just us?"

"Easy enough to find out," a clearly fuming Cranston said. He took out his phone and hit a button. Suddenly the embattled politician was replaced by a slap-on-the-back good fellow. "Senator Cranston for Senator Fineman... Harry, George here. Watching TV? Of course, aren't we all? Did your people catch that data stream? Yeah, us too. Yeah, that's what it looks like to me. Look, Harry, sorry to pry, but it looks like my data is correct, yours too? That looks like an official White House code to you? You talked to Katie and Paul? Both confirmed? No, I haven't talked to anyone else yet. Yeah, yeah, there are going to be a lot of pissed off Senators tonight." He disconnected and stared at the inert phone. "It's all true. The entire country is seeing this. Not everyone will be decoding it immediately. But it's all out there."

"Nice of them to share this, but couldn't SID have timed the release a little better? Like before, polls closed," Maggie said.

"Maybe the idea is not to influence the election. Maybe it's a warning," Sean said.

"What kind of warning?" Lilly was still trying to grasp what she was seeing. Spying on the Senate needed more time.

"SID is warning Ailes that they have hacked his most secret databases."

"And why now?"

"Well, what else would he like to keep secret? What's his most important secret?"

"The actual election returns." Cranston's words were like a chisel to a stone.

"Exactly. We have always thought that the White House channeled all district results through their own system to be adjusted before entering the official record. This is how our voters disappear. It's easier and more secure to steal the votes in a central location than in each district. SID is telling Ailes that whatever he steals, SID can steal back."

Mei the pessimist grumbled. "Great, so now we can be robbed by Ailes and SID."

"Or saved by SID," Sean countered, "Maybe SID will play Robin Hood and steal data from the rich and give it to the poor."

"We don't know who or what SID is! How can we put our fate in the hands of something like that?"

Cranston sat quietly, mentally moving his chess pieces. "I don't recall being asked."

CHAPTER 84

"**I**s this stuff fake?" Hayden asked.

Ailes was also looking at his chess pieces. "No, it's the real thing. SID has hacked the White House."

"SID? Why not Cranston? This clearly helps him."

"They hacked the *White House*. How could one person break through the most secure system in the world? Besides, if it's Cranston, then why not release this yesterday, so that the last day of the campaign would be 100 screeching senators? It's SID, they have some motive other than winning the election."

"What could be more important than winning the election?"

"Seeing that we don't know exactly who they are, it's a bit hard to gauge their motives, except that they want to stick a knife in my back."

The Chief broke in. "Mr. President, something else is happening."

"What?" He spat the question as he turned from Hayden to the screen. It was still showing the official result piling up, but the narration disappeared. A computer voice from past decades came through the screen. Voice recognition was so advanced that it was difficult to distinguish human speech from a computer's voice. But this voice was clearly computer-generated. A stilted, unnatural cadence like something out of a very old science fiction movie.

"Shut It Down. Shut It Down. Shut It Down."

"Shut it... S-I-D. It's SID. SID is 'shut it down'!" Hayden said.

But what's "it"? an aide dared ask.

Ailes growled, "'It' is me."

Like the White House and every other house in the country, the Cranston household was seeing the same thing. "Shut It Down. Shut It Down. Shut It Down."

Elena mulled it over. "Shut it down... S-I-D... SID!"

"Shut what down?" Nancy asked.

"The government! The election! The fraud!"

Sean agreed. "Exactly, the data on the Senate was a warning shot. SID is telling Ailes it has the true vote count, daring him to put out the fixed numbers. Shut down the fake vote count."

Maggie was trembling. "George, we have to use this."

"Someone is breaking the law." Lilly countered, "What do you propose we do?"

"Grab this gift with both hands."

"And do what?"

Cranston jumped up, barely able to control his excitement as he uttered his favorite word: "Win."

CHAPTER 85

The cozy atmosphere of the private quarters were long behind them. Ailes, Hayden, the Chief and a clutch of 360s had dashed to the Situation Room, leaving spouses and other aides behind. A table usually occupied by military personnel was now occupied by civilian computer experts. The screens that would normally show the planet and plots of troop movements and the paths of ships and planes were now showing the electoral map and a shell-shocked elderly man. Arthur DuPont had been given the plum job of Executive Director of the Federal Election Commission. His official responsibilities were to oversee national elections, prepare the ballots, maintain the integrity of the computer system against hacking, verify the results from each district, and certify the winners of the presidential election. In reality, his job was to do what Ailes said. It was a plum job, usually the last post before a comfortable retirement. That changed 20 minutes ago, and DuPont was not ready for it.

"Is the network secure?" the President demanded.

"Here, sir?" DuPont asked. He was still having trouble grasping the reality that he now had a real job to do.

"Of course, with you! I'm in the Situation Room, for God's sake!"

"Oh, absolutely. Absolutely secure, absolutely foolproof." DuPont immediately regretted using that word. Fortunately, Ailes was occupied elsewhere.

"You've seen this crap coming across from SID?"

"Yes, Mr. President."

"We have reason to believe it they are trying to hack the vote count."

"Yes, sir, we have come to the same conclusion. We are secure. Our people have set up extra defenses and we are trying to track the source."

"So are we." Ignoring the sweaty man for the moment, the President turned to Rampour, his senior 360. "Anything?"

"No, sir, decoy after decoy. We just traced it to a UN satellite, the De Marco."

"The UN is screwing with us?" Hayden asked, still a beat behind. Ailes was beginning to regret his choice.

"The De Marco went out of commission three years ago. It's a dead hunk. SID is bouncing the signal off of it. It's using any number of sites to cover its tracks, including the Golden Gate Bridge and General Hayden's house."

"We're coming up with the same thing," DuPont interjected before realizing that keeping his mouth shut was his strongest position.

Ailes whipped back around to DuPont. "Forget about SID," he warned, "We'll handle this. Your only priority is to keep control of the vote count."

"Yes, Mr. President."

CHAPTER 86

Cranston's exuberance was not contagious. Lilly sat, brooding behind a desk in a side office. No monitors, no phones. Only Elena sitting silently across the desk, knowing that whatever she said would be wrong. Without ceremony, Cranston walked in and headed straight for the desk. Elena sprang to her feet while Lilly barely raised her eyes.

"Elena, a moment, please." A classic you-don't-have-to-ask-twice moment. Elena looked a final time at Lilly for no good reason and left, making sure they both could hear the door shutting solidly.

"Well?"

"I'm not even sure if this is legal."

"I am a candidate for President of the United States. For all we know, I could have just won the presidency. 'I'm not sure' is not an option."

"Aren't you worried that we will be damaging democracy? That we could be destroying what we are trying to preserve?"

"Damaging democracy? Have you been asleep for 30 years? Do you think Ailes and the Doctrinists have been acting like tender, mother hens, gently cradling fragile democracy in a nice warm nest? Do you think we're foxes sneaking in the dead of the night? Do you think if we do nothing, precious democracy is saved?"

"We can't prove anything."

"There is nothing to prove. I'm not going to charge anyone with anything. All I want to do is ask Americans to act like Americans. Are you going to stand with me for that?" She said nothing, and Cranston couldn't resist a poke. "You know you weren't my first choice as a running mate. I didn't select you for your political acumen, because God knows you don't have any. You do understand my reasoning, don't you?"

Repeating a phrase, she has heard many, many times, she said, "Because I appeal to key demographics."

"Because you appeal to the future. We're the same age, but I'm today yesterday and you are tomorrow. I didn't know you when you were in college, but I thought maybe that Lilly McDowell was still in there. That Lilly McDowell would help reinvent America one more time. We're lifting ourselves out of the worst catastrophe in human history. We are finally reaching out to the stars. That destiny is now in your hands. You choose to sit on your hands and bow your head, fine. Do it. Go back to teaching see what they will allow you to teach. Go back to lecturing see where you will be allowed to speak. Write to see who will publish you. That is your choice. When you said yes to me, you said yes to a course of action. It's nothing less than reclaiming American democracy. You want to say no now, fine, but don't you dare weep for democracy."

Another perk of permanent Washington was that the elites had their own home studios this way it was harder to pull the plug and easier to block interference. The small studio contained only the essentials: one camera, enough lighting, a few microphones, a director and minimum crew. The "stage" was a projection screen that would show a detail from a slowly waving US flag Cranston's team had spent a week settling on just slow the flag should wave. Two minimalist lecterns were set up. The set had been ready all day. The plan was that Cranston would make his concession or victory announcement here. Keeping with the solidifying tradition of presidential candidates minimizing their public appearances, Cranston would only attend the public rally if he won. If he lost, he would make his concession speech and turn out the lights. The only change in the set was that a second lectern had just been added for Lilly.

"We're live in four minutes. Should I remove the other lectern?" the director asked.

"No," Cranston said.

"I don't think she's coming," Maggie said.

"She's not coming," Mei corrected her.

"She's coming." Cranston corrected both of them.

"Even if she does, what is she going to say?"

"I don't care."

"What? How can you say that? She could destroy us," Mei said.

The director broke in. "Three minutes."

"The election ends in four minutes, no matter what she says. Or what I say for that matter."

"George..." Maggie began.

"No. No second thoughts. SID or whatever has handed us the last, absolutely last, opportunity. I'm taking it with both hands."

"Two minutes."

With that, the door opened, and Lilly entered, followed by Elena. Lilly acknowledged no one but Cranston as she headed straight for her lectern. A make-up artist blotted the sweat and applied a bit of powder. There was no time for anything else, and it was unlikely Lilly would have allowed anything more. Once again Team George was out gunning Team Lilly.

Elena looked at Maggie and Mei and the wall they had put up against her, so she discreetly found a spot off to the side. Sean came over and held her hand.

"One minute."

Lilly turned to Cranston as if she was going to say something. Cranston looked back but waited for her. She said nothing, but instead looked down at the lectern. Neither of them had notes or a monitor.

"Twenty seconds! Quiet on the set!"

Ten, nine, eight, seven, six, five.

Cranston looked up, directly into the camera. It was his classic "are you sure you want to cross me?" look. If it wasn't a camera, it would have blinked.

Four, three.

Then Lilly looked up. She couldn't have copied Cranston's stare if she tried.

Two... The camera light went on.

"My fellow Americans. I am Senator George Cranston, the Federalist candidate for the President of the United States. As we all know, some extraordinary things have been happening this evening. We have seen proof that President Ailes has violated the most private lives of all the United States Senators. Think, if he can and will do this to the Senate, what has he done to you? Add to this the events of the past few weeks the Chinese Device, the scandal at the Pentagon, the near disaster with the *Roosevelt* how can we, as thinking, reasoning beings, ignore what we are being told. How can we not see what is directly in front of us?"

Lilly didn't see Cranston look at her, but she knew.

"I'm Dr. Lilly McDowell, the Federalist candidate for Vice President of the United States. Please listen to Senator Cranston. We stand at a unique moment in the life of our country. You all know the story of the Expendables," she held back a gag as she said the word "Ours is an American story, *the* American story. America's greatest strength from the start has been its people. We invented our country and we re-invent our country, and our country repays us by being as strong and dynamic and as good as we are. This is my country. I owe my life to my parents and my country. In other countries, I would be nothing, maybe even dead. I am alive because of my country, and I stand here tonight to fight to repay that gift. If we are weak and cowardly, our country is as well. If we stand up as a united people, our strength is insurmountable."

Cranston resumed. "Here is what I'm asking of you, my fellow Americans. The Doctrinists want to steal your vote. You've voted, but we cannot be sure your vote will be counted. We've seen enough for years, right up to tonight, to doubt the count will be honest. So, we are asking you to vote again, not to the polls that would be impossible and illegal. We want you to vote not by doing something, you can be stopped from doing something. We want you to vote by doing nothing. Stop. Just stop. Turn off all your electricity lights, phone, computers, cars, everything. For ten minutes. Let them monitor the power grid and watch the usage fall. They know what is in my bank account; they know when you are using electricity. Show them what you think by doing nothing for ten minutes. Starting in one minute. Stop for ten minutes and let the White House see what you think."

The pair were on the screen in the Situation Room. Hayden had an opinion. "Sedition."

"Can you monitor the power grid of the whole country?" he asked Rampour.

"Yes, sir, we have that protocol. Programming the computer now." Then began a very long two minutes. "Mr. President, we are getting reports of the power grids all around the country powering down."

"Show me."

"Yes, sir." The electoral map was replaced on the main screen with a blank map of the United States. A new set of colors began to blink in, slowly filling in the map. "I'm calibrating now. The white areas show current power usage or rather usage five minutes ago now as I enter data…" As he spoke, some of the white lights turned yellow, a few orange. "… the yellow indicates a ten percent or less drop in usage, orange up to 20 percent decrease." Most of the map was still white.

"So, anything in white means people are, not, listening to Cranston," Hayden noted optimistically.

"Most likely, yes. Minor fluctuations are normal, but I've programed the computers to ignore that and focus on steady drops as of six minutes ago." The white continued to be replaced by yellow, yellow replaced by orange. Maybe a third of the country was yellow with a few specks of orange in metropolitan areas.

"Any idea of how many people we are talking about?" the President asked.

"No, sir. I just made these calculations, I haven't had time to sort out the differences between private, business and public usage. A large drop could be half an apartment building shutting off or a business powering down their building for the night."

"What about red?" Hayden asked. Ailes looked up. There hadn't been any red lights before, but now there were a few scattered around the country: New York, Seattle, Austin, Huntsville, Chapel Hill, Chicago, Minneapolis, Albuquerque.

"Up to 50 percent power drop."

"Hmmph, fly specks," Hayden said dismissively. As if to taunt him, fields of red popped up all around the country.

"And there's no way of knowing how many people could be involved in this?" asked the President.

"No, sir. We're always collecting data, but it would take a while to sort out that specific information and analyze it. Obviously, a red light in the middle of Kansas doesn't represent as many people as one in New York."

"Chicago just went red!" Hayden cried.

"And Seattle, Buffalo, looks like the countries southeast of Denver," said Rampour.

"Good Lord, look at California," Hayden said. There was no white left in the state it was brilliant orange with freckles of red throughout.

There was no good time to say this, so Rampour simply forged ahead. "Mr. President, I've tried to calculate the number of people this could represent. It's very imprecise, many variables..."

"Tell me," he ordered.

Sixty-five percent of the people of the United States have cut their power." They all stared at the map. They were only six minutes into the ten and orange was still turning red.

"Is DuPont still on the line?"

"Yes, sir."

Ailes had very few moves left. "Tell him to stand by."

The candidates were back in the Cranston study. Lilly's husband, Worth and a few others were now present. No one dared speak. Only Sean was sitting. He was working on a map of the US as well. Their map was color coded as well, but less sophisticated than the one in the Situation Room. Instead of white/yellow/orange/red lighting, there were red dots of varying size across the country, roughly corresponding with the orange and red areas on the Situation Room map.

"Chicago is on our side..." Sean detailed, "New York of course. Not doing well in Washington..."

"They don't like that we're disturbing their slumber," Maggie snarled.

"Most of Colorado except Colorado Springs as well... Albuquerque..." He stole a smile at Elena. "Texas Gulf coast... nearly all of Oregon..."

"Is there any way of knowing how many people that represents?" Cranston asked.

"No, sir. You'd have to know which buildings are cutting power, how many people in each building... more data than we have."

"More than half the population," Mei said without looking up from her computer.

"How do you figure that?" Cranston snapped.

"I've overlaid Maggie's congressional map onto mine. Sean, give me the controls." As Sean complied, Maggie's congressional map with its green and purple patchwork appeared. "Ignore cities, towns, whatever, focus on congressional districts they all have roughly the same population." With that, she superimposed her new map. Now the red swallowed up their electoral green and a considerable chunk of purple as well. "It's not an exaggeration to say that maybe sixty percent of the people in the United States did what you asked."

Maggie had been doing her own calculations. "She's right, I've got the same thing." Then she flashed the biggest smile of the night. "Looks like you've got your mandate."

———

DuPont was desperate to give the President some good news. "There have been no further attempts to penetrate our systems, sir."

"Are you thick?" the President roared, "Do you think I care about that now? You saw what happened just now across the country? You saw what those damned hackers just did? You think I care if *your* systems haven't been penetrated? They penetrated *my* god-damn systems! And Cranston just pulled a coup." Finally, after nearly 12 years, Ailes was out of moves. "Call it."

"What? What? Call what?" the almost president asked.

"Release all the votes. There's too much out there we can't control. Call it."

"You can't…"

"You're the soldier. Do you attack if you lose control of the battlefield?" Hayden didn't answer, but Ailes didn't care. "DuPont, I said call it."

"Yes, Mr. President."

CHAPTER 87

The ten minutes had ended three minutes ago, and the country was scrabbling to catch up and see if their doing nothing had changed history. People were madly searching for news. O'Brien and America's Network were trending water, they had no idea what they should do. Other sources were collisions of confusion and rapture. The Andersons had kept their power off for three extra minutes, just in case, so now they were behind the rest of the country. The Lopez family was nervous and feeling a bit guilty. Obviously, they couldn't cut all the power in their house, Papi's room couldn't do without. So, the couple dashed around the house, unplugging everything individually. Was it enough?

Cranston's team was essentially standing at attention when Sean told them the ten minutes were up and they saw the map lose all its red.

And then, without ceremony, the seal of the Federal Election Commission appeared, followed by DuPont's image. No amount of makeup could disguise the fact that the man had collapsed inside himself. After too long a silence while DuPont worked to speak without letting any panic rise in his voice, he finally plunged ahead.

"The Federal Election Commission has the following announcement to make. With 98 percent of congressional districts reporting, the Commission has determined that the Doctrinist Party candidate, General Jack Hayden, has 204 electoral votes; the Federalist Party candidate, Senator

George Cranston, has 216 electoral votes. Therefore, we hereby declare that Senator George F. Cranston, Jr., is the president-elect of the United States."

The Cranston townhouse levitated. The roars, cheers, cries and gasps overloaded the air in the building as it caught fire. They sucked the power out of the computers. George Sr. started spraying everyone with champagne. There was nothing chaste about Elena and Sean's kiss. Lilly hugged her husband wordlessly, terrified. Mei compulsively started pounding Worth on the back. "We did it! We did it! We did it!" Worth the only person in the room who could have taken that beating stood there and shook the hands of every aide who passed close by. Cranston and Maggie did what they had never before done in public.

After the cracks in the walls grew a bit more, Cranston managed to regain control of the room.

"Family, friends. I cannot tell you what a debt I owe to all of you. We are no longer knocking, hammering on the door of history. Tonight, we have made history!" The room cheered as Cranston continued. "Lilly Madame Vice President, please." Lilly walked towards Cranston slowly, as if she felt she should now be walking differently. He reached out and grasped her around the shoulders. At a saner moment, everyone would have realized that this was the first time Cranston had touched his running mate.

"I've got a speech to make right now, but my God, after that, are we going to party!" But before he got to the door, sweeping Lilly up with him, he turned to his father.

"Dad! Did you waste all the champagne?"

"Hell no," he said as he reached behind his chair. "I've got this one." And he passed it to his son.

The president-elect studied the label. "1997. The year you

and Mom got married." George Sr. flashed his magical smile as the champagne cork went flying to the ceiling.

CHAPTER 88

The Zhidoi laboratory was as calm as the Cranston household was exuberant. General Xi was the only person in the room not wearing a lab coat. Technicians were staring into their monitors, seemingly oblivious to the massive machine on the other side of the glass. Xi stared right at it.

"We're at 23 percent power," said the scientist sitting closest to the general.

"How much is needed for detection?"

"68 percent should be enough. Station two, what is the position of the *Roosevelt*?"

"175 degrees west, 38 degrees north."

"Over the Pacific. Timing is just right," Xi noted with satisfaction.

"38 percent power."

"44 percent power."

"51 percent power."

"59 percent power."

"65 percent power."

And then, from another station came the report: "The *Roosevelt* is over Chinese space."

"Captain, we're getting abnormal readings over southern China."

"Zhidoi?"

The *Roosevelt*'s helmsman was the same, but Hightower was gone. Instead, Navy Captain Catherine Foster was standing behind the helmsman.

"Possibly. Power reading exceeding previous reading by 38 percent, 40 percent."

"Pinpoint the abnormality."

"Confirmed, it's Zhidoi."

"Show me the readings." There was no question as to what she needed to do next. She flipped on her private transmitter. "Priority One message for the President of the United States from Captain Foster of the USS *Roosevelt*. We can confirm with 100 percent certainty that the Chinese Device has powered up. To be clear, the Chinese Device is online."

Thank You for Reading

THREE DEGREES
The Tempestas Series — Book 1

If you enjoyed this book, please consider leaving
a short review on Goodreads or your website of choice.

Reviews help both readers and writers.
They are an easy way to support good work and help to
encourage the continued release of quality content.

Connect with Jim Wurst
www.jimwurst.com

Want the latest from the Brooklyn Writers Press?
Browse our complete catalog.
www.brooklynwriterspress.com

BROOKLYN
WRITERS PRESS